S0-ADV-071

Emancipating Elias

Family
What a
wonderful life
God has given us!
Please enjoy this gift
and Merry Christmas.
Mark
&
Joni

Emancipating Elias

Mark Williams

Emancipating Elias

Published by Wheatmark™
610 East Delano Street, Suite 104
Tucson, Arizona 85705 U.S.A.
www.wheatmark.com

International Standard Book Number: 978-1-58736-955-1
Library of Congress Control Number: 2007935524

Cover images: Paul Campbell at pljacks@plcampbell.com.
Content Editor: Nancy McCurry, All About Books at AllAboutBooks.net
Text Editing: Stacie Griffith

Dedication

I want to thank my family and friends for their support and encouragement in this project. They provided a living demonstration of safety and love that enabled me to write about just that.

Foreword

Mark Williams is my friend. Odd thing about friends. They have your back no matter what. But if a friend tries to attempt something significant or out of the ordinary-like lets say-*write a book*, friends don't know what to do with you. You think, "I mean after all, the guy's my friend. And *my* friends, well, they work in cubicles and do spread sheets and coach Little League teams. They don't go to the moon, run for president...*or write novels*. Those folk all live on Martha's Vineyard and have children with names like *Guthrie* or *Nadine*." Your friend could hand you a modern day equivalent to Of Mice and Men and you'd respond, "Well, it's a little slow and the characters all sound the same. I don't think it'll sell."

So when Mark told me, eight years ago, that he was going to write a book, I thought, "Well isn't that nice. My friend's entering mid-life crisis and wants to write a book. At least he won't have to shop for gifts next Christmas. Good for him!" ...And I forgot all about it. But he kept writing. He fell in love with the story and couldn't let it go. At first, His sentence structure and syntax was like a drunken man scribbling on a napkin his apology for coming home late. But eventually he got his story out. It was clumsy and meandering for pages at a time, but at several spots I laughed out loud and twice I cried. By the time I finished, I put down the manuscript, shook my head and said out loud, "Well, I'll be darned. My friend has a written a classic story." And so he has.

There are themes in literature that convey truths so beautifully magical and hopeful that they reach in to touch the deepest part of our souls. It makes us hope in life bigger and better than what we've seen. The characters are still grimy and their stories often unfinished, but their lives are afforded dignity and importance that might not get seen otherwise. Suddenly you can see an unseen hand moving disheveled appearing lives along a perfect course. We think, "I want my story to be told like this. I want life to be like this." Mark has brought us this kind of story.

My friend is very much like one of his characters-"Bull": a tough guy with a heart of gold and a great sense of humor. If I am ever held captive in an Iraqi prison Mark will find me and free me with an intricate series of MacGyver-like maneuvers and indiscriminate explosives. Pulling me from the smoky wreckage of my cell he'll exclaim: "I gotta warn you, there isn't a good Italian restaurant within 80 miles of here."

This book sneaks up on you, catches you off guard and leaves you undone at the surpassing power of love. It is not the slick formula of books pounded out for a publisher's contract by assistants long after the author has stopped writing. This book is the sacred sacrifice of a real person, like you and me. He might live in your neighborhood. You could watch his kids grow up with yours. You could watch how his family responds as they live through his wife's cancer. You could sit and have a glass or two of whisky with him…I know I have. Enjoy!

JOHN LYNCH

YOU KNOW.

1120-1-5-0

He was odd. There were only a couple of people who were still around that remembered when he arrived years earlier. There was something more to the fact that he was just "slow" of mind. The way he blinked. One eye was quicker in shutting and opening than the other. Or, on cold winter days, one foot seemed to drag a little longer than it would with a normal stride. His head had an odd shape. One side of his forehead was larger than the other and his scalp was off in its design around his face. He had some birth defect or maybe it was a surgery years ago that allowed for the malformation of the man's head. No one knew. The man was getting older. He was not a large man, with the exception of his arms, particularly his hands. They were larger than one would expect for an aged man of his height, even for a man who had worked with his hands for decades; the type of hands that one could feel great strength and protection in. Maybe it was the way you felt after you shook his hand? You were always careful not to let him see you wipe your own hand on the back of your pants because his were always wet from perspiration, always. But after a few days, people began to set it aside as their own buried prejudice. Still, when you looked into his face, you always had a tendency to see your own reflection in his eyes; but then it happened, a spark, a flash, something inside the windows lit up, then it was gone. He preferred you called him "Tony," not "Anthony" and would correct you gently, but firmly, if you erred.

He had been the elementary school's janitor, gardener, and crossing guard for as long as people could remember. He could be seen every morning patting the small ones, "his charges" he would call them, on the head with those huge powerful paws. But there was something. After a while; people would sign off their curiosity to wasted time. He became invisible to the new teachers and staff. He disappeared and became just someone else on campus. Maybe they didn't really want to see the product of the world's sin, blunders, or things that go bump in the night. Invisibility, remaining in the shadows and out of the eyes of those around us is accepted in many areas of society. People didn't mind looking or even interacting with those things as long as they stayed at an arm's distance. Every year, shortly after the start of the new school year, people would settle into a routine and forget about those things that hide in closets. It wasn't fear that people felt. Society had come too far for that. Someone of his mentality looked physically different. Still today, people were uncomfortable, almost embarrassed to be seen with him. They'd never admit it. But the world had come to recognize those in the shadows and they had all been mainstreamed and woven into the world where the rest of us live. He had gentle eyes and a disposition of soft stuffing from a favorite pillow. Still, there was something odd about him.

The bitterest tears shed over graves are for words left unsaid and deeds left undone.

Harriet Beecher Stowe (1811--1896)

An early September morning

She could hear the music play in her dreams. The repetitive sound of two notes on the keyboard repeating like rain drops hitting crystal. Hanna had a reoccurring dream of a little girl. It was herself as a child. She could see herself in the dream, like she was watching a movie. The girl was always young in her dreams, especially the ones she had recently. In this one, she was about three, Hanna guessed, but probably closer to four, but definitely not older than four. The girl always wore the same thing. She had on a dark dress with small white designs on it and a dark-colored ribbon for a bow. She thought the designs were little white berries. The grass was tall and the light breeze stirred it around as it did to her shoulder length long hair. The sun was full with an occasional cloud blocking the sun.

The dreams were almost always the same. There was some variation in sequencing and sometimes she started the dream at different points. She was sure she had other dreams but none that she really cared to remember, with the exception of the occasional dream of going out for a Dairy Queen Blizzard, with Tony Bennett.

"Mother, you made me dream about Tony Bennett," she said to her mother about four months prior to when the dreams had started. The two of them had watched a re-run of an old John Denver special with Bennett and Olivia Newton-John. Her mother loved Tony Bennett.

She always made her daughter report any new contacts with

the man. "Okay, so what was he wearing this time?" Mother would ask. Tony was always wearing the same thing, a slate gray turtleneck with a darker sports coat. He ate his Blizzard with a straw after making sure to get her a spoon and three napkins. "Oh Tony," Hanna would say to him. "You are so sweet to me." She could see herself saying it. She was on a date—at the Dairy Queen—with Tony Bennett.

"Did you drizzle on your chin again dear?" Mother asked.

He wrapped the cup with two of the napkins and gave her the third because she always drizzled some on her chin. He always thought that was cute, her drizzling. She had thought that Tony being in her dreams was an offshoot of the divorce. He started showing up about the same time and she really couldn't figure out why him. After all, her mother loved him, not her. He was significantly older than she was but then again, she thought, she was significantly old. At least she felt that way sometimes.

"Why Bennett? Why can't it be Harry Connick Jr.?" She would ask her mother. Even though he had a great voice, she always thought that Harry Connick Jr's voice was much, much better. She tried to always, when she did dream of the Dairy Queen, weave Harry into it. The closest she got was one time Harry Bellefonte showed up working behind the counter. After that, she gave up and just dealt with the dreams at hand.

Her dream of herself as a little girl took place in tall grass. She saw herself pause and look up into the sky, as if looking for the sun. It was bright on the little girl's face. The girl in Hanna's dream was back to something away from the vision of the dream. Hanna couldn't see what the child was looking at but she was definitely looking at something that made her smile. She felt herself wanting to look. She couldn't see any farther than where the girl looked, as if she was trying to turn her own, young head. Hanna's younger self wore a content smile; sometimes breaking into a giggle as she walked toward whatever it was she was looking at. As always, just before the dream ends, the little girl smiles and then she stops in her walk. She sees something. The smile spills over into a laugh that only children that young can have, as if she's getting tickled; but she was alone, at least Hanna thought she was alone. As always, the little girl of three, or maybe it was four, but definitely not older than four, began to walk again. This is where Hanna always woke up.

Hanna Jarger was a forty-one year-old, recently divorced, only child, elementary school teacher, now living back with her sick, sixty-two year-old mother, who also was a school teacher. They found themselves now teaching at the same school. She was back in her childhood home, with the exception of the short time she went with her mother while she taught on the Indian reservation, sleeping back in her childhood bedroom, maybe even on her childhood mattress. She was divorced from her husband and her mother, who was getting older, was now ill. She was still working also as a teacher, but age was catching up. She was having a re-occurrence of the cancer that started several years earlier in her left breast and then begun to travel.

Hanna's move home a few months before was not necessarily as a respite from her life, although that played into it, but truly to be with her mother. For most of her life, it had just been the two of them. One of the benefits of her move was the peace that it brought. She had spent the last two years struggling with the divorce, the illness, and basic life in general. Now that her mother did not appear to be getting better, it was time to move. It seemed right. She took a position as a teacher at the same school her mother had been teaching at over the last forty years. It was the same school she went to as a child, literally steps from her front door.

First, her eyes opened and focused on one sliver of light that was leaking through the string weave in the Roman shades next to her bed. The dreams always seemed to end just as her alarm went off. The country radio station had "Tim and Willy in the Morning" waking her up with the 5:30 traffic report. "There's back up again on the east bound 10. With delays that stack…." It was the same report, different day. The report was no longer an issue for her. She smiled as they recited the accidents and obstructions on the same road she use to travel. She was home, the home of her youth. It brought a row of mixed feelings to her, anxiety as to her mother and her future but also warmth of peace.

She lay there for a moment, taking inventory of how good the bed felt and how much she hated waking up. The cool pillow under her head and the two she cradled with her arms and between her curled up legs made her feel like she was wrapped in a cloud. She felt sore and realized it was from the fact her body hadn't moved in hours.

"God, I love my bed," she said into her pillow. Her memory foam mattress and the cool twelve hundred threat count sheets she bought through Overstock.com just before she moved in were her new lovers. It was the best $99 she had spent and every night it called her by name. She thought for a moment about bedding being her lover and if that was socially wrong. That's what a guy might think. "Yep, that's wrong," she said out loud. "I can't be dating my bed." But, maybe it was her friend she thought as she laid there, cuddling her pillow. It couldn't be her best friend. That was still her mother now that she herself was grown. She rolled on her back. She thought for a moment longer. A friend would do what this mattress does. It listened to her thoughts at night, held her while she cried herself to sleep; laughed at her while she tried to name her new cow slippers her mother gave to her as a welcome home present as they rested next to the bed. Her friend took care of her during those hours when she couldn't take care of herself. At least a third of her life she would share with this friend. It was wonderful. It gave her rest and she enjoyed its company. Her dear friend didn't eat, need unguarded or unwelcome comments on its figure or political beliefs. In many ways, and at this point in her life, it was even better than having a romantic liaison. She thought that there were no misinterpreted meanings generated by a night of passionate, physical, rolling and tumbling and then of getting up early and leaving under the fog of "Sure I love you. Sure I want to spend the day with you. I'm just running home for a minute—honest. Make some coffee and I'll be right back," she said almost in an audible tone. Words that played in her mind from a memory of a different time. Her friend accepted her the way she was and gave to her what she needed—rest.

The radio was just loud enough to break her sleep. "Again, we are down to one lane on the east bound I-10 so you might want to think about alterative routes to the central city," the voice on the radio said. Traffic to her was an issue at the last school where she taught fifth grade. Listening to the traffic was a habit she would keep for a while, she thought. She at least could smirk a little at all the other poor slobs who had to deal with it.

Since she moved in with her mother, she could walk to work. She was back in her old room. Her mother had painted it and redecorated it but there were still some pictures and knick-knacks from her youth that could be found around the room.

She rolled from her back to her side again, still looking at the sunlight through the curtain. As the traffic report rolled into Tim or Willy, one of them began to talk, which she knew would lead to more music. Her green eyes lazily scanned the room. They landed on nothing in particular and merely rolled from one inanimate thing to the next. Each of them, triggering a memory in her mind. Strange memories came back as she let them.

There was the bed she slept in and probably on the same mattress; she couldn't remember at that particular moment if her mother, Gwen, had purchased a new mattress for her or not. She needed to remember to ask her. She did have her memory foam friend, which was really all that was important. It caused her to sigh.

Her eyes fell on a Madame Alexander doll on top of her dresser. She remembered having doll parties underneath her bed with her Barbies, Madame Alexander, and another doll with a great big head. That doll was her favorite. She lay in bed thinking about where she got it and what the doll's name was. After a minute, she figured it didn't have one. She liked it more than the other two because that doll was more real to her. She remembered hanging Barbie and Madame upside down by their feet from the slats under the bed and Huge Head doll would pretend to play tetherball with the other two. Her eyes came across the old bottle of Ciera perfume on her dresser that her mother let her borrow her junior year for the prom; she had never given it back. She had to move it to put the nineteen-inch Sony television she brought when she moved back in. Finally, her eyes stopped at the nightstand. On it was an old, faded, black and gray picture of her father, her mother, and her. Her father was holding her. She could make out her mother and recognized herself but her father's face was heavily shaded and darkened by time. The image of herself in her dream was the same as in the photo. She figured that was probably the reason she was so familiar with the little girl. She had her picture in her room. She was about four and her father was in his Marine utilities. She reached up and pulled it to her. Lying on her back, she stuffed one of her pillows under her head and propped the picture on her stomach. With her finger, she traced the outline of each of them in the photo.

"It's five forty-five and time for a quick check on the traffic," she heard Tim or Willy say; she could never tell them apart. It was time to get up.

"Mother," Hanna called from her bed to her mother who was somewhere down the hall.

"Yes, dear?" The muffled voice of her mother came back. She must be in the bathroom, Hanna thought.

"Tony Bennett was in my bedroom last night—"again." There was a smile on her face.

"That's wonderful honey. You should have woken me up. Any luck with Harry Connick? We could have double dated."

Hanna laughed. "No, mom, that's weird. A mother-daughter date is not in our future—"ever."

"So, Connick?"

"No, just Belafonte—again."

"He's too old for you too. Why are you dating all my guys?"

Hanna's smile was large as she again yelled down the hall, carrying on the conversation instead of getting up and walking down to where her mother was. Her bed was too comfortable to get up. "It's because I'm so much younger and better looking."

She rolled her legs off the side of the bed, let out a sigh as she reached to shut off the clock radio and slid her feet into the new cow slippers. She looked at them as she sat on the edge of the bed, holding one leg out straight with her feet pointed to the ceiling as well as the cow's face, then the other leg. She sighed again. She noticed that her legs needed shaving. Once a week probably wasn't enough, she thought.

"Oh well, who's going to see them?" Her new friend, the memory foam, didn't seem to mind. She toyed about names for the slippers. One could be Elsie after the famous cow on milk cartons and one could be Nadine, but she quickly voted that name out. She was saving it to name one of her future children and the idea of naming her child now after a left footed slipper really took the beauty out of it in her mind. Of course, the thought that she was ever going to have children was, by each day, fading from her thoughts. She sat on the edge and pondered her slippers again. "God, if I name these slippers, do I have to name the mattress as well?" she said, as she turned the left slipper with the toes on her left foot. She concluded that was taking this issue way too far.

She had thought that she was actually starting to lose her desire to have children. She could see marrying someone with children, older children, and non-diapered children. Children she could carry on an adult conversation with. Some time when the two of them could sit on the veranda of their fictional estate, the child sipping some fresh lemonade and she, a Mint Julep. "So, Fauntleroy, I see what you mean when you say that Lord Tennyson was erroneous in his transcription of the piece. But, if he was alive today, would he really be a Chicago Cubs fan? I think not, Fauntleroy—I think not." She smiled. "Where the hell did I come up with 'Fauntleroy'," she said to herself.

She liked that idea. She stood up, reached over, pulled open the Roman shades, and allowed her childhood room to be bathed with the morning sun. She slid into her large, white, bathrobe, found the tissue she left in the pocket from the night before, wiped her nose one more time, and then tossed it in the wastepaper basket on her way out the door, first to the bathroom.

The 1949 Womack home was built in the era following the

war; it was the traditional wire cut brick home, three-bedroom, one bath, and one car garage. Over the years, everyone in the neighborhood had added a second bathroom and converted the garage into another room, usually a den. She had lived within its walls until she finished college at the University of Arizona with her degree in Education. Most of her life growing up, it was just the two of them, Hanna, and her mother, Gwen. Gwen lived in the house since her and her husband, Elias, bought it in the mid-sixties, just before he went to Vietnam.

Hanna could barely remember her father. Most of the memories she had were found in the now dark and faded pictures her mother had around the house in photo albums and the one on her nightstand. Gwen said Elias died in Vietnam on a warm spring day in 1969. Every day in Vietnam was warm. Hanna was five. Her father was a young Marine gunnery sergeant in charge of a platoon in the Mekong Delta. She had heard the story many times of how he lived and how he died. She didn't like hearing those stories anymore.

Hanna moved back home after her six-year marriage to Bobby Jarger ended. She stayed in the townhouse she bought with Bobby for awhile but then the issue with her mother became more than she could handle at the traveling distance she was plugging away at. That was the reason she gave to others. In her heart, she was seriously wounded by the betrayal of her husband.

"I'm fine mother, really," she told her mother shortly after the smoke settled on the formal divorce.

"I don't have time to dwell on pain. Really, I'm fine. I have school; I have you dealing with your stuff. I think I really am fine. I'm over him." She felt she couldn't tell her mother anything else. She said it enough times, she almost believed it. There were two weeks after the final divorce decree that she would come home, crawl into bed and replay her life. Then, after a few minutes had passed, she crawled out of bed, took two of her pillows, curled up in the corner of her room, and cried.

She had accidentally opened an envelope addressed to him from the Insurance Liaison Department at United Health Care.

The tragic effects of the divorce were made even worse by a miscarriage just three weeks before she found this envelope. A baby they hadn't planned but caused her to feel joy and she thought Bobby felt it too. It wasn't the envelope that rocked her but what she found in it. Thinking it was a statement on a recent doctor's visit, she was a little more than surprised to find a letter on scented, eggshell white paper addressed to "My Lover." It went on to thank Bobby, in graphic detail, for all he did for her the night he was supposed to be at a supplier's meeting in north Scottsdale. "I loved they way you touched me that night. I'll never forget it. I had to write to you. I know it's a risk but I can't help myself. When I think of you I…." It was signed "Keli" with an "i."

At first Bobby tried to deny what Hanna was incoherently ranting about. "You got this all wrong. I have no idea who this woman is."

He said it was a wrong address or a wrong "Bobby." Then his defense moved to someone trying to frame him, "Those guys at work, gee, what kidders!" he actually said to her. Finally, he admitted his guilt when Hanna told him she had called United and asked to talk to Keli with an "i". Hanna hadn't really called, but lying seemed to work. He buckled.

"I did-did spend time with her. It was a fluke thing. We met and…" He then proceeded to tell her he hadn't loved his wife, who stood in front of him with her arms crossed, for a while.

"How long is 'awhile' Bobby? How long is it? A day? Week? How about a year? How long is 'awhile' Bobby? We've only been married six years."

"But we dated for a few years before that."

"Oh, crap," she said.

"A while," he said.

"I know. You said that. How long is that?"

When he told her "About a year after we got married." She, in turn, buckled.

She went down the check list of things she might have done or should have done differently. They all seemed to orbit the physical. What did this woman look like? She imagined Bobby and this woman having sex like they use to have when they were dating, everywhere in every way with a couple of exceptions. Her mind played with its own insecurities. God, maybe she should have done those exceptions, not limiting him, giving all of herself to him. When she first found out about Keli, she blamed herself. Images and ideas were coming so fast that her mind spasmed. She couldn't focus on any one thing, just the images of Bobby, and this woman doing things, naughty, freeing, loving, things. She walked around the house looking for something that put every thing in its place; that made everything all right again.

While he went out to the hardware store, she searched his desk, checked his e-mail on his laptop, and searched his trash file as well as the 'sent' folder. His password was the same as their ATM password, which also doubled as their every other thing password. There was nothing in the e-mail folder. It was empty. She went to the trash can in the computer.

There was an e-mail from Keli, apparently from work. It was less than a week old. He never was good at taking out the trash. He must have assumed that she trusted him so much that she would never check his computer, she thought. They were romantic, erotic, daily letters back and forth, some explicit, some mundane. Hanna's face began to flush. Her hands were cold and wet from sweat. She couldn't read them but she couldn't stop reading them.

"Oh, Bobby, you were so..." she read it as if she was addicted. She hated it and couldn't stop it at the same time. She clicked from one to the next, reading, and scanning each for words of intimacy from the man the two women now apparently shared. There was mail with pictures attached. Hanna took a breath and opened it. Her palms were shaking; her heart was pounding in her throat. She didn't want to look but she had to. She clicked on the first one. It opened.

Numerous people standing next to what looked like a waterfall, maybe Niagara.

She turned it over— "Niagara 2004." She was right.

There were ten pictures in all and there was one dark haired woman throughout. Crap, she was young, with a nice body and—

young. Hanna scrolled through each. They appeared to be travel photographs, pretty harmless. Then she opened the ninth picture and there they were. Taken from the side, Keli with an "i" appeared to be holding the camera out to the side and Bobby's head lay on her naked chest. They were in a bed somewhere and both were smiling. She felt faint, angry, nauseated, and unable to focus. She stood up and walked around the room, then reversed direction. She looked down at the screen and their faces, smiling, exhausted. They must have just finished. She stood next to the desk and reached down and closed the screen. It went back to the original letter and she clicked on the tenth one. It took a few seconds and Hanna held her breath. There, in living color, was her husband lying on his back in bed, looking up into the camera lens. From the position of the camera, the photographer must have been straddling him. He was naked from the waist up with the tops of someone's knees beside him. Her knees, Hanna suspected. His hair was tossed and touching the headboard. Hanna stopped. She pointed to the screen.

"That's our headboard. They're having sex in our bed," she whispered. That was their headboard, bought as a wedding gift to each other. That was her husband in her bed with another woman straddling him, taking his picture. Her husband was having sex in the only bed she and her husband had ever had. That piece of furniture, with their scent on it, was just a few feet away.

The image shoved her as if some unseen force pushed her back. The image sat on the screen of the computer, staring at her. She didn't know how long she had sat there, three minutes, three hours. But when she pulled herself back to the desk, she loaded the printer with color photo paper and printed the two pictures. After about a dozen of each and having to change the color printer cartridge midway between print eight and nine, she began to tape them up all around the room and throughout the house. She had saved one, the one with him lying on his back looking up. She went to the garage and got a hammer and a huge nail. She took the picture into the bedroom and pushed the nail through it, directly between the eyes. Then, she hammered the nail into the headboard-hard. She missed and swung harder, hitting the nail or missing it. Large hammer marks left holes in the wood. The picture became imbedded as the hammer missed the nail, hit the picture and then forced it into the wood. There must have been forty impact marks by the time she stopped. A light sweat had started on her forehead as she knelt on the bed. Her breathing was labored. Her arms finally folded to her side and she looked at her work. Then, without taking her eyes off the picture, she slid her ring from her left hand and slid it over the nail head.

She pulled the sheets off as she left the room. She went into the closet and pulled out his clothes, emptied his dresser drawer. Anything that reminded her of him went on the sheet. In the end she had filled the two sheets with his crap, including his Ty Cobb, Willie Mays, and Don Drysdale baseball cards that he kept in clear glass containers. He loved those cards. He loved baseball. He loved all sports, including bowling, watching it avidly. She played a tape back in her mind of a time he had actually hushed her when she came in the room. Hushed her! She opened the sheets and searched through the clothes until she found Ty Cobb and took it into the kitchen. She opened the plastic shield and removed the card from the container. Bobby had left the original plastic wrap on it to give it extra protection as well as value if he ever wanted to sell it. She carefully cut the seal and slid the card out and cut Ty Cobb into fifty-seven pieces, taped him back together and placed him back into the plastic wrapping, sliding him carefully back into the clear plastic housing. She then took Ty, Willie, and Don and placed them back on the shelf where the pictures lived. She finished by dragging the sheets to the edge of the driveway. A flash came into her mind. An image she remembered, when she told Bobby she had miscarried. She remembered his face, the look on it. He was relieved. There was a look of absolute relief. It made sense now. It was then she came back into the house, sat on the couch, and burst into a sob. She thought she was done with the hard crying until she found herself in the corner of her room, curled up, hugging her pillow, and audibly sobbing.

After the divorce was final, she lived for a while in the town home the two of them had bought. She first made sure most of the items of furniture that played a role in the vision she had between her husband and that woman were removed from the house. Her salary as a teacher at Estrella Elementary wasn't a lot but it was enough. She sat on the patio listening to the wind chimes. The ones he said he bought her at a convention in San Francisco. She wondered if that woman helped him pick them out. She pulled them down and threw them in the trash.

The days following her discovery were filled with changes between anger, hate, fear, relief, and even envy. She envied the romance she knew he felt with the new woman. It was new. After nine years, the newness of their life had worn off and they were just "doing life." The things she found so cute when they were dating now caused her to roll her eyes at him and question his reasoning. She knew he saw it. But she was sure it was the same for him. If he stayed with this woman, she knew it would happen to him again. It tired her to think of it. With all the fear of the unknown; the finances; the responsibility for the house; the car payment, and who was going to get it; along with their collection of Fiesta ware—with all those things, she thought that there was a chunk of her that was relieved that it was over. She had sensed something since even before they were married. She stuffed it and told herself it was the wind or something like the wind. But she knew it was something. Now she was certain.

There were other dreams she had. Dreams that, with the passage of time, became less frequent, but dreams that still could wake her at night or stay with her for the rest of the day; dreams that were more of a movie of past events.

She still replayed the last time she and her husband were intimate with each other in her mind. "Why? Why do I do this," she said to herself. They had gone to a beautiful dinner at an upscale restaurant in Scottsdale for their anniversary. One of those places with candles on the table, linen tablecloths and napkins. Few places in Phoenix had a dress code let alone one that required a sports coat or jacket. He had planned it. She looked beautiful in her dress and he wore one of two suits he owned. They held hands across the table, drank too much wine, and danced slowly on the open dance floor. They went home and spent the night in each other's arms, laughing and holding each other as young lovers would, not a married couple after so many years. She remembered it well. The next day, when she woke, his side of the bed was empty. He left a note saying he had to go to a meeting a meeting at United Health Care—on a Saturday morning.

The dream had faded with time. She could relive it with her morning coffee or ice cream after dinner. It was right there. Still, after months had passed and other events had entered her life to distract her, with her mother and the job change, she could still twist her stomach in knots thinking about her husband being with another woman. It was not her face he saw, but the other woman, the younger, prettier woman. She heard her say to herself. "Never again. I will never feel pain like that again."

They never talked about why things moved in the direction they did. She never found out the answers to all the questions, the why, how, when. She wanted to hate him, but couldn't. Her stomach knotted just thinking about it. "Never again."

Looking back, she did love times at the town house before the discovery and collapse of her marriage. It was only a two-bedroom but it was a large, two bedroom with a fireplace and a two-car garage. The best part was the back patio. It was completely shaded from noon on by a large set of ash trees in the common area just outside their back gate. They had set up a small fountain and she would go back there on the weekends and set up her easel and paint with water colors or just read. She could hear the water hitting the small pool in the fountain in the complex's common area and the wind would move the limbs of the fifty-foot ash gently over her head, as if the old girl were trying to fan a breeze down on her. At night, when Bobby was away at a conference or working late, she would play some Jim Brickman and open the windows and let the music come out to her on the patio where she sat, curled up in an old padded wicker chair that she found at a yard sale two houses over, sipping on a glass of Stelzner Merlot and reading a trashy novel in the light from the kitchen. It was a quiet, comforting place to her. Now it was gone.

A little over a year later, she sold her place and moved in with her mother. She had always been close to her Gwen, but time with Bobby had tested their relationship. Gwen had seen the things that Hanna didn't discover until it was too late.

"Hanna, there's something about him I just don't—," Gwen would always catch herself. They would have discussions and Gwen inevitably would bring up her concerns. Hanna waved off her mother at first, but as the years passed she would get angry and accuse her mother of trying to control her relationship with her husband. Bobby would sense Gwen's wariness and fan the flame of discontent with Hanna. It stained their relationship. Instead of talking to her mother every day, she would skip days to try to punish her. It was Bobby's idea and one that Hanna followed because she knew that her mother could not be right about the man that she thought she knew so well. But when the marriage imploded, it was Gwen who was the first one Hanna called. Since the divorce, Gwen had never told her daughter she'd seen it coming. In the time since the divorce, they had re-galvanized their friendship and care for each other. There was a day, an early morning; Hanna woke up to no pain. She didn't have anger either. She was healing. The scars were crusting over and life was life again instead of feeling like she had a dark suffocating blanket pulled over her head. She was breathing again. This began to work the relationship not only into a bond of a mother and daughter loving each other, but it also was preparing them for times to come. Gwen was getting old. She was extremely ill. Everyone knew the cards on the table.

Hanna moved home after her mother called and said the doctors had found a lump in her breast and it wasn't benign. The surgery and reconstruction changed Gwen. First—"fear. It caused fear to melt into resolution and resolution into hope. It worked on both the women. Gwen had moments of severe depression but also tremendous hope and an almost "squirrelish" happiness Hanna called it when her mother was on a high moment.

"You're a squirrel mother. One moment, you're on the ground and the next minute you're somewhere in the tree tops."

"It could be worse dear," her mother said. "I could be doing a swan dive off of a high bridge."

"This is Arizona, mother. We don't have any high bridges here, just bridges that are high enough to permanently put you in a wheel chair and eating out of a tube."

"Maybe that would help me lose a few pounds."

"Yeah, Mom, that's not an over-reaction. It wouldn't do anything for your weight but it would definitely affect your height." That, brought a smile to Gwen's face.

Hanna, in the beginning, saw this as another ton of bricks falling on her since her divorce. She didn't hold it against her mother; at least she didn't think so. She did, however, get depressed herself. She wallowed at home, sometimes walking from room to room in the empty townhouse before it was sold. She found temporary solace in staying up late and eating Ben and Jerry's Karmel Sutra, which she always thought was an oxymoron for her life at that time. Even though her mother allowed herself to show her emotional state to her daughter, Hanna didn't feel the same freedom. She needed to be strong for her.

In the early rounds, Hanna took her mother to chemotherapy once a week. Gwen walked into the clinic with smiles for everyone. She moved a little slowly and all her hair fell out. Still, she had enough strength and good nature to wish people well. Hanna, on the other hand, didn't. Her face was flat and her shoulders slumped. After they went into the treatment room and Gwen got settled into the chair she looked at her daughter. The dress was long with an olive green background and some kind of fruit on it. She wore a darker green sweater. Gwen thought it resembled one her mother had worn. When the nurse left she turned to her daughter, "What's going on with you?"

"What do you mean?" Hanna said with a sigh.

"I mean look at yourself. You look like crap."

"Why thank you mother, thank you very much." Hanna raised her head off the high-backed chair to look at her mother. "I've had a few things on my mind."

"Yep, you have, but the way you look isn't one of them," Gwen said as she put her head back to rest it. She closed her eyes and continued. "Look, I know you've had it tough recently. I won't take that away from you. But you've got to get up. You've got to get back into the life around you or you will miss the whole show."

"Mother, what the hell are you talking about?"

"Look at the way you dress."

"What's wrong with the way I dress?"

Now both women had their heads resting on the backs of their perspective chairs.

"You don't care about life. The fire in the furnace is gone."

"Hanna, you look like a dork," Gwen said raising her head off the chair and looking at her daughter.

"A dork?"

"A large whale dork, yes." Gwen was resting her head on the chair but was still exchanging looks with her daughter. "Look, it's not just your looks. You have lost that fire that used to fill you. You look sick. I can't remember ever seeing your hair like that. When was the last time you washed it? Honey, this isn't you. It's not just the clothes."

"It sure does sound like it."

"No, they're just the symptom. You've seemed to have given up on who you are. Don't give Bobby that power. He was a piece of something you want to scrape off the bottom of your shoe, baby. I'm looking at a daughter who won awards for her teaching."

"Mother, that was a long time ago."

"Not that long ago." Gwen paused for a moment. "Four years. The point is, you have value; you have worth. Your identity isn't wrapped in him but in your own mind."

Hanna rolled her head to face her mother. "That's part of the problem; I'm having trouble knowing who I am. You're married, welded to someone for years and you can't help but become a part of them and they a part of you. I hate him for what he did and I have to tell you—."

"You still love him, too," her mother interrupted.

Hanna smiled at her mother and nodded her head. "Yeah, the bastard. There's still a part of me that does."

The nurse came in and checked the I.V. then left before Gwen spoke again. "You've got to learn to love yourself again. I believe that in the destruction of every relationship there is blame to be had on both sides, whatever it is, gambling, adultery, alcoholism, there is some that both sides have to own. Now, don't get me wrong, one side usually wins the prize for being the biggest dork," Gwen said with a smile. "I like that word. Maybe that will be the word for the week with my kids—"

"You can't do that."

"Why not?"

"Mother, it means a whale's penis."

"I know."

"You can't give that word to a classroom of fourth graders."

"It's scientific—part of biology—I can't understand—,"

"Mother, focus."

"Right, the point is we can beat ourselves up about anything. I'm sure there was something I did to contribute to this cancer. I didn't eat something that I should have or I ate something that I shouldn't have, I don't know. Maybe I could have checked myself more often. But I do know that I have to move on and forgive myself. You have got to move on or you will grow into a bitter, miserable woman." She put her head back and closed her eyes. "You'll love again. You'll stick your neck out again. You can't crawl in your shell and stay there for the rest of your life. It's too pretty of a day."

Hanna paused. "You really think this dress makes me look like a dork?"

"A Blue whale, grandmother dork, yes," Gwen said with a smile. "Other whales would point their fins at you and ask the name of the thrift store where you purchased that dress."

"I never told you I got this at a thrift store. How did you know I—."

"Dork."

Hanna laughed. Gwen laughed. The nurse came in and asked what the two were laughing at. "She looks like a whale's dork,"

Gwen laughed and pointed with her thumb at Hanna, who was laughing.

It took time. There were good days and bad for both women. Hanna had to work at opening her eyes to life again. She just had to look a little harder at the world around her to see it. Simple things caused her to laugh out loud and sometimes cry. The girls in the franchised lemonade and corndog shop at the mall's food court always made her smile. She never could remember the name of the place but they always had to wear a yellow, blue, and red outfit with a matching pope hat, right out of the sixties. She thought how bad it would have to get for her to work at a store where you had to wear a pope hat like that. The National Anthem still made her cry. The poor on the street, especially the occasional mother with a child, made her sad. She missed dancing. She missed singing and watched *American Idol* while she slopped the occasional nail polish on her toes. Her emotions, although deeply buried and protected with emotional sandbags, were coming alive again. She went for walks and then jogging, and then back to walking; she bought some new clothes not on sale. She washed her hair. She seemed better every day. Fear, however, was still very real.

Hanna attended to her mother's needs during and after the surgery. The treatment was almost as bad as they'd heard about. Hanna continued to go with her mother as often as she could to the treatments and check-ups. The driving distance was tiresome. Eventually, the peace of the townhouse was replaced with the convenience of being closer to Gwen.

She was also lonely. Even though Bobby was gone and Hanna truly was content now with that outcome, she missed the company. Fortunately, the back yard of the family home had its own habitat that Hanna found to be as peaceful as that of the townhouse.

As she scuffed down the hall trying to wake up to the day, she could hear Gwen now in the shower in the master. Hanna had the run of the hall bathroom. That's the one she always used, even as a child, except when she would come in and watch her father shave in the morning. The fear of getting hurt, after a while, was not a controlling factor on a daily basis. It was hidden behind high walls—"Never again." But living back at home did have its own comfort. She found herself calmer. Every room had memories of happy times.

She stood in the hall for a moment and placed her hand on the bathroom door. Her mind was filled with an image. She would climb up on the clothes hamper and sit with her knees pulled up to her chin and her arms tucked around them to help keep her warm in the chill of the winter mornings. She'd watch as her father would repeat the same steps every day; lather up the warmed wash cloth, scrub his face to all four corners including inside the ears, rinse the wash cloth, squeeze it out, and hang it on the towel rack to dry. He'd then get out his Gillette safety razor. If it was Monday, it would get a new blade, set it on the sink while he, with three fingers only, put on the Gillette Foamy. Starting with the side burns, just in front of the left ear—no—it was the right ear, she sat on his left, and he would take the first stroke with the blade, rinse, and repeat.

She remembered it as if it were yesterday. She would hear her mother in the kitchen scrambling some eggs and when she had seen enough of the Dad Show, she would wander into the kitchen, hop up onto the counter by pulling out the bread drawer, second from the bottom, and use it as a step ladder to get her onto the counter. Gwen still kept the family bread in the same drawer.

Hanna walked into the kitchen. Her mother had made a pot of coffee, as she did every morning, even when she was living alone. Hanna was happy to see her mother finally get rid of the old percolator. If the thing hadn't finally worn out it would still be on the counter making its millionth pot of dark Folgers. Her mother left the coffee pot plugged in, waiting for her to get up and have a cup.

The coffee maker wasn't replaced with any fancy thing. It was a standard drip coffee maker with no timer, no chrome, and basic white. When Hanna asked her why not get something fancier, Gwen smiled and looked at her and said "Your father would like this one." She sighed and poured herself a cup after putting in the 2% milk and the non-sugar sweetener. Wandering back to her room, she heard her mother humming.

It must be leg shaving day, Hanna thought as she sipped. She remembered her mother showering and putting her leg up on the edge of the bathtub to shave. It was one of the only times she ever heard her mother hum. Humming was saved for gardening and leg shaving. She remembered when she was doing chemo, her mother didn't hum. She didn't have any hair. She'll go through that again with this next predicted round of drugs.

The house was nice but the water pressure was for the late forties and if one person showered no one else could, or even flush the toilet for that matter. And if someone flushed the toilet while one was showering, look out. Someone was going to get scalded and the other was going to get yelled at. Hanna knocked on the door to the bedroom. "Hey Mom, hurry up, I still need to shower."

"Okay, I'm almost done. How are you feeling today?"

"Fine," Hanna called back to her. "Hurry." Hanna walked back to her room holding her cup with two hands. She glanced at the doorjamb and saw, written in pencil, small hash marks with dates written next to them. They were hers. Over the early years her father would place her back to the doorframe and mark off her growth. After about age four there was a space of time and then about halfway up the doorframe the hash marks started again but this time it was in a different handwriting.

By the time Hanna got out of the shower and dried off, her mother had already left. All her life she remembers her mother leaving early, sometimes even before the sun broke the horizon, and in the winter time is was still dark when Gwen went to work at the school. It wasn't the travel. The house was half a block from the school. Down a quiet street of homes that at one time were mirror images of each other to keep the cost down for World War II veterans. But now they had grown into homes that at first glance, appeared unique, almost custom.

Hanna finished dressing after pouring herself a second cup. She returned to the kitchen, popped an English muffin in the toaster, and glanced at the newspaper her mother left on the table. Gwen didn't read the paper much. She said it was too full of sadness and "gluttony," one of her mother's favorite words for the kids to learn every year.

Gwen had lists of favorite words. She would take them to school and make her sixth graders use them in sentences and study them for tests. Words like "trepidation" and "asphyxiate," were a couple of her favorites. Since Hanna had requested transferring over to Borman Elementary, she had seen her share of Gwen's students take their new found power in the words that were shared with them and heard used around school. None of the teachers on campus ever asked the children where they learned to use a word with four syllables. They all knew.

She sighed at the headlines, something about Washington being in the red, and another headline talking about a group of illegals found in the desert, barely alive. She went deeper in the paper to the sports page, 'Diamondbacks lose the third of three with San Francisco,' "God, Mom was right. It's all bad," she said stuffing the last of the muffin in her mouth and turning to rinse out the coffee cup before putting it in the dishwasher.

She grabbed her backpack and carried it in her hand to the front porch. After locking the door behind her, she turned towards the walkway before she slung the bag over her right shoulder as she stepped off the porch. She took in a deep breath as she stepped out and down the path.

Some days, her past and future looked blurred to her; as if all the weight of all the things in the past had blended with all the things in the future. None of it, not a drop of it, looked promising or even hopeful. Since the divorce, she appeared to have recovered. "I'm all better," she would say to people at school, sometimes even her mother. "I'm in a really good spot now. I wasn't before but he's got his issues and they have nothing to do with me. He'll do it again to someone else. I'm just glad I got out when I did. No, really, I don't think I've felt this good in years," she heard herself say in a tape recording that played almost automatically in her brain. She remembered when she first said it. She thought it was a good way to end the inquisition. Now, as the days and months slid by, the lie she told was now the lie she convinced herself to believe.

All of her problems and fears and dreams and nightmares; all of them, were stuffed into a bag and hung on her shoulder and for the rest of her life she would walk these same steps she had walked so many times before. She had thought those steps were a thing of an overall pleasant past but now they rose up to haunt her. Now, on some days, they pounded their way into her; reminding her of the failure that she was. They gnawed at her and drew her complete focus. She could not see left into Mrs. Hammon's front yard and the last blooms of the beautiful Palo Verde tree or right into Vi Nygen's yard who lived two doors down and the new fat stone Buddha statue that reminded him of the one in his village when he lived in South Vietnam.

She could only see the sidewalk, which would always lead to the life she felt destined to live because of her life's failures. She could not see, nor could she fathom, the change in her life that was about to roll over her like a huge breaker that wallops you off your feet from behind while you are turned staring at something on the shore. She had no dream left that was able to lighten the bag that now cut into her shoulder with the weight of its contents. She couldn't see it. But it was coming. If she could only look up for a moment, she could see the rains on the horizon, the cleansing, fresh, dampening rain. It would make her smile. It would make her cry tears of joy; if she could only look up.

Pleasure in the job, puts perfection in the work.

Aristotle (384-322BC)

The trip to work was six hundred and thirty-seven steps. She counted them as a child and later, as a college student on her way to the community college, another quarter mile past Borman, to the south. She quit counting when she got to the corner of the school, which is where Tony Jackson, the school's crossing guard, worked. September in Phoenix was already very warm at 7:00 a.m. She walked down the sidewalk to school. The same sidewalk from her youth where she raced her Schwinn with the white basket against dopey Johnny Childers on his Stingray with the metallic blue banana seat and the shiny metal flakes in it. Hanna hated every time he won. So she would try twice as hard the next time.

The monsoons had tapered off early but the humidity was taking its time to leave. Hanna had a bead of perspiration in the hundred yards she had walked to the corner. She started to cross the street towards the rising sun and turned south to cross Borman Street, which ran east and west in front of the school. Tony stood in the shade under a large Chilean mesquite tree on the school side of Borman. When she got to the far corner he saw her coming and waved to her, as he did every morning. As she started across the street, Tony pointed his stop sign at her indicating he wanted her to wait and not cross as a car approached the intersection. "Oh, come on. I don't have time for this," she mumbled to herself as she stepped back on the sidewalk. She waited for the car to clear the intersection before Tony would allow her to pass. "I'm not in the mood to deal with the old, simple crossing guard with the odd forehead this morning," she said as if she was talking to some other self. The bag she carried was heavy. She was hot.

Arizona heat, this late in the year, always made her grumble about anything. She wasn't usually so negative and she felt bad about the words she used to describe him that morning. He had always been nothing but kind to her and she remembered those acts of kindness. But there were other times as well.

She always thought that being so hot so early in the morning was absolutely wrong. She had nothing against Tony that morning and yet everything against him. He was just the wrong person in the wrong place. She had known him most of her life and the man hadn't changed. Her mind churned on the idea that he was still a stickler for his mundane job. She was not one of the kids. Her life had been a train wreck but at least she could cross the street by herself. "Come on Tony, I can do this," she said with a sigh.

Tony was simple. He had the mind of a young adult. Every day, she saw Tony standing on the corner with his big red "Stop" sign hustling children, including herself, across the street to the safety of the school. Gwen had him as a renter for years, for as long as Hanna could remember. He lived in the converted garage in the back yard. She had watched his short, dark hair turn silver over the years. The kids were his "charges" Gwen would say. He would smile and wave at most of the cars and children as they walked by. His smile was genuine, as if he was seeing you for the first time, every time. He especially liked Hanna and would grin and smile his now yellowing teeth at her every time he saw her. He helped around the house and took care of the outside, doing any repairs that might show up that Gwen didn't feel comfortable fixing. Gwen invited him for birthday parties and Christmas.

"He's got no one else other than us," she told Hanna. No other family claimed him. As she got older, she began to feel the embarrassment of having a man, especially a man of Tony's demeanor, living with them. Even though he lived in a separate house, he was still on their property. And kids her age could be ruthless.

When they saw her at school, some of the kids would say "Hey, why's your daddy living in the shed?" It wasn't every day but when it did come, it was always at the worst and most embarrassing of times.

Toby Etcher would lean over and say just above a whisper. "Hey, Jackson, I see your retarded daddy got promoted to crossing guard. What's the matter, things didn't work out as a brain surgeon?"

She would roll her eyes and tell him with clenched teeth. When they were out of earshot, she'd seethe, "He-is-not-my-father," It wore on her whenever he was helping with things around the house, assembling or fixing Hanna's bikes or wagons, maybe putting her Barbie bed together. On her fourteenth birthday, she had a dozen friends over from school for pizza and Gwen was going to take everyone to the arcade and goony golfing. Gwen had invited Tony.

"I don't want him to go."

"Oh, Hanna, he loves you and wants to celebrate your birthday with his—."

"I am not his daughter," Hanna said loud enough so she was sure Tony could hear out back where he was setting up a tetherball set. "All the kids at school make fun of him living in our back yard and call him 'my retarded daddy'. Well he's not my daddy, so stop calling him that. I wish he'd move," she shouted.

Gwen held her as she cried. The teasing had taken its toll. She held her daughter and looked up. Tony was wearing a tie and a nice shirt standing at the back screen door looking at her. His hair was combed and he had a wrapped present in his hand. The two looked at each other for a long time. He then nodded and turned away, walking back into his room in the garage.

After Hanna's birthday, Gwen never referred to Tony as her father. She dropped any discussion of Tony playing fatherly roles. Even though Hanna and Gwen never talked about it again, the change was there. Even years later, when she was going to college, Tony, a little grayer and beginning to slope in the shoulders, slipped with Gwen and said "my daughter," referring to Hanna. Both Gwen and Hanna looked at him. He caught his words and corrected them. "I, I mean Hanna."

Tony's daily job never altered. In the morning, while he was working as the school's crossing guard, he took it very seriously. He always entered the street and made sure that his body and sign stood between the cars and the children. He always seemed to make sure he walked next to Hanna in particular as if he was shielding her as they came across the street every morning. He would eclipse the morning sun as she walked in his shadow. Sometimes she would look up at him when she was young and see nothing but his silhouette.

He was strict as well. If there was a bike rider anywhere near the crosswalk, they needed to get off their ride and push it well before the intersection. It didn't make any difference how old they were. Boys, especially older boys going to high school, would try to push his strict sense of right, especially if they were riding in pairs with a friend. Occasionally, a couple of boys would try to cross at the intersection. They would talk under their breath about the "idiot." Somehow, he could hear what they were saying, but he never gave any indication to them that he was listening, until they tried to cross the street without getting off their bikes. It was usually both bikes that were stopped at the same time with Tony grabbing the back of each seat. The boys tried to stand full weight on their bike peddles but couldn't move.

"Hey, let go of my bike, retard," one would say.

"You have to walk your bike across the street," Tony said. He had heard those words before from students and even adults. His face showed no emotion. There was no indication that he was ever wounded by those words.

"I don't have to do crap. I don't go to this school, you retard," the mouthy one would say, still trying to peddle. Only Tony wasn't moving. He wasn't going anywhere. Tony just held the bikes and actually started to pick them off the ground, lifting them by the seat.

"You have to get off your bikes and walk them across the street," he repeated. The boys eventually did what they were told, talking to each other under their breaths.

When Hanna started going to college she would ride her bike

a quarter mile south of Borman to Phoenix College. When she got to the intersection his smile again turned to discipline. She would try to sneak by while he was busy with the children but sneaking a woman and bike among fourth and fifth graders was not a great plan He would look at her with a 'Get off that bike,' and punctuate by pointing the stop sign at her. After she got to the safety of his sidewalk, his frown turned to a toothy grin followed by a loving "Thank you." Hanna still looked at him as a trespasser on a part of her life and even though she was kind and friendly, there was a part of her that came to the surface with the scars that she held him to be partially responsible for. If one knew where and when to look; one could see it. She could logically work through it all now. She was older and knew it had nothing to do with her or even him. That was just the way things worked out, she thought. But the wounds from her youth scarred her heart. Just like the wounds from her marriage making her quake at the thought of another relationship the idea of Tony, and the memories he brought, were right under the surface.

What worries you, masters you.

HADDON ROBINSON

The school was a single story brick building. The classrooms opened to the interior court on the south with large overhangs covering the walkways that passed in front of the doors. On the north side of the classrooms were walls of windows looking out onto grassy areas between the rows of classes. The sun had not yet broken the horizon, so the colors of the day were still bathed in shadows. The lawns were manicured and the bushes that bordered them were always trimmed. That was Tony's job when the yard guys from the district couldn't make it over or were backed up with other chores, which was most of the time.

Hanna walked east from the intersection and headed for the front door of Borman. Mrs. Barbara Gaven, the Principal's secretary and backbone of the school for the last thirty years, was already there and working. Mrs. Gaven was a small, thin woman in her mid-sixties, always perfectly dressed and her hair always perfectly coiffed. Prior to coming to work in education, she had spent her early years in the Army folding parachutes for the Rangers. Her father, a career Army NCO, caused the family to travel, changing bases about every eighteen months. She was the ideal secretary and public relations person to meet and greet the public. Her smile drew people in and made them feel comfortable. But she could swear like any sergeant. She smoked black cigarettes; long, thin, black cigarettes that smelled like wet, dirty hair on fire. They were from Azerbaijan, just north of Iran. When asked why she smoked them she'd draw from the black stick, and savoring it in her lungs for a moment before exhaling said, "full bodied smokes."

She claimed there was less nicotine because Phillip-Morris didn't make them. Still, there was that burning hair smell.

She was two years older than Gwen but had been in the district three years less. They had developed a friendship. They loved each other as sisters, with an edge of juvenile delinquency bubbling just below the surface.

"Did you tape all the desk drawers shut?" Gwen asked.

"No."

"I thought..."

"Shrink wrap."

"Excuse me."

"I wrapped the desk in shrink wrap."

"Holy-," Gwen said.

"Yeah, I think we outdid ourselves on this one. That teacher will never want to announce her birthday again."

"You dork."

"Thank you; new word?"

"Yes."

"You going to teach it to-,"

"Hanna says I can't."

"Fuddy-duddy."

"Exactly."

Gwen went to Barbara after she'd been diagnosed. Barbara took her out for dinner and bought margaritas. They sat and talked and at some point, somewhere between pitcher two and three, Gwen acknowledged the fear approaching. Barbara just nodded. Gwen wasn't much of a drinker. Barbara use to win drinking contests, so it came to no one's surprise that between the two, Barbara had to drive Gwen home.

Nothing took place on the campus without Barbara Gaven knowing about it. She broke in more principals than any other secretary in the district. Like a Master Chief on a warship, Mrs. Gaven ran the school, with the authority of the Principal. "No, the principal is not here. I'm his administrative assistant and I'm telling you that delivery has to be today."

Every principal knew their success would rise and fall around the secretary they had. That is what Barbara did—"if she liked them. If she didn't, they would mark their year and their contract as a principal would not be renewed. She had been married twice. The second husband she has been with for thirty-four years. He was now retired as an electrician and stayed at home dabbling in the garden.

She worked to keep their health benefits. Plus, she really wouldn't know what to do if she didn't work. She loved her job and the kids and drew energy from them.

She had smoked for twenty-nine years and for the last two and a half she had been trying to quit. She had convinced almost everyone that she had. All the signs were there. She didn't sneak out onto the teacher's patio anymore and smoke. She didn't smell like burning hair. She was putting on weight. The ruse was broken late one afternoon. Gwen was driving a student home from volleyball practice and saw Barbara walking around the block sucking on her smokes from Azerbaijan. She apparently had cut back to only her neighborhood, Gwen thought. She could be seen, right after the dinner hour, rain or shine, hot or cold, casually walking around the block, waiting until she was out of visual range from her husband before she lit up.

Every morning her face greeted staff and children alike. She was secretary to the principal, counselor to the teachers, mentor to the staff, and mother to six hundred children every year. It seemed she never got tired of hearing the same stories, the same excuses time after time. Her mind was still just as sharp as the day she started. It was her body that was beginning to feel the time. The mornings and hours of standing on her feet had taken their toll on Mrs. Barbara Gaven. She was looking to sit down. She knew her time at this stage of her life was about to change. There was a part of her that welcomed retirement and a part of her that feared it. She welcomed the thought of slowing down. Maybe taking that cruise with her husband sometime other than summer when school was out. Maybe she would even take up painting, she thought. She always wanted to paint. She could even spend more time with her grandchildren. She could not bear the thought that that her husband might go before her. Losing him would be devastating, as if losing half of her self. Living to old age was not a dream of Barbara Gaven's, it was a fear.

When Hanna walked in, the first face she saw was Barbara's. Barbara gave her a smile and a standard, "Good morning Mrs. Jarger," Hanna smiled and said "hello" while she worked her way to her mail box to pick up her memos, calendars, notices, and anything else people found worthy of passing out. As she walked back out towards her classroom, she was able to see Barbara full length. She was busy reading the contents of a student's folder and Barbara didn't see her watching. Her hand trembled. It was slight and almost unnoticeable, but it was an unmistakable tremor. Hanna wondered if it was early Parkinson's. It didn't shock Hanna as much as startle her. She had been so in tune to her own problems with life, as well as her mother's, so she didn't see what appeared to be so obvious. Someday, she thought, this could be her. Her gaze was broken when she saw Darrel Horton walk in.

Our doubts are traitors and make us lose the good we oft might win by fearing to attempt.

Shakespeare

Darrel Horton was the principal of Borman Elementary. He was an auspicious fellow. He had worked in the district for years, moving with his family to Phoenix from Kenmore, New York, just north of Buffalo. He was tired of shoveling snow. He had taught back east and received his degree from Cornell University as well as his Masters after a five-year tour with the Navy, where he met his wife, Cindy. They moved out west after a conference in Scottsdale one January.

Naturally, he fell in love with the weather and called Cindy and said he was going down after dinner and jump in the pool and hot tub. "I love you," he said.

"Yeah, love, well since you've left, we received twenty-six inches of snow on our driveway and the schools are going to be closed for the next couple of days," she said.

He apologized for his luck, told her he loved her and to kiss the kids for him, and that they needed to come out here forever. He quickly finished the phone call with a kiss and an "I love you," while standing in his swimsuit with a towel around his neck. "The staff here says we really should come out here in a few months. You know, to get a feel of a real Arizona summer," he said. He thought about that as he sat in the hot tub, leaning his head against its edge while holding his second margarita served poolside by a young Samoan named Carlos. He could not figure that an Arizona summer was anywhere close to a Buffalo winter.

When he brought his family out the following summer, it was

late July. He remembered looking out the window of the plane at the huge thunderheads forming north of the city and feeling the plane hit some unusually aggressive turbulence he didn't remember from January. The family was fine until they carried their bags out to the curb to catch the shuttle. When the automatic doors opened, they stopped in mid-stride when the rush of the heated Arizona air blasted them.

"Oh my God. Is this the heat we've heard about?" Cindy said as she carried one of the two boys on her hip and dragged a carryon in the other hand. Beads of perspiration began to gather on her forehead before they walked to the hotel shuttle curb.

"No," Darrel said. He was struggling with the two other bags and the garment bag draped over his shoulder while herding the five year old in front of him. "I actually think it gets a little worse. We're in the shade?" He saw Cindy look at him over her shoulder with a combination of fear and amazement in her eyes. He said, "It'll be fine at the hotel. We'll get our suits on and have dinner by the pool," trying to soothe the fear in his wife's mind.

Cindy's mind calmed when she got into the shuttle and the air conditioning blew over her sweaty body and cooled her down. Her body relaxed as the van pulled north onto Scottsdale Road. "How bad do the storms get?" Darrel asked the driver while pointing at the front windshield, the view of which was filled with the dark gray of the clouds north of town. The driver recited what sounded like a well worn phrase that Arizona was in the middle of their monsoon season and the clouds might roll down from the mountains where they form and give the valley a "light rain" that night.

"See honey, they get light rain out here. It'll be a nice light rain," Darrel said to his wife.

Cindy remembered what the driver said, but more importantly, what he didn't say when she was trying to keep her two babies from being blown away as they got out of the pool in response to the forty mile-an-hour winds and a nearby lighting strike. The concern for their safety and the size and shape of the storm diminished while scrambling inside. Darrel asked one of the passing pool attendants if this was common. "This storm?" the young man responded. "Oh, yeah, this time of year it's not quite every day. You'll be able to go back into the pool in an hour or so. Soon as it blows itself out. We might even get a little light rain out of it," he said with a smile. "We sure could use it."

"Light rain," Darrel repeated.

Sure enough, within an hour, the rain had stopped and the clouds had pulled back to show a moon and a black sky full of stars.

The following year, Darrel applied and got a teaching position in the Scottsdale District and eventually worked his way into the principalship at Borman. Cindy grew to love the city and actually enjoyed the weather, even the storms.

He had been head of Borman for eight years. Life had settled the former naval officer. A body frame that once was taunt and sinewy now carried the weight of fatherhood and a life that needed and deserved relaxation from hours of daily fatigue. But the dimpled smile was still there and greeted staff, parents, and students every day. He could be tough, sometimes even harsh when he had to, but he enjoyed it when he had reason to smile.

"Someone shrink wrapped Mr. Hershey's desk and left a note that said 'Birthdays are for sissies'. Do you know anything about this, Barbara?" Darrel asked in a whisper.

She looked at him over the top of her glasses. "I don't know anything about a note."

He smiled.

He trusted Barbara Gaven with every aspect of the management of the school and had confidence in his own abilities. He was a calm man. Not a whole lot upset Darrel. "Mr. Horton," Barbara called from her desk. She could pick up the phone and call but why, she thought.

"Yes, ma'am."

"The Superintendent's secretary just called and wanted to know if you could come an hour early to go over those reports before the meeting."

There was a pause and then Darrel came out of his office to Barbara's desk. "Tell them that would be fine. I should be done with all eighteen holes by then as well." He winked at her and she smiled. "You going to be around then? You're not going off campus for lunch or anything today?"

"No, I'll be around."

Yeah, tell them that'll be fine."

She was tested every time one of the rookies came up with a question. Even if it was a good one, and even if a teacher had been teaching for years, Gaven's patience sometimes tore at its moorings. She would talk to them slowly and more loudly than normal, as if there was some physical malady that kept them from understanding. Jessica was one of the worst because she didn't recognize Mrs. Gaven's behavior for what it was: pure sarcasm. The Army sergeant wasn't going to change now.

"You need to fill this out and then let me copy Katie's immunization card for her file. Her name should be on the board over there under her teacher's name," Mrs. Gaven said to a child's parent who was at the counter, pointing in the direction of the board on the wall with the information that the parent needed.

Jessica asked Barbara as Barbara turned to work with another parent, "Mrs. Gaven, have we received the updated rosters for the ESL students yet?"

She responded in a slow deliberate tone after she turned to see who was asking, "No, Mr. Horton hasn't heard back from the District Office yet. I know he called them twice already. I'll call the D.O. here in a minute and see if I can't light a fire under them,"

"You're my hero," Jessica said as she turned and left, bringing a fake smile to

Barbara's face, which quickly washed away as Jessica turned and walked off.

"You saw the cape under my dress," she mumbled to herself as she watched the young teacher walk away.

"A positive attitude may not solve all your problems, but it will annoy enough people to make it worth the effort."

Herm Albright (1876--1944)

Early morning in late September

Police Officer Packard "Bull" Thornton was the school's resource officer—"SRO" for short. He was a high and tight man in his early fifties finishing up his twenty-seventh year as a police officer with the city. He had pulled almost every duty the police department had and now, while others with his seniority were at the command staff level, he chose to stay on the street. It wasn't because he was 'brave, clean, and reverent,' as the Boy Scout Creed goes; he was heard to say to people who asked. He just liked it.

Bull was a friend to many, yet didn't have many friends. He was the guy you wanted around. Calm in a storm and yet, when the time was proper and conditions called for it, he was a storm himself. He was not too old to chase a fleeing burglary suspect down an alley. He never caught them like he did when he was a young rookie but he still thought he was a young rookie sometimes. From a distance or even close, he walked with a cadence and confidence step of a gentle man. It was a walk as if he knew where he was going. As he got older, his steps slowed, not because of age, but because he was trying to slow down and see life go by. A man who had an air of confidence, tipped with humbleness. His uniform included a baseball cap as part of the police daily uniform but he always take it off as he entered a building; a rule from his marine days. He would also do so if he was in the presence of a woman.

There was a blue-collar edge to his face and hands, one he didn't hide. He always seemed to have a band-aid on at least one finger all the time. But he was educated, including a master's in Political

Science. He was not beautiful but handsome in appearance. He had the body of a fit, late middle-aged man. A slight paunch to his belly but he wasn't fat. Yet, if he were lost at sea with just a hat and a smile, he wouldn't starve to death for weeks. He was not one you would want to mess with on the street.

"What can you tell these new recruits, Officer Thornton, that they will remember as new officers guarding our streets," one of the training lieutenants made the mistake of asking Bull when he was teaching a course at the academy on defense tactics.

Bull looked into the young faces.

"Cheat," he said.

He was never asked back to teach another course as long as that lieutenant was there.

He fought dirty when he had to fight, which was rare, even for police work. The days of getting into knockdown, drag-out fights were over, not by forced choice, but by wisdom. He didn't get in foot pursuits, other than those down alleys trying to see if he could recapture his youth; he drove his car. He didn't force his will but spoke his mind and convinced those that needed convincing that he had the better way. He compared himself to a Silverback ape he saw on the Discovery Channel. Not because of his crown of silver, but because of the wisdom the elder ape would hold in his mind and let spill out when the time was right. He was a good man, a caring man, a child of God. He was a thief, a collector of orange construction cones.

He was a stealer of stuff. His specialty was orange road cones. He would collect them from sites all around Phoenix, usually from city road construction sites; he'd only take one. He wasn't proud of this thing that he did, this act of weakness that he had totally justified in his. He could afford to be picky. Some of the cones would be new; some, he felt sorry for. He wanted them to feel someone out there wanted them, no matter what they looked like. He applied the same rule to cans of beans or corn in the store.

"Ah, little dented can of beans," he said as he did his weekly grocery shopping. "No one wants you. I'll take you home and give you meaning." If it was dented, he would buy it so it felt loved. The worst part of Bull Thornton's hidden life of crime was what he did after he gathered his cones. Packard Bull Thornton was a man who hated handicapped parking spots.

Not all of them. It was the volume of slots that he took exception to. There was just no way to justify row upon endless row of empty parking spaces. He agreed that each store or mall needed a certain number for those people to park close. He never had a problem with those folks who needed a little extra edge to live life. He figured he was going to be there soon enough and liked the idea of having a front row seat to anywhere. He even took a great liking to writing tickets to those who parked in a slot when they didn't have a license plate or a sticker hanging in their front window.

For the last five years, as a game that only Bull played, he would take several stolen cones from his garage and load them in the trunk of his patrol car. Then, under the cover of night, Bull Thornton would drive into an empty mall parking lot and place a cone in front of four or five handicapped parking spaces, as if some official had marked those slots for service. Then he would bet with himself about how long it would take for someone from the business to figure out that something wasn't right. The longest was always a Wal-Mart where almost two weeks passed before one of the manager's elderly grandmothers circled the busy lot for almost forty-five minutes, not that she couldn't find a place to park; there were a dozen open handicapped slots.

At night, as he was on patrol during third shift, he would find an excuse to go to the headquarters building. Late at night no one other than the custodians and a few detectives occupied the sixth floor building. He would place one of the newer cones in front of the Chief's parking space—just because.

He would steal your last donut or eat your last bite of pie when you got up to use the restroom. He would land in the middle of fire and thunder to save your life after you made him leave the tip for the donut he himself had stolen. Afterwards, he would eat the French fries off your plate while you did the paperwork. He would borrow fifty cents for the soda machine just because he didn't want to break a one-dollar bill. And then, later that night, he would leave a food box with toys and new white socks on the doorstep of a child from the school whose family he knew was struggling.

He would squirt water on cars driving down his street, which appeared to him to be driving too fast through his neighborhood while standing in the front yard watering the lawn in tattered shorts. "Slow down, ya miserable bastard," he'd yell at the fading tail lights. Later that day, he would go to the city building, water billing department.

"Officer Thornton, it's good to see you again today," the girl at the counter would say. What can we do for you?"

"Here to pay a bill."

"Who is it this time?"

He would arrange for the water and power bill to be paid for a different family whose father had been injured and couldn't work, sometimes paying it himself and no one knew.

For a man his size, he moved well among the shadows. Most people thought they knew Packard Thornton. They claimed him as their own and called him "friend." The Silverback smiled and just moved again. Bull was just a man. He had flaws, many flaws, and was often the first one to mention them. He drank hard liquor with a good cigar, could swear like a sailor after nine months at sea, and ate too much pie. But in peaceful times and in heavy seas, there occasionally comes someone who will stand watch on a quiet Christmas morning outside the door, so the rest could sleep in. He didn't mind. He was always seen on patrol, not only Christmas Eve but also the next morning. He had convinced himself he actually enjoyed it. It was his gift. Those who called him friend didn't know what they were saying. While other officers his age approached their retirement, Bull had not thought of retirement, not quite yet.

The nickname "Bull" was given to him when he was still in the Marine Corps as a Marine pilot redeployed as a flight instructor to NATO troops in Europe. The Marines and naval NCO's formed a competitive soccer team to challenge the French troops that were stationed at the base. They got tired of beating each other up in pick-up football games and the European countries had no interest in American football. So they formed their own soccer team to represent the United States against their host nations.

The camaraderie on the warrior level was always a little tense towards the Americans but always professional when it was time to be professional. The first game the Americans had was against the Italians, who beat the Americans badly 6-0. With their "skinny Italian arms and their skinny legs sticking out of their silk shorts," was the way Bull described them, the Italians took the American team to school. Bull hated it and it was embarrassing to him to be beaten by the Italians in anything, let alone a sport. They even had an attitude about it. Bull explained it to others as if it was like the skinny neighbor kid beating you in a bike race and then never letting you forget it.

Packard stood just under six-feet, two inches, but it was his sloping shoulders and neck that caused the Italian players to call him "il Toro" or "Bull." They would bark about his lack of grace and inability to move the ball. They laughed until during one game, one of their players and Bull were both going for a ball and Bull gave the opposing player a forearm to the side of his head which caused him to flip one-hundred and eighty degrees with his feet straight up in the air. The game got fun after that. The nickname stuck.

He was a sergeant during his seventeenth year in the job but went back to a patrol officer after he allegedly hit a lieutenant. He thought he probably should have been fired or at least given days off but the lieutenant, according to a friend of Bull's on the disciplinary review board, really needed to get his "clock cleaned" and Bull was just the one to do it, was reflected by the panel's vote. Command knew both officers and after reading the Internal Investigation Bureau's report, it was clear to the Chief what happened. The Chief of Police was always the final reader of disciplinary reports. Bull found out what the Chief thought, that the man was so bad as a leader, that had Bull not broken his nose, he would have been killed by his own men, found in a trash dumpster, somewhere among a pile of dirty diapers. The Lieutenant was given an incentive to take an early retirement and Bull was given 5 days off—with pay. He spent it on the beach in Cabo San Lucas, Mexico.

He had been a School Resource Officer, SRO, for three years. He had great hours and could earn all the overtime he wanted, a desired goal for officers close to retirement. What he would retire to was a topic of endless talks around the morning coffee maker. Retire to what?

He was on the Neighborhood Response Unit, officers that could respond quickly to high threat events and buy time for the Special Assignments Team to get set up with their bazookas and long guns. He was married and had a child once, but an accident claimed one and put the other in a care home. He would talk about them only to those closest to him, which you could count on one hand; Gwen Jackson was one finger, Barbara another.

When he came back from Mexico with his wife, Beth, dead and his daughter in a coma, time stood still. He froze in his life.

He had taken his wife and child to Cabo when he was given the five days. It would be fun, just the three of them, he thought.

"Let me get this straight," Beth said on the phone when Bull called her from work with the idea. "You hit a lieutenant in the face."

"Yes ma'am."

"They're giving you time off."

"Yes, ma'am."

"With pay."

"Yes, ma'am."

And you want to take us to Cabo, a place I have wanted to go since we've been married and have been begging you to take us there. Do I have this correct?"

"Yes, you do."

Beth was smiling on the phone because she could picture her husband on the other end with a large, Cheshire-cat like smile on his face. "Do I want to know what you did?"

"I'll be happy to tell you, as we sit on the beach sipping mango margaritas. What do you say?"

"I say we're going to Mexico," was Beth's excited response.

It was a nightmare that he would carry for the rest of his life. After his wife's funeral he spent days in the house with the lights off and the curtains drawn. He sat in a chair, alone. A week had gone by without a word and Gwen went over to see him. She knocked on the door, then the windows, then the back door. Finally, a shell of a man came to the door. He was wearing the same pants and shirt that he had worn at the funeral. He hadn't shaved, bathed, and from what Gwen witnessed, there wasn't any proof that he had eaten anything. He said nothing but merely turned around and went back in and sat in his chair. Gwen said nothing but followed him in and sat on the couch next to the chair.

After a few minutes, he slid out of his chair to his knees. She simply watched. He turned and bent back into the chair, as if the chair seat was an altar and he was praying. He buried his face in the crease of the seat with the arm of the chair and gripped the seat cushion with his hands. He then began to cry. He sobbed. His body would wretch with the sobbing and arch uncontrollably. She knelt down next to him and laid her hand on his back and then his head. She wept as well. Her friend was in an excruciating amount of pain and there was only this that she could do for him, to comfort him, just to be there. He would sit and then cry, sobbing into anything that was handy. She just sat with him. He was so tired and weary from sadness he just turned and sat on the floor, holding his head. He knew that he was responsible for the lives of his wife and daughter. Gwen said very little. She just was.

An hour passed. "I'm going to make you something to eat."

"I'm not hungry."

"Don't care, you have to eat."

He said nothing. He didn't move. She went in and found a can of tomato soup, heated it up and brought it to him. After she got him in his chair and a bowl in his lap, she went through the house and began to open the curtains, letting the world back in.

"It's too bright," he said, shading his eyes.

"Don't care, world's coming back in." She stood next to him for a moment before she continued. "Look, you gotta let people help you. That's all we got. It frustrates us on the outside to just stand around. So, shut up and let me love you."

It took time and patience but Bull was able to pull out of the nose dive that was his life. He found himself first wanting to live for his daughter, Cheri, who sustained permanent brain damage. But guilt continued to rain down on him in those quiet times at home. So he stayed busy. Between work and his daughter, there wasn't room for anything in the year after the tragedy. Eventually, he was able to breathe again. But there was still deep scarring that even he dared not look at.

He never told Gwen the deepest of the secrets. He never told anyone. He didn't tell them that he hadn't loved Beth as much as he thought he should have. He was pulling away in their last year together. There wasn't anyone else. There was just the three of them. But he felt a distance between them and he knew Beth felt him pulling away. The trip to Mexico was his way of trying to work at falling back in love with his wife again. He never had a chance to see if it worked. His guilt was full of the idea that his wife died with the knowledge that the man who was supposed to be her best friend and lover was struggling with the idea of the whole life the two of them had. He never found himself telling her he loved her anymore. He did. He just never said it. He couldn't remember if he had told her that day in Mexico that he did love her. There were times that he found himself wanting to live for life itself. There were women. Not many when he stopped to count them in his own mind. But there were enough to neutralize the pain. It was through his friend at school that life came back.

"Bull, you can't be free of the guilt as long as you hold on to it so tightly," Michael said. He was a man that Bull respected. A man, Bull thought, who had experienced pain like his.

Having met Gwen a few years earlier, she requested Bull specifically to be the SRO for the school. At first, Bull wanted nothing to do with "baby sitting a bunch of runny nosed little lemmings," he said after he approached her and asked to use her influence with the Commander. A request she refused with a smile.

"Come on Gwen, I don't play well with others; especially when the others don't come up to my knee." After being reminded by the Commander of the forgiveness granted him by the department for the little lieutenant incident, the fact that Gwen was well liked by members of the department, and the fact that he could still work NRU and virtually unlimited overtime, he decided to give it a try after the Commander explained it to him. They weren't lemmings anymore, those children. He looked at them as if they were a salve for a heart that had been broken almost beyond repair. The excruciating pain he had felt for so long was fading. "I'm smiling at you, Jose," he would yell at one of the boys across the quad. "You're just going to have to tell your gangster friends that you have a middle-aged white cop for a friend," he followed. He said it loud enough, always loud enough so others could hear when he was talking to any child. He was marking them as adopted, and in his mind, he didn't care who knew it.

Bull bellowed as he entered the front door. "Good morning, Beautiful. How are you this wonderful morning?" as he waded through the sea of children, seeing Barbara Gaven. The older children would wave and smile and the new students would stop in their tracks as the battleship of a man, in full uniform, would walk into the lobby.

"Good morning, Officer Thornton. Are you ready for another day?" Barbara said.

"Mrs. Gaven, the sun would fade and the moon could fall from its mooring and I would still claw my way here to spend another day in your presence," Bull responded, holding his hand over his heart.

"And you sir, are living up to your nickname—Bull," Gwen said with a smirk as she stood behind the counter next to Barbara.

"I am aghast at your accusation that my sincerity is less than—well, sincere."

"Officer Thornton, you do make me smile," Barbara said.

"My joy in life madam; my simple joy in life," Bull said with a slight bow.

At that moment, Hanna walked out of the mailroom. As she came around the reception desk, she could see only her mother.

She remembered about the coffee. "Mom, you left the coffee pot on again; one of these days you're going to burn the house down."

"That's why I have you," Gwen replied with a smile. Hanna didn't see Bull just around the corner by the desk. When she turned to walk back to her classroom she walked straight into Bull. He had reached out to her with one hand to stop her or she would have run dead into the center of his chest. It startled her. She quickly said, "Excuse me" and walked around him but as she did she shook her head as if it was his fault he was standing in her way.

The two of them watched as Hanna worked her way to the door and out to her classroom. "Your daughter seems distracted," Bull said with an air of curiosity.

"She always is these days. I should probably introduce you. We have been in school for over two months. It's probably about time."

"That should be—fun," Bull said with a smirk.

He felt a light touch on his shoulder and turned to see Jessica Farmer. Jessica had been a teacher at the school for seven years. She was thirty seven, but Bull thought she had the body of a twenty-five year old. She had been married twice, both times to wealthy men who had taken care of her financially. Rumor had it that she was from wealth, her daddy being an oral surgeon and having patented a treatment for recessive gums. It was theorized that every time someone got their gums scraped a little cash register bell went off in the Farmer home. Her first marriage was to a wealthy lawyer. It was a "match made in the checkbook," Barbara Gaven once said. The divorce was quick. Her second marriage didn't make it that long.

She married a doctor, a plastic surgeon, the second time. Her "augmentations" started about six months into the marriage, and she was divorced in fourteen months. "Irreconcilable differences" she said in court papers.

It was here that many thought she started to dabble in real estate.

"Geezus, she must be investing all of Daddy's money," Barbara said once when she heard about Jessica passing the real estate exam. As a teacher, she worked the real estate end on her off time. She was good at it and no one at the school could figure out why she did the education thing and not real estate full time. She had told other teachers that she was through with men, at least the marrying part of them. She dated well; sometimes being picked up at school on a Friday afternoon by a chiseled man one week and another handsome man the next. Each time the gentleman appeared significantly well off, expensive bouquets, jewelry, and on a couple of occasions they showed up in limousines. "Geezus," Barbara said as she peeked out the blinds from the front office. "She's towing a damn suitcase this time," as she watched Jessica walk across the parking lot and get into the car. The office staff would stop and watch her leave. Another "Weekend at Bernie's," Darrel would say. Why she was picked up at school and not at her home was anyone's guess.

Shortly after Bull started at the school, Jessica had made several comments to other teachers that Bull was her next target. Bull figured she was just "slummin'" and wanted a cop on her "Things to do" list. He did like the attention and realized quickly that his rejections of her advances drove her crazy. She was not familiar with rejection. She thought that receiving it from someone who should really appreciate the fact that someone like her would be attracted to someone so much older and unsophisticated as himself went against all that she knew to be true. She wanted him even more. "What do you mean you don't want to go to Newport with me? It would be fun."

"Nope, don't like the sand. Newport Beach has sand—hence the name 'Beach'."

"We wouldn't have to spend any time on the beach."

"Sure we would. Why else would you go to a place with the word 'Beach' in it?"

It had grown to a conquest competition and she had lost but couldn't admit it. One of the advantages that Bull noticed as he got older was he mellowed in his youthful craving for sex. Not that he lost his interest or desire, but it counted more. He was still emotionally tied to his wife. It just meant more. The fluff on relationships for him was stripped away. He was too old and too tired for games unless it was touch football, darts at O'Flattery's, or best score on the shooting range.

"Hello, Bull. We get the pleasure of your company again today?" Jessica said, looking up at him through her tinsel blue eyes. "Aye lass, you get to share me today with so many others." Bull said in his best Scottish brogue. "Jessica, you look and—" Bull paused and sniffed Jessica's hair "—smell just as good as always. You washed your hair this morning."

Jessica giggled one of those fake giggles. "Silly Bull. I always wash my hair. So it's silky soft," she said tossing her hair like she would in the shampoo commercial she quoted.

"Bar soap," Bull said, rubbing his head and turning back to the counter and taking out his pen.

"Bar soap?"

"Yea, bar soap. That's what I use. Wanna sniff?" Bull said as he bent over.

"You watch yourself, Bull. You're not getting any younger. Your bones are getting brittle," Gwen said from behind the counter.

"I think he has nice bones," Jessica's voice came from behind him.

"Jeeezus," Barbara said from her desk as she looked over the top of her glasses, shaking her head. Bull thought that he dare not make eye contact with Barbara.

"That's what I love about you, a keen insight into the inner working of a Cop's mind. Wasn't your degree in Psychology?"

Jessica giggled again while flipping her hair back over her shoulder. "Oh, Bull, you know I majored in Dance. I taught you the Electric Slide, remember?"

Gwen walked out from behind the counter with her arms filled with papers and books she had gotten from the mailroom. She had been talking to Tony, who had come in to drop off a purchase order for the principal to sign.

"What are you doing?" Barbara said under her breath so the students couldn't hear but with a firmness of an educator who has witnessed years of stupid things. "We have people all over this campus waiting to help you. You know you shouldn't be carrying this stuff." She began to take the papers from Gwen's arms just as they started to slip. The pencil behind her ear fell to the ground. Gwen looked like she was working on a juggling act as she followed Bull to a nearby counter to land the pile. Jessica followed them over, first picking up the pencil.

"She's right Gwen, you need to let some of us to help you," Jessica said after handing her the pencil.

"Guys, I'm not dead yet. I'm all right, really. I can do this. If I can't, I better get out of the business," she said looking back and forth between the two women. She was a little out of breath as she tucked a strand of hair behind her ear. She then smiled at them. She was a woman who believed in Grace. She had learned the long way that people needed to feel important. It wasn't enough to be strong. She told Hanna once that "It was desperately important to allow people to love you." Sometimes, it was the only way they could participate in the person's pain. Sometimes it was the only way they could show anyone that they cared and mattered to them.

Bull got in close. "Shut up and let us love you." He smiled at her and she smiled back.

It finally sunk in years ago when she was going through her first round of the cocktail adriamycin and cytoxan for her breast cancer. The doctors had gotten a pretty good handle on the nausea with compazine but the treatment left her weak. Then she heard about the car wash. The kids and teachers at the school were having a car wash for her to raise money for her medical expenses. She didn't need the money. The district had great insurance that paid for just about everything. Her expenses were nil and she had more than enough sick leave. Besides, if she did actually need the money to pay her medical bills the money the car wash would generate wouldn't be enough to pay for even one round of chemo, a few hundred dollars at the most. She at first told Darrel with all the sincerity that a fake smile could transmit that the offer, although sweet, was not truly needed, but to thank the students anyway. She remembered what the man did next. He reached out and touched her arm and focused her eyes on his so she would hear and understand what he was about to say to her.

"This isn't about your needs now, Gwen. It's about the needs of the students and staff. I know you don't need this money. They need to do this. I know you have a lot on your plate but this is one thing you have to allow these people to do. You have to let them love you. They are frustrated with the course of events. It is human nature for people to want to act. Let them," Darrel said.

"I love you guys. I really do. You're right Jessica; I do need to let you help. Just keep reminding me, okay?"

Bull's smile always brightened her day and his presence made whatever was going on around her seem not as important. He knew her history as well as she knew his. They were friends in the truest form. There was no romantic tie but there was love. He would take a bullet for her and she knew it.

"Good morning, Bull. It's good to see you." After Barbara and Jessica had secured her things she walked to the other side of the counter out of earshot. "Everything would be fine if these loving people would just let me do my job."

"They love you, dear," Bull said as he watched the two women walk away. "Some of them around here might have their helmets on a little too tight but for the most part they just want to take care of you. You've done the same if memory serves—several times." Bull still had his arm on Gwen's shoulder and she had turned to face him. He looked at her for a moment, sniffed her hair, and looked at the ceiling as if he was pondering something. "Did you shower this morning?"

"Hell, yes, I showered this morning," Gwen said in a low voice and lightly slapped Bull's chest.

"No, you look pretty good," Bull said with a sincere look on his face. He looked her over again.

"I look like crap."

"No, Pal, you really look pretty good. Chemo patients aren't supposed to look this good. They're not suppose to smell this good either. You must be using Jessica's shampoo. What is that remarkable perfume you're wearing?"

"You know it's Absorbine—for my knees."

"Ah, I thought so. In what fine store do I find a delicate sample of it being offered Sports Authority?" He said with a smile, "You really do look good."

"You think I look pretty good?" she said with an edge of seriousness in her voice. "Have I ever lied to you?"

"Yes, you have."

"I mean when you didn't want me to. Have I ever lied to you when you needed me to tell you the truth?"

Gwen realized that Bull hadn't ever lied to her–ever, except for one of her birthday parties where they had a monkey that stripped. That was a disturbing party and one that set the stage for the establishment of "party boundaries." Then he would let her know that he knew what her birthday presents were and for a price he would tell her.

"Look," he would start. "Everyone has a price and my price is...." He would tailor his cost for information to the person. He even sold information on birthday presents to the students, in exchange for part of their lunch pudding cups; after all, he was human.

She finally had to admit, "No, I guess you haven't."

He took his hand and turned her face towards the light. "See, you even have color in your cheeks." He took his thumb and started rubbing it as if it were paint.

"What are you doing?" Gwen said as she grabbed his hand to make him stop.

"Just checking to see if you painted it on today."

"You bastard," Gwen said under her breath with a smile.

"Packard Thornton at your service, Madam," Bull said. "Did you have anything to do with this party their throwing me this afternoon?" she said as she brushed her hair out of her eyes.

"You know this is supposed to be a surprise?" She knew everything that went on at the school before it actually took place. He knew she hated surprises and was not surprised at all when her illness came back after being in remission. He was in her room when she got the call from the doctor's office about the blood test results.

Her face was calm and one of expectation. She thanked the doctor for calling and hung up. He remembered her looking at him and simply saying "It's back." It took him a moment to realize what she was even talking about. The picture of that moment will be with him forever. "You better act surprised when you walk in or they're going to be pissed."

Hanna walked in the back door. She saw the two talking and stopped and listened.

"I told them I didn't want any fuss and look what they did."

"Yeah, its terrible people love you so much they want to celebrate your existence. What could they be thinking having a party for you? They should be flogged," Hanna said as she walked by.

"You know what I mean," Gwen said to both of them.

"We have had this conversation," Bull said.

"So you know what I mean."

"We've had this conversation a lot."

"Bull!"

"Gwen!"

"Mother," Hanna piped in as she stepped forward. "Look, I know you think they're doing this because you're sick. Guess what? You're probably right. I got to tell you sister, you've got the easy job. The rest of us have to stand around sitting on our hands waiting to see if this is the big one or if we still have some time—again." There was strength in her voice; firmness in what she said, a confidence.

Bull noticed the change in tempo of the room when she spoke. She wasn't a young know, nothing woman. She was mature in her thoughts and calm in her response. He had seen her around and knew her enough to say 'hi' but they hadn't truly been introduced to each other.

She had some practice in dealing with this subject before, he thought. She seemed to have been down this road with her mother before. She put her arm around her and hugged her.

"How do you know about this—,"

"I'm my mother's daughter, remember?"

Gwen turned from Hanna to Bull. "Bull, I—"

"I know dear, it scares me, too. But we just do what we can do and move on." He pushed her back so he could look at her. "Promise you'll be surprised? You know they'll think I told you, and then they won't talk to me for weeks. You know how cold Farmer can be when she's mad. I think I got a real chance with her." He looked over at Hanna and winked. Hanna just stared.

Gwen snorted into Bull's vest. "The entire FBI has a 'real' chance with her.

"Good point."

The meeting of two personalities is like the contact of two chemical substances: if there is any reaction, both are transformed.

Carl Jung (1875--1961)

Having a husband and a wife teaching at the same school isn't as rare as one might think. John and Stacey Tripoli were a young, childless couple who happened to teach at the same school. When Darrel did their review, he wrote the same thing for each of them, that they were strong and quick with their discipline of distracted children but equally as quick with their praise for them. "Come on, people," Darrel would say to them regarding "Public Displays of Affection," PDA's, the acronym usually used for teenagers who have allowed their hormones to spill over onto each other in school hallways. They were often seen making "cow eyes," as Mr. Horton called it, to each other.

"Good morning, Mr. Tripoli," Stacey said as she came up from behind him standing at the teacher's mailbox. She patted him gently on the bottom as she approached, snuggling up close to him while pretending to look into her own mailbox.

"And good morning to you, Mrs. Tripoli. Did you have a good weekend?" he asked.

"Oh yes. I had a wonderful weekend. And you? How was your weekend?"

"What did you do?" he asked as he pretended to look at the attendance sheets in his hands.

"Well, I got to sleep in on Saturday-,"

"Uh-huh."

"-then I went for a drive with this extremely handsome man out to the lake for a picnic lunch that he surprised me with."

About this time, Darrel walked into the copy room side of the mailroom; his attention was broken at the familiar sound of the Tripolis. He shook his head, and then pretended he was looking at the paper while he stood at the copier, not wanting to turn it on because it would drown out his ability to hear what they were saying.

"He sounds like a very considerate man. Did he bring all your favorite foods?"

"Very considerate and yes, he thought of everything. Then we walked around the lake for a while and he tried to teach me how to skip stones but unfortunately, I wasn't very good at it."

"I'm sure he didn't care. He probably thought you were so cute that there was nothing you could do wrong."

"Oh, my God," Darrel said as he rolled his eyes and started the machine. He had heard enough.

"He then took me to a wonderful restaurant and we dined and danced and later, well, that was wonderful as well."

"Wonderful, huh?"

"Hugely."

"Hugely?"

"Immensely."

"People, please," Horton broke in, "Not on a Monday. I'm breaking out in a sweat over here," "Sorry boss. Stacey and I were just—."

"I know, I know. But please wait until I finish before you go any further, okay? My heart can't take it."

"So uh, how was your weekend Darrel?"

"It was wonderful—hugely." The two turned and looked at each other and smiled. The Tripolis attracted the love of children. Children were drawn to them. As they walked out of the room they almost stepped on Dorthea, a small fourth-grader from the Sudan who fled the civil war with her parents, two brothers, an aunt, and uncle when they crossed into Ethiopia just outside of Bikori. That was where her uncle drowned while carrying her across the last river before they crossed the border. There was some unofficial rumor from the counselors who had worked with the family that the uncle was eaten alive by a river crocodile but no one really wanted to confirm that. To look at her was to believe that only God could make something so precious, Stacey once said. Her skin was so dark it was almost purple, offset only by her beautiful smile with her two front teeth missing, and ebony eyes.

"Hello Dorthea, are you back with us this year?" Stacey said while giving her a big hug and John looked on. "That makes me so happy."

"You have more gaps than teeth this year," John said, looking on. "I bet you have fun using a straw. You don't even have to open your mouth, huh?" Dorthea covered her giggle with her hand while Stacey was crushing her with a hug.

Darrel came out of his office and sidestepped the Tripoli's and Dorthea and walked up to Barbara. "Mrs. Gaven, I have tried three times now to get those ESL amendments from the D.O., can you call them-"

"Yes, sir, I just got off the phone; they're sending them with a runner right now,"

Darrel stopped in the hallway halfway between his office and the counter. "How did you get them to move so quick? I've been trying for the last day and a half."

"I told them I had an irate parent who was a lawyer and wanted to know why his child was not listed. I told him we couldn't place them because the list was at the District Office and that he wanted a name of someone there that he could come and talk to about it." Barbara looked up just long enough to say 'good morning' to Tony then put her head back down into her work.

"Good morning to you Mrs. Gaven," Tony said as he shuffled by.

"Are they still buying that line? How many times have we used it this semester?" Darrel said with a smile.

"I used a Bosnian accent this time. They thought I was a parent volunteer."

"Oooh, nice touch. What does that sound like?"

"Don't ask," Barbara said.

Darrel turned back to his office and saw the Tripolis. "Is your committee set for Mrs. Jackson's party this afternoon?"

Stacey and John both looked up. "Yes sir, Mrs. Holtfield and Miss Sonet are all set with cake, ice cream, and the plaque you ordered," said Stacey.

"Did they collect enough in donations? I'll cover the shortage if she went too much on the plaque," Darrel said.

"Cost wasn't an issue here. Gwen's done so much for this district, and each of us; it isn't enough. It's not fair that-," John said joining the conversation.

"I know, I know," Darrel responded with a sigh.

"Why did she even coming back this year?" John asked.

"She's been here over thirty years. She wants to stay as long as she can work, as long as she can teach. This is her life."

John grew quiet in his question. "How long? Did you hear anything about what the doctors said about how long it might be?"

Darrel looked up from his paper. "No one knows—or they're simply not telling. She's been in remission twice. This third time, I don't think she'll beat. But that's why there's not an MD after my name. But if you talk to her, it's just another walk in the park. Of all the people I know, she is the last one I'd wish this on."

"Keep true to the dreams of thy youth."

Friedrich von Schiller (1759--1805)

The smell of the fresh-cut grass drifted in the propped-open door of Hanna Jarger's 4th grade classroom. The walls were covered in cabinets and whiteboards and the desks were lined in neat, straight rows facing the front of the class, which also contained Hanna's desk, next to the window. Hanna had her back to the door. She pulled the last few items out of a box that she hadn't had a chance to get to at beginning of the year. She put down the picture of her family she'd taken from her nightstand.

She decided that morning she wanted it at school where she could see it all the time instead of at home. She didn't know why. Her father had not been around for decades. There were times in her life that weeks or even months would go by and she never thought of him. But since she had come home, there wasn't a day she didn't wander into a thought about her dad. It was odd, really. She didn't even tell Gwen because it felt like she was coming up with something to feel sorry for. There were times throughout her life that she would have ideas and questions about him, his life, what he did, or didn't do. If Gwen couldn't answer the question, which was rare, Hanna remembered spending days trying to solve the question—whatever it was. She remembered when she was twenty and she went to a Halloween party. She dressed up like a Marine sergeant, complete with a plastic machine gun, face paint, and the traditional chewed-on cigar. She threw the cigar away shortly after she got there because it was making her sick to her stomach.

Hanna grew up liking competition. Her mother was heard on

more than one occasion telling her that she was her father's daughter. After shellacking Johnny Childers and his Stingray, there were other victims. She loved sports, playing and even watching them. She played all the sports in grade school and high school that she could, but softball was her favorite. There was a part of her that seemed free and natural when she played. She told herself that she was good at this. Some of the happiest times in her life were when she was on the field. She was fast and strong but still kept a woman's figure and personality. She was still Hanna, but when she was playing a sport, she became someone else.

"Hey, batter batter, hey, batter batter," she would say in unison with the others on the field. When she thought about, she became someone that she thought her father would love to have around, a daughter and a son, rolled up in one.

It had been years since she had seen the mitt that she used all through high school. The last she'd seen of it was when the Lynches' golden retriever, Girly, was shaking it like a rag doll after Hanna laid it down on the Lynches' front lawn next to the crosswalk in order to get something out of her backpack. She had loved that glove. She loved the smell of it, sweaty leather. She used to walk home from practice with the mitt open and resting on her face. She breathed in deep lung-filling vapors of cowhide and the sweat from her hand. Tony, when he was standing at the crosswalk, would place it on her head as a hat while she crossed the street. She had broken it in and used to keep it under her bed with a softball in it and rubber bands wrapped around it to hold it in place and give it a natural form. Tony had taught her how to do that. As the dog ran away from her, she chased and finally cornered her, pulling the mitt from its mouth. The laces had been shredded along with half of the webbing and large holes had been opened in the thumb. She walked home crying as Tony and a few other high school students she was with watched her and tried to comfort her.

She gently wiped off the picture and placed it on her desk after she removed it from her backpack. A slight smile came to her face. She had a few of the windows open, allowing a gentle breeze to move across the room. Between the traffic outside dropping off children and being focused on her task, she didn't hear Tony walk into the room through the open door. The man entered gently, remembering to take off the well-worn baseball cap with the faded name of "Borman" stenciled on it. He stood there to see if Hanna would turn around and after a few moments cleared his throat to make himself known.

"Morning, Hanna, I mean Mrs. Jarger."

Hanna looked up and smiled. The memory of the crossing was still there but she still came across the room and hugged him. He had always been a presence in her life, around the house, at this school, on the street corner, talking to her mother or on her way to college. He was grayer now. His walk was a little more labored. Sometimes she noticed it more than other times. The look of the simple man in the brown eyes seemed a little simpler now, she thought. Not as quick as before, but then she thought, he never was. Her mother told her since she was very young that Tony was "special." His mind was injured years ago but he was able to land this job with a forward thinking district, which prided itself on hiring the "handicapped." He was a phenomenally loyal employee. The school could always count on Tony.

"Tony, oh it's good to see you this morning," she said while she gave him a hug. She remembered the man who would hug her every morning after she crossed the street. She had seen him from the house in his small apartment out back but they hadn't really talked for the time she was away in the townhouse. And since she had been back, all their brief conversations have been short, cordial but short. They waved to each other as Hanna was going out or coming back. When she was living in her own place, she saw him hardly at all, even when she came home to visit her mother or to take her to the doctor. She could tell when he saw her around the house that he wanted to stand and chat. She just wasn't up for that, not with him.

"I'm just a little bit older than the last time. Moving a little slower too," he said. His smile was a little heavier on the ends and one side was higher than the other. The crow's feet around the eyes were more distinct, wider than the last time she saw him; when was it? She thought to herself. Was it this morning or yesterday? His eyes were still the twinkling brown set on a clear white background. Tony was still in there.

"I think we've all changed, Tony. You're still looking just as good as always. How long

has it been since the last time we talked?" There was awkwardness in her voice. She knew she hadn't talked more than just saying 'hello' to him in the morning, for a long time. It was as if she was trying to avoid him, an impossible task in such a small environment. She was wondering why he hadn't come in sooner.

"Four months and three weeks since you moved in," Tony interrupted with a smile.

"Four months and—,"

"—Three weeks. We've talked a little bit but you've been busy." There was a look on his face. He looked at her as if he didn't remember or even notice that she had been avoiding him. "Three weeks," she repeated after him. "Well, you look just as good as ever."

"We talked a lot when you were younger—when you walked to this school—and when you walked from your mother's house to go to West High School, too," Tony said.

"And West High," repeated Hanna.

"And Phoenix College," Tony said.

"—and Phoenix College. You were my protector. You even worried about whether I was dressed warmly enough, and if I had remembered my lunch."

"You just lived four houses from the corner of the school Mrs. Jarger. You had to cross the same corner for all of those schools. I didn't help you cross when you went out to the University because you were driving by then and you didn't need me to help you cross the street. You were driving by then," Tony repeated while shaking his head as if he knew the answer.

"Nope, you're right, I was driving by then. But sometimes I would come home this way and you would make me stop my car so you could cross some children."

Tony smiled at the memory. "Yeah, and sometimes you would

stay and talk to me and tell me about your day at the University. And now we get to work together."

"We sure do." Hanna smiled at the memory and then glanced away. "You always made sure I was safe," she whispered. Tony looked at her as she appeared to be working on memories. "Your mother sure is happy that you are here and back home. So am I."

"Oh, I don't know about that. Mom always liked being independent and now I'm back in with her. I think she was getting used to having me gone and now her baby has crawled back home."

Tony was staring at the desk while she talked. He picked up the old picture of Hanna, Gwen, and Hanna's father, Elias, holding Hanna in his arms. The man held Hanna close and Elias and Gwen were looking at their daughter. He put the photograph down when she was done speaking and turned to look at her. "Your mother has been talking of nothing else about you coming to live at home again. She is usually very smiley but when she found out that you were coming home; she was like a mother bird with its nest. Who do you think she talked into helping paint?"

Hanna smiled. "You? Oh, I'm sorry. You really think she wants me home? It really is making a difference with me, too. I've had—,"

"Yep, your mother had me working like a Trojan slave," Tony interrupted with a smile.

Hanna paused and looked at the picture that Tony had just set down. "It's been a tough couple of years for me."

"Your mother knows," he said, softening his voice.

Hanna changed the subject. "So has it been a good school year for you so far? You've been doing this so long you should be able to do it in your sleep, huh?"

Tony smiled, "Yes ma'am. They made me assistant custodian three years ago. I get to help Lyle around the school during the day."

Hanna smiled with surprise, "That's right, I heard about that. I saw him. He's gotten a crown of silver like you."

Tony smiled while rubbing his hands through his hair. "Oh,

Mrs. Jarger, he is ten years younger than me. He's real smart too. He is my friend."

Hanna knew Tony's simplicity. Tony was just "Tony" to her. But for the first time she saw him as a man getting older and with age she had a flash of worry that he was now becoming vulnerable to the world outside.

"I used to come out early in the morning and wait to cross the boys and girls. I wanted to get the signs out early so the cars know it's a school day and to be careful. I still get the signs out early so the cars know it's a school day. It's a little harder now days because I'm still sleepy when I put out the signs. But the kids need me to have the signs out and I need to be there early so the kids can get across the street." Tony paused to catch his breath. "I remember seeing you down in front of your house with your Momma. She would walk you to the sidewalk and see me and wave. I would wave back and keep my eyes on you until you got to me and then make sure you got tucked into school safe. You liked to come play in the gym with the other kids who came early remember? Your mother would let you come to school early and play with the others."

Hanna openly laughed at the picture of her mother walking her out to the sidewalk. "You did that even when I went to college. I remember I would ride my bike and you would make me get off and cross at that same corner. What was that saying you would always tell me?"

"Look left; look right; no cars coming."

Hanna smiled with a snap of her fingers "Yeah, that was it. Even in college when I was late for class you would still stop me. Sometimes, I have to admit, I'd get so mad at you."

"I know, but it was my job to keep you safe. It still is." He paused for a minute. He was back in time. "Sometimes the other kids would get mad at me too. They would call me names and say bad things to me. I got sad sometimes because they would say them in front of you. I didn't want you to hear those things."

Hanna remembered those words and those moments. They were fresh in her brain. That rattled her. She never thought he heard or at least she never thought he cared. "Ah, but I'm all grown up now, Tony," Hanna said.

"I know. Everyone grows up and grows old. But you will always be a little girl up here," he said as he pointed to his head. I have to get back to work now. Is your mother in her classroom?" Tony said as he turned to leave.

"I think so. Are you going to go see her?"

"He doesn't have too," Gwen said as she entered the room.

"How are you feeling this morning, Mom?" Hanna said, peeking around Tony. Gwen was carrying a stack of files and loose papers in both arms. Her reading glasses were down on her nose.

"About the same as when you asked me this morning before you left the house, and yes, we're all set," Hanna said as she moved an empty box from her desk.

"Good morning, Tony," Gwen said, placing her head against his shoulder because her arms were full. Tony gave her a quick hug. "It's always good to see you in the morning."

"Good morning, Mrs. Jackson. I was just saying good morning to our Ms. Jarger here," he said as he pointed his thumb towards Hanna. "Excuse me ladies, I have to get to my corner. My charges are coming." Tony turned and left the room as quietly as when he entered.

"You always said that, too," Hanna whispered to her mother.

"Said what dear?" Gwen asked.

"'My charges'. He always called us his charges."

Gwen moved across the room towards Hanna and saw the framed photograph on her desk. "You still have this old photo." Gwen had a look of surprise on her face. "I thought we lost this. This was taken two days before he went back to Vietnam."

Hanna stopped loading the fourth grade reading books on the shelf and moved back to her desk next to her mother. "That was a long time ago. About four months before he died, you once told me."

She paused for a minute and looked at her mother. The lines around her eyes, she hadn't noticed how deep they cut, how much more pronounced they were. Her hair showed even more silver.

Hanna knew there was a difference; doing life, her illness, the job, were all taking their toll.

She found herself becoming the mother in some regards as their lives now intertwined again. She found herself saying things to her mother that only a mother would say to her child. "Did you take your medicine? Don't stay out late on your walk." She would check on her during the day and ask her if she needed to rest or if she wanted her to cook dinner, or breakfast, or lunch. She would write her notes to remind her to take her pills or to follow up with the doctor and call him if she felt any of the dozen symptoms that went along with the cocktail of medications she was on. This wore away at Gwen but she silently accepted it.

"Do you still miss him?" Hanna said as she looked at the picture.

Gwen's smile left her face. She glanced over at her daughter then back to the picture. "Sometimes. Some times are worse than others. Then there are times it's like he never left."

"You think about him a lot?" Hanna asked almost in a whisper.

"'Every damn day' as your father would say. It's silly," she responded as the smile came back to her face.

Hanna was puzzled by the smile. "What?"

"I can still smell his cologne—Aqua-Velva."

"When do you miss him most?"

"You'll think this is silly."

"No, I won't."

Gwen smiled. She was lost in the memory. "When I go for my walks at night; that's when I feel him the most. It's like he never left." Hanna could see she was there, reliving that moment and then as quickly as it came, it was gone. "I have to get back. The kids are starting to arrive," Gwen said as she turned to leave. "Let me know if you need anything, dear." She stopped when Hanna spoke.

"He's a funny guy," Hanna said, looking out the window at Tony crossing the children at the crosswalk.

"Who is, dear?"

"Tony," Hanna said as he pointed out the window with a nod of her head. "How long has he been here?"

Gwen stopped and looked out the window. "Tony got here some time after I did."

Hanna paused and then asked, "Has he always been—slow? I mean, I've always known him this way but when he first came here, has he always been—," She paused for a minute. "It seems like he's getting worse."

Gwen looked at Hanna and then out the window. "For at least as long as I've worked here." She paused and looked at her daughter. There was firmness in her voice. "You have always been embarrassed by him, living in the house out back."

Hanna stumbled a little with a response. It seemed like there needed to be a response, one that would cover her feelings. She didn't know they had been that obvious. For years, she thought, she put up a pretty good front. Now, she felt like she needed to either justify her actions or defend them, minimizing them. "I wouldn't say that I was 'embarrassed,' that seems a little strong."

Gwen just nodded her head. "You have been since you were fourteen. It was even before then, remember? Even when you were tiny. He loved you like a daughter, or as close to a daughter as a man in his condition could love. Even after that day, he hasn't changed, except to protect you."

Hanna looked at her mother. "What do you mean?"

"I mean that—," Gwen paused and looked out the window. She watched the man. She was thinking, thinking hard, Hanna noticed. "For years he has noticed yours and others' treatment of him. He heard every word spoken about him by the children, by the adults, even by the teachers. He has heard you respond to the hardness of those students when they spoke to you about him, about him being your 'Daddy'. He knew how bad it hurt you to be associated with him. There was a time when you were young; actually, you were college age. You tried to avoid him all together. He noticed how you sometimes took the other side of the street so he couldn't cross you. He noticed how you would look away when he waved to you, pretending you weren't able to see him wave." Gwen grew quiet.

"He knew, he absolutely knew, you thought he was stupid." Then Gwen smiled. "But he still fixed your bike when the tires went flat so you didn't have to walk." Gwen turned to her daughter. "You probably don't remember this, but when you were younger you got sick—real sick, and I was at work. The doctor called in a prescription for you but I couldn't go get it. Tony walked to the pharmacy for me and got the medicine and came back and gave it to you."

"I don't remember that." She paused. "Wait, yes I do."

Gwen nodded again. "He stayed and made you some chicken soup and sat in the living room and listened for you. When I came home he was standing in the doorway watching you. I asked him what he was doing and he said he was watching you breathe—to 'make sure you kept breathing' he said. You were thirteen and it wasn't long after that you told me you didn't want him going to your birthday party. You didn't know it but he was standing on the back porch, directly behind you."

"God, what an idiot."

"It didn't end there. You still find it hard to be around him. Problem is, he knows."

"Why didn't you ever tell me?"

"Tell you what, honey? Tell you something that you already knew? The fact is, we all knew it. He and I both knew how you felt." She paused again. "He said it a long time ago to me and I told him I didn't believe that you would eventually feel the way you did. But he was right."

Gwen didn't say anything for a moment. She just looked out the window. Nothing was there, Tony, cars, children, nothing moved. "Don't ever judge a person by their appearance on the outside. The core of who they are is under their skin and that man is a walking example." Her eyes softened again, as if she was catching herself. "His heart has always loved this school. He took a special interest in you, ever since you were young. He's always asked me how you were doing." She paused again as she watched Tony come back into view. A small smile came to her lips. But there was sadness in her eyes. "Do you know how you can tell he is worried about something?" she said to Hanna as she turned to look at her then back to Tony. "He walks with his hands behind his back and his head down, like he's in the middle of some great thought process." It was almost inaudible when she spoke. "He always asked me how you were doing."

Hanna and Gwen watched Tony through the window, neither of them saying anything. Tony stopped for a moment on the far side of the street and looked up and down the road for kids. The sun broke the tree line of the houses down the street and lit up the top of his head. He shielded his eyes from its brightness and stood still for a moment. "He still stops to watch the sun rise. Tony's mind, a lot of people think, is the mind of a child, but it's not. He's just slower than most, but his heart—he'd give up life itself for someone he loves."

"Does he have any family?" Hanna asked.

"I think there's someone," Gwen said. She smiled, "Get ready for your class, honey. I prayed that we could some day work together. I just wish it was under—,"

"I'll take what I can get," Hanna said smiling. They hugged; Gwen turned and walked out of the room, "I'll see you at lunch then," speaking over her shoulder.

Without friends, no one would choose to live, though he had all other goods.

ARISTOTLE, 384 BC-322 BC

Late September

The "surprise" party was set for lunchtime. Bull had the assignment of bringing Gwen to the teacher's lounge on whatever excuse he could create. Gwen normally ate lunch in her classroom so there was concern she would not come unless someone could persuade her, like Bull. As the lunch bell sounded and the children bailed from their classrooms to scramble to lunch, Bull swam against the tide of little ones and entered Gwen's room. They sat together for a few minutes, giving an impression to those in the teacher's lounge that she was struggling with Bull's request to come. After a couple of minutes the two walked down to the lounge, took a deep breath, and entered.

Everyone, except those who had playground duty, was there. Everyone yelled "surprise" and Gwen did the best she could to pretend it was for real. All the other staff and a few from the District Office also attended. The group jumped right in singing "Waltzing Matilda," a song that Gwen made the mistake of saying she liked several years prior and now has become her "theme song." She never could admit she liked Kenny Loggins' "*Danger Zone*" from the movie "Top Gun." That admission seemed out of character for her. When Kenny, whom she had a secret crush since he and Messina did "*Pooh Corner*" sings "*Spreading out her wings tonight*" it still gave her goose bumps. She was half Scottish. "Matilda" was Australian. But she guessed no one knew any Scottish songs or even Irish, so they went with Matilda.

"Thank you everyone," Gwen started. "I don't think I have ever heard that song sung so badly in all my life. Bruce," she said as she pointed to Bruce Holinger, standing in the corner next to Tony, "You really stink. No, I mean it, you're really bad, but I love you anyway." She bit hard on her lower lip as she looked around the room. Hanna had come up to her side as she entered the room while Bull stayed back next to the door. He grabbed a Diet Pepsi, popped the top and took a healthy swig.

"I know why we're having this today and not at the end of the year when I actually do retire. We're not kidding anyone knowing that my last day may truly be my last day. I've spent many years at this school, longer than some of you have been alive. I have earned my retirement points years ago. I've worked alongside every one of you. We've disagreed from time to time. We've even argued and then made up. But we've never, for one moment, forgotten why we're here: the babies." She looked at Hanna as if to convey something unspoken. "These are inner city kids we have here. They used to be upper middle class with a stay-at-home mom and dad with a retirement plan. Now, we're lucky to see one parent, sober, and not on food stamps or high on drugs. Every one of these kids is our babies," she said emphasizing the word 'our' to make the point. "We have to give them back at the end of the day, but for a cherished eight hours we can pour our hearts and souls into them. We can teach them more then math and suffixes. We can teach them right from wrong, good from evil, and we can soak them with love." She looked around the room, her eyes falling from one staffer to the next, including Hanna, Tony, and Darrel. "Ever since my husband, Elias, left us, Hanna or I have been at this school. I love each and every one of you; you have loved both my daughter and me. I would love to be able to tell you all that I'm positive I'll beat this thing. I can't do that. But I can look each of you in the eye and honestly say that I am one of the most content people on this earth. I get to teach the kids I love with people I treasure and now I know I get to do it all alongside my own daughter. I am truly blessed. A toast, to the babies!"

Everyone raised their glasses and responded, "The babies!"

Bull and Hanna both walked up to Gwen at the same time.

Just as Bull reached her, his pager went off. Both of them looked at it. The number was known to Bull. It was his Sergeant's cell phone number with a "10-8" after it. The number was code to let Bull know that there was a need for him to respond. They were scrambling the Neighborhood Resource Unit before the city's tactical unit SWAT team. Although they didn't have all the guns and other toys that the SWAT team did, they were quicker to deploy and most of the time, they were enough.

"You have to go?" Gwen said.

"I'll see you tomorrow," he said softly to her as he kissed her on the cheek.

"You better. Oh, Bull, before you go, I want to finally and formally introduce you to my daughter, Hanna Jarger. Hanna, this is Packard Thornton. He's our school resource officer, or SRO. He is a man of many talents. Bull, this is my own baby."

Bull reached out to shake Hanna's hand. His smile was not reciprocated. There was anger in her eyes. Something was wrong with this picture. "Hanna, your mother has spoken of little else. I know we've said 'hi' around campus but it is a pleasure to finally meet you."

"I've heard a lot about you too, Officer Thornton. I hear you're pretty tough on these kids," she said as she finished shaking his hand. Gwen felt the tension level between the two. It surprised her.

"Hanna, I don't think that is—," Gwen started to say.

Hanna kept on talking as if her mother weren't there. "Don't you think these kids need love more than they need a storm trooper standing on their chest?"

"Hanna!" Gwen said looking around. No one else was listening.

"It's all right, Gwen," Bull said softly to her without taking his eyes off Hanna. "It is truly a pleasure to meet you, Ms. Jarger. I have heard a lot about you and I'm sure I speak for the rest of the school when I say we are all looking forward to working with you this coming year." He turned and kissed Gwen on the cheek again. "I got to go. I'll talk to you later." He left the room as quietly as he'd entered, patting Tony on the arm on his way out the door. No one but the two women heard the conversation.

"What was that all about?" Gwen whispered to Hanna after Bull left.

"I've just seen so many men like him. They think they know everything and they try to bully the whole world into conforming to their way of thinking, including these kids. I know you—," Hanna stopped when her mother put her finger to her lips to hush her.

"You have, have you? Well, Officer Thornton is my friend, my good friend. You stick around and watch what he does. He has some prejudices to overcome. We all do and he does it well," she whispered to Hanna while her eyes moved around the room looking for a sign if anyone was picking up their conversation. "I don't know where this came from but you need to flush it–quickly."

"Mother, come on, you know as well as I–," Hanna responded, also looking around to see if they were being watched. Hanna had realized that she had spoken her thoughts when she should have kept them to herself. She realized too late that she had stepped into something that was going to stick to the bottom of her shoe like a wad of children's bubble gum until she fixed it.

"I know he is a good man. Until you get to know him, you don't qualify to judge him. I never taught you any differently. You learned that somewhere other than in our home," Gwen said. Her eyes had caught a couple of teachers looking at her as she finished who smiled and waved her over. Hanna looked past her mother and out the wall of windows to the parking lot. She could see Bull walking out to the police car parked under the peppercorn tree on the far side of the lot, still carrying his soda.

He was talking into his hand-held radio microphone that hung from the shoulder strap on his shirt. The other end was connected to his radio on his belt. He climbed into the car and put the can of soda carefully in the drink carrier on the dashboard. He put the keys in the ignition and started the car. His computer, MDT, or Mobil Dispatch Terminal, came on line and he typed in his call sign and punched in "10-8." He snapped the seatbelt, put the car in gear, took another large slug of his soda and drove slowly out of the parking lot. When he got to the street he flipped on the lights. When he got to the main street, away from the homes, Hanna could hear the siren come on. She shook her head indiscernibly; never again, she thought. She then walked over to where her mother stood.

Pale Death with impartial tread beats at the poor man's cottage door and at the palaces of kings.

-Horace 65 BC-8 BC

When people ask a police officer where the bad parts of town are, they get a wide selection of answers. One of the answers would have been the area in and around 1253 W. Jackson Avenue.

1253 W. Jackson Avenue housed a man, his common-law wife, her two pre-teen sons by two different men, and their infant daughter. Bull would say the house and family fit the profile of why society has a social services division. The division exists specifically for families like this one. They had received assistance from almost all departments, from food stamps to pre-natal care, to anger management and drug counseling. The two older kids attended the K-8 school three blocks down and twice a day, once going and once coming back, walked passed the hazardous waste recycling plant. They got used to the air burning their eyes, especially in the afternoon. Their father worked, sometimes; drank most of the time, and beat them in between. This was the place that Bull was called to.

He pulled his car up to the scene after passing the outer perimeter check point and the officer there waving him through the taped-off road. Up ahead, he could see at least a dozen patrol cars and the police response van. Overhead, the helicopter kept an orbit over the house that he could not yet see. He pulled up next to the van where the bulk of the officers were standing at the opened back doors of the van. Bull smiled as he recognized the sergeant standing on the steps just inside the back doors. "This should be good," Bull said to himself as he drained the soda and got out of the car after popping the trunk. There was a moment he thought of his daughter. It came in a wave sometimes. He didn't know when it would show but all of a sudden it was upon him. "Get your mind on the game boy," he said to himself. He knew these thoughts could bring him to his knees. What if he died? His daughter would become a ward of the state. He had dreams of watching his daughter wheeled out of her room and moved down the hall to a closet because he wasn't around and the insurance lapsed because he wasn't alive to pay it. It was always the same thought. He was able to stuff it away. He knew he couldn't be thinking about 'what ifs' while he was trying to figure out the reality in front of him. He closed his eyes and breathed slowly until the wave ebbed.

He went to the trunk and pulled out his jump bag and unlocked the Remington 870 with the collapsible stock and the cut down barrel. It was the perfect weapon for violent people in close quarters. There was never a lot of discussion as to the finer points of life when someone evil was taking a round of OO buckshot at two feet. The debate was pretty much over at that point. The weapon's operator didn't have to be much of an aim either. They just had to have it pointed in the general direction and be able to pull the trigger faster than the one they were pointing it at.

Bull shut the trunk and walked up to the crowd of officers and began to listen as Sgt. Stan Garrison began the briefing of the situation. On the inside of the back door to the van was a white board and what looked like an outline of the house and its rooms. Garrison was an old salt like Bull and the two had actually been partners years ago before Stan went one career direction and Bull went another. Both were former Marines and Bull was godfather to Stan's son. Stan had a head of stubbled silver hair like Bull's and talked in a groveled voice from years of smoking "El Presidente" cigars.

"Well, hot damn, we can start now. Officer Thornton has blessed us with his presence. Good to see your fat ass here, Bull. I hope we didn't pull you away from anything real important. We just have a 918 threatening his family and shooting up the good citizens of this neighborhood," Stan said, sliding the cigar to the side of his cheek and then rolling it with his lips. As he spoke, he would occasionally take the cigar from his mouth and point with it. This always caused a spit string to drape from the end of the shredded end to be drawn out to his lips and inevitably break like a vine in the jungle.

"Stan, you know I love you more than all the other sergeants and want to spend every available moment in your reflective sunshine. Please continue with your wonderful dissertation." He finished transferring his radio to the vest pocket of his Kevlar vest and stuck the tactical earpiece into the end of the radio after removing the hand mike. He then pulled his helmet out of his bag and zippered the bag shut. The helmet had a built-in mike, which also plugged into the radio. He left the helmet unbuckled until it was time to go.

"All right, as I was saying. We have a distraught father slash ex-boyfriend holding her and their common law child hostage in the house. He's pretty three-ninety; he's been hitting the bottle since about nine this morning as far as we can tell. From what we can gather from the limited phone contact with him, the last thirty minutes or so, she's pregnant again and he doesn't think it's his. Every once in a while we can hear him put the phone down and go over and hit the woman. She's crying, the baby's crying, everyone's on the edge. They have two others in school as far as we can tell. We need to try to pacify this thing until the Special Assignments Unit shows up with the negotiators. Also, it sounds like another male is there. From what we are gathering from the relatives, it's the drunk's cousin from El Paso. He's wired as well and it sounds like he is encouraging the other guy. We are probably not going to be able to wait for SAU. We think they're going to plant the woman and the kid and do a suicide by cop thing." Garrison pointed to the white board on the door with the lay out of the house drawn on it.

"Here's the layout, as best that we can gather from the neighbors, of the inside of the house. We hope to hold this until SAU shows but we need to be prepared quickly to go if it gets worse. We think the woman and child are in this room." Garrison pointed to a room in the center of the house, just off the living room from the front door. “The Shit’ums are here,” Garrison pointed to the living room in the front of the house. “Behind the living room is the kitchen, then a short exit to the back door. Down the other side of the living room are the bedrooms, and another exit to the back yard. We think the kid’s in here,” Garrison points to a small alcove. “The woman’s either there or in here.” He stubbed at the living room with his cigar. “From the gunfire that we are getting, it sounds like they got a Mac Ten and what we think is a 357.” The team looked at each other and shook their heads. “The guy can’t afford food, or to pay the water bill, but he can afford a thousand dollar weapon. Shit, he probably has a big screen in the living room.”

“Not for long,” someone quibbled.

“Don’t kill it unless you have to,” Garrison said, pointing with his cigar. “Tarnelli, you and your team take the front with me. Boswick and Cramer, you flash bang at this window here,” he said, pointing to a window around the back of the house on the white board. “Make sure you rake that window really well to draw them back there. Only do it when we give you the go- ahead. Bull, you and your team will key the back door when we do the front after Boswick does his thing. Any questions? Okay troops, we’re on channel 10. Let’s move like we have a purpose,” Stan said as he shoved the soaking wet end of his unlit cigar back into his mouth.

The team quickly began to deploy around the house, crouching down, trying not to provide a good target to the men in the house.

They moved through neighbor’s yards, coming up on the rear of the house through a back alley as well as the blind side of the front of the house, using the garage as cover. As Bull’s team moved through the alley, the odors that were cooking with the heat of the day started to make them gag. The alley itself buzzed with flies, and had been used as a toilet for the homeless. Dead kittens dotted a space just off the road and down the alley about fifty feet. The men moved through the alley as quietly as possible but each house seemed to have its own pit bull that began barking as they entered the throat of the alley where it met the street. In back of the house, the yard was exposed to the open alley through a chain link gate. There was a broken wooden fence on both sides that went to the neighbor's yard. Bull and two other officers got to the back gate and opened it just enough to slide through. Bull had carried the entry bag which contained tools like bolt cutters and laid it down behind the shed where he took up a cover position. The team found a spot behind and just to the side of the shed. The yard was all dirt with a clothesline on the far side, opposite from the shed. There was a car up on blocks and another that looked like it might actually run, parked next to the shed. From under the short back porch came the sound of a chain moving. "I hear a chain," Bull whispered. "That could only mean a dog." There was only one kind of dog in these neighborhoods: a pit bull. It drew all three officers' attention, especially after it cleared the porch and started towards the men with a growl that rolled into a bark.

"Tommy, snuff him," Bull said to the officer to his right, who was already moving to do so. The officer pulled out a can of pepper spray and hit the dog with a stream of spray from about twenty feet. The dog stopped in its tracks, blinked and then began to sneeze and wheeze rubbing its face with its paws as it stumbled to the side of the house at the farthest reach of its chain. Bull could hear in his earpiece Stan calling the units deployed around the property to check in as soon as they were in position.

"Sam thirty-two. All units, check in once you're twenty-three," Stan said in a matter-of-fact tone. Bull could hear the individual team members' call signs begin to report in as ordered.

"Charlie three-forty-one, we're twenty-three."

"Paul thirty-one is twenty-three."

It was Bull's turn. "Four thirty-two Adam is twenty-three." He turned to Tommy Slovel, who was crouched behind the house after spraying the dog. Bull put his hand over his mike and turned to Tommy. "You know what I don't like about these operations?" he started while adjusting his chinstrap. "Every time I do this, I have to pee."

Tommy just smiled and pointed to the alley. "You don't have to go far to find a toilet around here, that's for sure." Tommy paused and looked back at the house and then back at Bull. "Why the hell did you have to mention that? Now I have to go."

Just as the two stood up to go use the public facilities behind them, the back door to the house opened. The two quickly squatted back down behind the corner of the shed.

Bull spoke in a whisper activating the mike. "Four thirty-two Adam to Sam thirty-two, hold your positions, we have one coming out the back door. We're going to try to take him." Bull waited for Garrison's acknowledgment and then moved his people into position. The team had been together for three years and was well aware of each other and what each could, and more importantly, could not do. Individual strengths and weaknesses were always in play. From here, they moved with hand signals. A Hispanic man came through the door and stumbled down the steps. It was obvious to the officers that he was either drunk or high. He was carrying what looked like a .357-revolver in the front of his pants. He skidded down the steps heading towards the car parked just a few steps from the door. He had to turn his back to the men when he opened the door and sat in the driver's seat. Bull moved from his squatting position to the driver's door. He felt his knees creak and he had a low grunt of an ache. Tommy followed Bull and the other officer, "Flap Jack" Riggins, went to the passenger door. The window was down on the driver's door. As Bull approached, he slung his shotgun over his shoulder and then drew his Glock. The man did not have time to put the key in the ignition before the gun was pressed in the side of his face. "Mister, tell me one reason why I shouldn't operate on your brain stem right now," Bull said with his teeth clenched. There was something about this whole thing, the looks of the house, the alley, the stench, the drunken man in front of him, too many years working the street told him that this was not going to end well. The thoughts of the house and the mother and child filled his brain. No, this was not going to end well at all, he thought.

"Eat shi–," was all the man could voice before Bull shoved the barrel of his Glock into the man's cheek. He pushed himself on him, almost crawling on top of him in the car. His knee grounded into the man's thigh while his empty hand had the man's throat. "Wrong thing to say this week." The drunken man struggled for only a few seconds. Maybe it was the look in Bull's eyes. Something he saw as an indicator that right at that moment, he could die, that seemed to cause a moment of sobrietal clarity, the man quit fighting and submitted to the arrest. Or maybe it was the forty-caliber gun, with a bullet the size of a middle-aged man's little finger, traveling at just over one thousand feet per second, shoved into his cheekbone. In any case, he was pulled from the car, thrown on the ground and cuffed by Bull while the other two watched the house for any action that might be coming their way.

Bull cleared on the radio once they dragged the man back behind the shed. "4-32 Adam. We have secured one. We might want to go before this guy is missed."

"Copy, Four thirty-two. We just had another bad phone call. It's sounding worse inside. All units stand by for entry as planned." Bull turned to his team and gave deployment orders. Bull and Tommy would take up positions by the back door leaving Flap Jack to guard the prisoner and to give them cover fire from the shed. Tommy picked up the crow bar from the entry bag for the door. He carried his MP-5 and the crow bar to the door with Bull giving him cover. The other team that had the side of the house met them there. Tommy quickly slung his weapon and prepared to place the crow bar on the doorknob side of the door. The door opened out so the only way to open it was to pry it outward. It was a bar about four feet long and made of reinforced steel. It didn't bend but because of its length it had a tremendous amount of leverage. Bull had re-holstered his Glock and went back to his shotgun. He took up a cover position on the knob side of the door but back about five steps. If anyone opened the door to shoot any of the officers, Bull was far enough back to get a good shot and kill whatever was going to try to kill them.

Tommy set the bar in the doorframe and got ready to shove. He knew these older doors could be deceiving; sometimes they break in half or splinter. Sometimes they pop like a cork. The key was the rush. There was a team in front and their team in back. Tommy wondered, as they all did, could they get to the shooter before he killed the kid and the woman?

Phil Boswick and Joey Cramer were planted on both sides of what they thought was a bedroom window. Phil used a mirror to try to see inside the room. The light in the room was poor but he could see through the room and into a lit area on the far side. The area where they thought the shooter and the hostages were being held. They could see movement in the room. It was only a guess as to where the woman and the child might be in the house. Boswick thought an image just on the other side of the open door, lying on the ground, was an adult foot. It was dark, but in the man's pacing, he walked over in the direction of the foot.

"All units stand by," came Garrison's voice. Boswick and Cramer would rake the window they were standing at, breaking windows and then throwing in a flash bang, causing enough noise to distract the man inside. The team in front would break the front door with the ram or "Universal Key" and then throw in their flash bang. The team at the back door, Bull's group, would then enter. They had all done it many times before, but each time was always like the first time. The whole thing would only take a few seconds and then peace would be restored, for a while at least. But before the peace, for a short period of time, it would become very, very violent.

With a nod of the head from Boswick to indicate he was ready, Cramer would hit the individual windowpanes in the old steel case window with his expandable baton. Boswick cleared on the radio. "Paul-31."

"Paul-31," Garrison came back.

"We're in position. We have visual on the primary, the female and we think the baby is on the wall just to the left of front door."

"Paul 31, Sam-32, we need to expedite entry. The individual is becoming worse. We are not going to wait for SAU. Paul 31, we will go on your drop."

"Back door is ready."

"Front door is ready."

"Sam -32 to all units, we're go."

Boswick secured his radio and nodded to Cramer. As he did, he pulled a hand-sized object from a case on the side of his web gear. It looked like a can of beans without the label on it. When Cramer saw his partner open his mouth, he knew he was ready. The over pressure from the concussion would create a temporary loss of hearing. Opening the mouth helped eliminate that problem.

He raked the window with his baton, trying to make as much noise as possible, then Boswick tossed in the flash bang and both men went to their knees and covered their ears. The hand-held explosive had about a two second delay and then it flashed. The sound it made was deafening. Their sole purpose is to make a crisp, loud concussion, leaving just a puff of smoke and a growl in the belly. The violence began.

Bull and his team stood almost frozen at the back door. They heard the window and then the concussion. They began to pry the door. Within a second of the explosion they heard the Universal Key hit the front door and the yelling of officers making entry. The back door lock and knob fell off as the jam of the door was shattered by the pry bar and within two seconds after the front door seemed to explode with their own flash-bang, the rear team was passing over the threshold.

The house was filled with smoke and the smell of cordite. Screams of "police, police let me see your hands" were echoing off of the walls and bouncing off of the smoke, one never could really understand what was being said. It didn't really matter that the man didn't understand English. He had the universal sign of communication of men in black with guns stuffed in his face. He just needed to do what ever they wanted him to do. Bull's team arrived in the front room just after the front door team. They already had the man on his belly and his arms outreached. He was moaning from the pain of one of the officers kneeling in his back. Two officers were cuffing and searching the man and two others proceeded down the short hall along with Tommy.

"Sam 32, 4-32 Adam, we're code-four here."

"Sam 32, 10-4."

Bull moved to the right, next to the wall where Boswick thought he had seen a woman's foot. He was right. She was there, behind a heavily worn, overturned recliner. She was lying on her side and her dark hair was covering her face. Her body looked fine if you just stood over and looked down at her. Bull knew. His hand holding the 870 dropped to his side as he took a deep breath. It wasn't until Bull knelt down and brushed her hair away that he saw the massive wound where she had been hit with something that caved in the side of her head.

"We don't see the kid." Tommy came back into the room and looked down at Bull. "Is that the woman?" Tommy asked. Bull simply nodded without getting off his knee. He looked to the left and noticed the recliner was not resting flat on the shag carpet as it should. There was something underneath it. Bull reached under it and with a sweep of his left hand, righted the chair. There was the child. Its fate was the same as the woman's. The crimson colored hammer lay next to her little hand.

Bull was distracted for a moment at the noise the man was making. The man was angry, swearing at the dead woman in Spanish. The officers pulled him off the ground and lead him outside. As he passed the dead bodies he spit, hitting the woman. One of the officers grabbed his hair and jerked it back, resulting in another scream and more words of Spanish and English.

"Sorry, Bull," one of the officers said as he leaned his weight down on the cuffs on the man's wrists, bringing him back into compliance.

"Get him out of here before I cut out his liver and eat it," Bull said. There was no anger in his voice. He turned back to the two on the floor. The man and the officers pushed him through the front doorway and out to a waiting car. Garrison passed them on the front porch and walked inside and stood behind Bull.

"Shit, buddy, he did both of them?"

"Yeah, some time ago from the looks of the dried blood. You got homicide rolling?"

"I will now. Crime Techs are here already. They'll just wait for the dicks. You, ah, want to go and gear down?"

Bull shook his head. "I think I'll wait here until they process this one, then I'm going to take her myself." He then returned the chair to where he found it on top of the dead baby. Just the way he found it.

Stan nodded. "I'll wait with you."

Bull looked up at his friend and nodded his answer.

It would take the rest of the night, well into the early morning, before the detectives were done. The two men stood near the lifeless form of the baby for the entire time.

Life is pleasant. Death is peaceful. It's the transition that's troublesome.

Isaac Asimov

Later that same night

After taking showers, Gwen and Hanna made some broccoli-cheese soup with some French bread and a glass of merlot. By the time they were in their comfortable sweats and curled up on the couch with their bowl of soup, it was seven o'clock; their hair was still damp. Hanna was still brushing the tangles out as she walked into the living room carrying the mail from the other room and tossing it on the wooden coffee table in front of the couch.

"I made you a cup of tea. Come sit down and talk to me," Gwen said to her daughter after placing the glass of iced tea on a coaster on the coffee table. She had a file in her lap and placed it on the table next to the couch.

"Here's Kathy Cryer's engagement announcement." Kathy was one of Hanna's best friends and had actually taught at Borman for three years before Hanna arrived. "She told me the other day it was in the mail. I didn't think anyone had engagement parties anymore. Wow, look at this! It's at Mary Elaine's at the Phoenician. She didn't tell me that," Hanna said, opening the envelope while walking over and sitting down on the couch next to her cup of soup. Gwen picked up the invitation and began to look it over.

"Does her father still own that law firm?" Gwen asked as she propped the invitation on her lap while she took in a spoonful of soup.

"No, he sold it two years ago," Hanna said as she found her spot on the corner of the couch. She pulled her legs up under her and cradled her soup in her hands after placing the hairbrush on the table beside the file. She picked it up and opened it while her mother drank her soup. There was a letter from the Veteran's Administration regarding her father. Just above the salutation line on the letter was written 're: Wounds sustained in combat by Gunnery Sergeant Elias Jackson'. "What's this?"

"Oh, that's your father's file. I was looking through it for some social security information," she said as she reached for it. "I can't lose this. It has information I need when I retire."

Hanna handed her the file and Gwen put her soup down and took the file back into the other room.

The floodlights filled the room as the detectives worked methodically through the house. Bull stood over the body. He moved when the technician snapped the crime scene pictures of where the bodies of the girl and mother lay. But then he moved back to his position of standing over the girl. He moved again when they did their measurements and rectal body temperature. But then he moved back again. He moved one more time as they rolled the bodies to check for anything underneath them, just prior to placing them in the body bags.

When Gwen came back, she sat back on the couch and took up her soup. "He probably had to in order to pay for the party," she said as she sat down.

"She has at least nine months before they could get married because she told me once that she would need almost a year to plan her big day. She wants me to be in the wedding with her," Hanna said as she slurped her soup and tried to catch a small pug of juice with the spoon as it slid down her chin.

Gwen frowned as if she was trying to remember. "You taught with her at the other school before she moved to Borman didn't you? I don't know her very well even though she's worked at the school for a while. You and her go way back, clear back to preschool over at First Methodist. Her mother and I used to work the ice cream social together." Her eyebrows rose as if she just got the vision of the mother. "I remember her mother never liked to reach into the large pickle jar to get those big, whole pickles out. She kept getting her ring hung up on the side of the jar when she reached in. She had that huge diamond on her hand." She shook her head as she looked into the deepening bowl of soup. "That thing was the size of a finger nail.

Hanna's eyes also got wide as she remembered. "Oh, yeah, I remember. She was the first person I ever heard of that got a boob job. She was so flat and then about four weeks later I went over there and they were out to here," She gestured by holding her bowl out in front of her at the full extension of her arms. Hanna picked up her tea and focused on the glass for a minute . "There has always been something you do to this that makes it so good. It's different every time."

"When it's my time, you'll find out all my recipes. This one has just a pinch of peach schnapps in it."

"Mother!" Hanna said with a raised voice of surprise.

"Hanna!" Gwen said with a wide grin.

"Mother!" Hanna paused for minute and looked at the glass while smacking her lips. "This is really good."

"This was one of your father's favorite drinks. We used to sit on the front porch or in here on the couch and talk about the day. Sometimes we would walk down the street and back up the other side with you on his shoulders. Do you remember any of that? Ah, you were too young. Your father would put you on his shoulders and carry you until you laid your head down on top of his and fell asleep. You used to love to go for a walks, especially by those large bottlebrush trees that the Fillmores have in their front yard. If the sun was still up you used to say the trees 'shimed'. This was the first place your father and I lived in as a home. There are a lot of memories here." She paused and looked into her drink. Hanna could see the muscles in her cheeks flex as if she was clenching her teeth. Gwen began to blink rapidly—tears came. "I get scared, real badly sometimes." She paused again and two large tears streamed down both cheeks. Hanna watched. A wave of anxiousness moved over her and she moved quickly to her mother's side, almost crawling in her lap, holding her as she felt Gwen's head find the nook on Hanna's shoulder. "I'm tired of being sick. I don't want to get so sick I can't take care of myself. I hear about people who just languish in bed and die in their own fluids." Her lips quivered. "God, Hanna, I don't want to be in a diaper."

"Mother, no," Hanna said trying to reassure her, but she had thought of the same thing. If she needed round the clock care, how would they do it?

"I know you don't want to talk about this and neither do I, but I fear the end, if this is the end, who is going to take care of me?" There was a soft woundedness in her voice. Hanna thought for a minute that her mother heard her thoughts. "I've gone real dark with this."

"I know. So have I."

Gwen cried hard for a couple of minutes. Hanna had never heard her mother cry before. She had seen her shed tears, but she had never heard her sob. Hanna could say nothing to her. She didn't need to, she figured. Gwen felt she was seeing the last chapter of her life. She couldn't tell, but the events and the colors of the day appeared to reflect the last season. Hanna's thoughts reflected her mothers without the two comparing. They were both in the same mind set.

After a couple of minutes Gwen's tears slowed down. She pulled out a tissue and wiped her eyes, nose, and sat up again. Gwen struggled to recover her composure. "Wow, where did that come from?" she said as she wiped her nose.

"You've been storing that for a while," Hanna said as she held her mother's hand.

It was late. It had been almost eight hours since they broke into the house and found the bodies. There was one last set of photos that the Tech needed to shoot and then he nodded to Bull. The baby was dwarfed by the size of the body bag she was in. The Medical Examiner had a child's bag, but for an infant it was still oversized. The M.E. on duty came in to transport the child to the office. Bull just raised his hand and stopped him. "I'll carry her out." Their eyes met and the M.E. knew Bull needed to do what he was doing. It was simple, really. It was Bull's child. They're all his children, or sisters or brothers. He counts them all in his mind. Cops and firemen all count them as their own. Then they have to move on to the next one. Part of how they can exhale the exhaustion of the calamities of this life was doing just exactly this. If it was his child.

A few more minutes passed as the two talked about death. They waded deep into the subject as objectively as two people could. If there was going to be a funeral what kind did she want? Did she want to be cremated or buried? "Why would you ever want to be cremated?" Gwen said.

All the subjects that people who are so ill have to deal with but no one wants to talk about, they discussed in the next thirty minutes. It ended with laughter when Gwen told Hanna that she couldn't die because then Hanna had to take care of Tony. "Well he would be your tenant then," Gwen said. "You'd have to make sure your renter was cared for."

"Yep, you're not dying. I'm not becoming a slumlord," Hanna said and then got up and refilled her drink before she sat back down next to her mother.

"You think Daddy would have been sad when I moved out to the far side of town?" Hanna asked.

"Oh, your father understood—or would have understood," Gwen said catching herself with a slight smile. "Yes, I think he would have been sad. But he would have known that you were growing up and needed to go where the jobs are. He would have put on a good face for you. Your father loved you very much. What would have made him sad was that you were gone from him. He was so proud of you. He used to watch you sleep just for entertainment." She paused for a moment. "What about today, baby?" Gwen said as she too pulled her legs up under her.

"What about it?"

"What about it? What do you think about today?" she said repeating her mother's question.

"That conversation between you and Bull. Why so hostile?"

"I'm sorry mom; he just rubbed me the wrong way, that's all.

Cops just seem to have the attitude that they're bigger than life. They're so full of self righteousness and positive they know what's best," she said, trying to mean it. She wouldn't make eye contact with her mother and Gwen knew she was making it up. "They carry that big gun and that big badge and all that crap on their belt; they look like a bad Batman movie. I bet half of them are probably on the take."

"What late night show have you been watching? You sound like a bad Spike Lee movie. What's gotten into you? You never talked that way before. You've been around him for weeks and this never came up."

"I'm sorry. I don't know," Hanna answered softly. Gwen knew that wasn't her daughter and that something twisted her that afternoon at lunch. She waited until Hanna was ready. "Remember when Bobby left?"

"How could anyone forget that nightmare? Your husband walks off with some woman right after your miscarriage, and blames you for all the problems of your marriage, including his anger. Then he takes just about everything you own and had built together in ten years-"

"Nine and a half."

"I'm sorry, nine and a half, and left you with the debts of the marriage including the credit card he used to charge, among other things, two plane tickets to the Bahamas for him and—what was her name?"

"Keli—with an 'i.'"

"Keli. No, I don't remember when Bobby left," Gwen said with an edge of 'Could you ask a dumber question?'

"Alright, you made your point. I didn't really need a walk down 'Memory Lane.' It makes my stomach grumble. Remember what that officer said when we filed the report on the credit cards and the other stuff?"

"Oh honey, they're not all like that," Gwen said with a sigh.

"It's not what he said. It's not what he did. It was nothing. I needed compassion and he gave me stone coldness," Hanna said looking into her hands while resting her head on the back of the couch. "It was just a job to him."

"Honey, that was his job."

"Not like that," Hanna said shaking her head. It still bothered her and it had been years. Something small and seemingly insignificant touched and changed her and her mother saw it. "Maybe it was. I look back on that time and just shake my head. How could I have been so blind? How could I actually still love him, even after what he did to me? I really thought we'd make it."

He gently scooped her up in the large, stiff, bag and carried her like she was a sleeping child in his arms. He walked outside and down the sidewalk. He didn't notice the clicking of the cameras from the media line that had been set up. His face looked straight ahead, without emotion, without a flavor of what the man thought. He had done this too many times. The show never stopped. It went on, never ending. He carried her out to the Medical Examiner's van and climbed in, sitting on the bench seat along the side wall, next to the gurney that held the mother. She was in her own plastic bag. The tech shut the rear doors and tapped the van twice to let the driver know they were ready to leave.

"Baby, we all think we're going to live happily ever after. Life is kind of like that. It teases you with a dream and then changes course. The best you can do is ride with the changes, learn from them and grow to love your new life," Gwen said. "Don't give your troubles any special magic. Things will never be the same but if you remember that God is in it somewhere, the change isn't so bad. It can actually be good. It can open up a whole new world of opportunities. Bull was married once. They had a daughter," she said as her voice got softer, "They were down in Cabo a few years back and the three of them were swimming just off the beach at the hotel where they were staying. He came in from the surf to get a mask for his wife and turned back to find them being taken out to sea. There was an undertow. In that part of Mexico there are no life guards on the beach."

"What happened?" Hanna asked. Her eyes widened.

Gwen looked into her daughter's eyes. "He turned to another American there on the beach with him and told him to run for help. Then he went in after them. It took them twenty minutes to get a rescue team together, made up of mostly guests. By the time they got to him he was about two hundred yards out. He had his unconscious wife by the arm and he was giving mouth to mouth to his daughter. His wife died and his daughter might have, but didn't. She's in a care home here in the city, severe brain damage they said. He worked it out with the department to work the same area that the home is in so he can stop in and see her during his shift. He lives for that child .

"Does he ever talk about it?"

Gwen shook her head. "He only spoke to me about it once. He will be dealing with that for the rest of his life. He blamed himself for taking them there. Over the years, that demon has rested. It hasn't gone to sleep, but it is quiet now. We all have things we carry. We have to learn to let them go and accept things for what they are or we'll drown in them as well."

Hanna knew that her mother was talking about more than Bull. She knew it applied to both of them. She didn't know if she was ready to let go of the hurt yet. She had it for so long it seemed like it was a part of her. She denied it to herself. She had "processed" her marriage and the relationships that were left in tatters. It was good, she thought. Everything was just fine; sure, a little scar left on the old brain pan but that is what life was all about. Wasn't it? She would ask herself, sometimes daily. She had to change the direction of the conversation.

"Oh, come on. What about you and Dad? These last few decades, you haven't even gone out on a date. How could this have been good? How could God have been anywhere in this? You've lived alone for the last forty years," she said with determination and a frown.

"It's a heart thing, baby. I still love your father. I'm still married to him. I have no interest in any other man. Now don't get me wrong, I've checked out a few butts in the last few—,"

"Mother!"

"—years, but I have no heart for it." Her voice slowed and a smile came to her face. "Your father captured my heart a thousand years ago. He has fulfilled me, comforted me, and loved me for our entire marriage."

Hanna looked at her mother. She could see it in her eyes. Her mother was still in love with a man whom Hanna called her father but whom she never knew, at least not anything she consciously remembered. "I look at you and want to be like you. I want to have your heart." She started to choke up. "I don't know what I'll do if you die."

"Baby, we all have to go sometime. I'm not out of this yet. I'm kind of grateful to it in a sick, sadistic, way. It brought you back home to stay with me. See, that was a course change that was good for me. I think it will be good for you, too," Gwen said. Her voice was almost playful.

"This thing you got, it scares me. There is a great chance that you won't make it." There was firmness in her voice that Gwen heard as well. She could tell that Hanna had thought a lot about this. "Other than the fact that I would be losing you and that would be devastating enough, what about all the other stuff? I feel bad thinking about it, but the fact is that I don't know about living here. Can I pay the bills? Can I take time off work to drive you to the doctor? Who is going to take care of you during the day if you can't work? What the hell am I going to do about all of that? Doesn't that sound bad? We have to look at it. And the fact of the matter is—people do it every day. We'll deal with it when we have to deal with it. I just wanted you to know." She reached out and touched her. "We both will get through this, one way or another, and it'll be all right."

Gwen was calm. It was a conversation she had had with herself a least a thousand times since she got sick years ago. "It scares me too, but there isn't a whole lot I can do about it other than what the doctors are having me do. We have to go through the cycle. I don't plan on leaving you for a long time. But if God should have other plans, who are we to argue? I've just got to know that you will be all right. It's here. We can't turn this back. Hell, daughter, you get to keep all this," she swept the air with her hand, pointing at the house.

Hanna laughed and wiped her eyes. "He is pretty cute."

"Who is dear?"

"Officer Thornton," Hanna said with a pause and a coy look at her mother.

"You mean the one you just blamed the entire world's sins on? That one?"

"Yeah."

Her mother paused and smiled. "He is—very. I'm sure that if he heard that he would appreciate your split personality."

"You think?" Hanna said, laughing at herself.

"Oh, sure. I'm sure he doesn't deal with enough nut jobs in his line of work. He would love to come home to a wacko-space monkey like you. Besides, like I said, you get all of this," she said rolling her eyes.

"Please Mother, no dead joke humor."

"You can put me right up there on the mantle in an old coffee can. You can do a class project and glue little colored macaroni noodles to it."

Hanna giggled without lifting her head off the back of the couch. "That would look real bad—but appropriate."

"I thought so. Well, I'm going for my walk," Gwen said.

"Can't you miss one night? Stay here and sip tea with me," Hanna said as she held up her nearly empty glass.

"Wait up, I won't be long," Gwen said. Hanna laid her head on the back of the couch and closed her eyes. "Neither will I." The weight of the peach schnapps finally kicked in. She fell asleep sitting up.

Complaining is good for you as long as you are not complaining to the person you're complaining about.

Lynn Johnston (1947-)

An October day

Tony watched from the seat of the tractor lawn mower. He stopped working and sat with the engine off, his face expressionless. The glare of the sun caused him to squint just a little but his eyes, in a stare, fixed on what he was watching as if caught in its movement. The small ones would scream for no reason. Then they would hit or kick or push. Sometimes, one would get the other in a headlock and the two would fall to the ground, wrestling in the dirt of the infield, oblivious to the dust. This was the life on the playground for the inner-city kids at Borman, especially at lunchtime. Even though it was the second week of October, it was still warm in Phoenix. There was enough heat to cause the children to come in from recess in a sweat. The smell of child sweat, dirt, dirty feet, dirty hair, and the wafting smell of lasagna and garlic bread coming from the nearby cafeteria made for an interesting combination that greatly aided anyone struggling with their diet. Appetites were suppressed. After school, the kids had a choice. They could go home to an empty home and feed themselves until some family member would arrive, or they could stay for after school sports. It was not uncommon to have one hundred trying out for the eleven-man basketball team.

Bull started it. Whoever didn't make the varsity team automatically qualified for one of the six intramural teams. Bull teamed up with his friend, Michael Caris, a soft-spoken, six-foot six inch, one hundred and sixty pound Ethiopian who had literally walked to the United States through numerous refugee camps. Michael and his family had fled the famine by walking out of Africa. Somehow the family of seven stayed intact during the journey. They were able to stay together at a Catholic-funded refugee camp just inside the Sinai border. Other families around them had lost family along their routes either to disease or by being eaten while crossing rivers in Africa. They were in the right spot at the right time and when the agency running the camp asked them for any work experience, Michael's father, an electrician in Ethiopia, was able to land a job with an outfit setting up job training for the camp. Eventually, the family filed and was granted work visa status into the United States.

Michael went to school and was quickly plugged in as a center in basketball. He was able to market that into a college scholarship to Phoenix Community College and then over to Arizona State where he finished his degree in Education, bringing him to Borman. He had short hair, but not shaved. He was tall and skinny with fingers like straws and he was as black as ink. But when he smiled it was as if a light turned on. He loved the kids and loved basketball, as well as his fellow coach. Bull, on the other hand, didn't care a whole lot for the game, but loved watching the kids play. Michael knew the game; Bull knew the "hard" game tricks. The challenge for Michael was keeping a leash on Bull, who loved it when one of the kids was called for a personal foul during the game.

"This is not football, Mr. Bull," Michael would say in a thick English/Ethiopian accent.

"No, that's the unfortunate thing about this game," Bull would always say. The two men played off of each other's comments and over the three years they worked together had grown to respect and truly like one another. Michael had to come much further than Bull due to the fact that law enforcement in his country was corrupt to the point of death. He struggled trusting anyone in law enforcement. But after enough time, Michael realized his colleague was truly his friend.

"Miguel, que pasa? What's that you're wearing, my friend?" Michael said to a round sixth grader who was watching the practice from the side of the court. When Miguel heard his name he stopped picking his nose.

The kid pulled up his baggy pants. The belt he wore had an eighteen-inch tail on it and the pants dragged on the ground. The style was finally beginning to fade but when you didn't have enough money to buy anything else, you were stuck in the fashion past. "My pants," was his soft answer.

Michael looked at Bull and smiled. He had been around his friend too long and was contaminated by his humor. He looked back and smiled at Miguel and tugged on the side loop of his pants. "Brother, did your fat uncle die in his sleep or something and the rest of you ate him? Man those pants are big enough for three of me in there. You could probably only get one of Officer Thornton in them, but he's a lot older than I am, and when you get older you start to build another body inside the one you got—you know, in case you lose or forget where you put the last one. Isn't that right Officer Thornton? You got someone else in there with you, Chief?" he said to Bull setting up the play.

Bull looked at Miguel. "Mr. Caris is a wise man, Miguel. You listen to him and you too will be wise. He worked and studied really hard to pass the time while he was in that Turkish prison."

"I thought we were never going to bring that up."

Unfortunately for Miguel, he was about to start a journey he knew nothing about. Like walking into a deep forest and two of those monkeys from the Wizard of Oz used brooms and swept away any assimilation of a trail behind him. Once Miguel stepped into the world of these two, it would now be an E Ticket ride.

Bull began, "Brother, you just got done telling the boy that I could fill those parachutes he's got for pants. You're lucky I didn't tell him about your Momma."

"My Mother?" Michael said, using the proper form of the word. "I thought we had the same Mother," Michael said as he looked at Miguel, who was becoming totally lost.

"I keep telling you, how could we have the same Momma? I am so much better looking than you." Miguel had no idea what they were talking about. It didn't help that he didn't speak a whole lot of English.

"You are not better looking than I," Michael said as if insulted. "I—," he said placing his hand on his heart, "am the son of a great prince in the birthplace of the world. You, my dear friend, you—, cannot dance."

"Oh come on, Mr. Caris, don't lie in front of this boy—I know," Bull paused and looked at Miguel. "Don't rest on my opinion. We'll ask Miguel."

Both of the men turned to Miguel, reached out and gently grabbed his shoulders as he tried to turn to leave. He knew he didn't want to be a part of this conversation. Even though he didn't know what they were saying. He knew he didn't want to be around when it eventually came back to him. "Miguel, who do you think is better looking? Bonito?" Bull pointed at Michael and then himself.

Miguel began to laugh. "Uhm."

Bull looked at him with serious eyes. "That's not a choice, Miguel." Then quickly he reached out and grabbed the boy in a bear hug and began to tickle him. Miguel began to struggle and laugh and more stuff started to come out of his nose but neither the boy nor the man seemed to care. "Who—do—you—think—is—better—looking?" Bull said. Miguel could barely speak, he was laughing so hard. "He is, he is."

Michael stood watching with a great smile. "See, I told you, man. I am better looking. How could you doubt that with that big ol' booty of yours? Just for that, you are not my brother," Michael said with his best street black accent. He grew up speaking Ethiopian, English, and French fluently but he had lived in the United States long enough to get the idea. His street slang had a formal English overtone.

Bull took his hand and placed it over the boy's face and rubbed it, hard. "Well, it's pretty obvious that this child has a fever. You just did that because Mr. Caris smells bad and you feel sorry for him." The boy was trying to laugh but there was a paw over his mouth and leaking nose.

"I do not have an odor. The only thing wrong with that young man is that your big, pink hand is suffocating him. He has no idea where that hand has been and frankly, none of us wants to know," Michael said.

"Oh yes—you smell bad," Bull said still roughing up the boy by pulling on his ears and putting a gentle arm bar on him.

"No, I do not. I smell like Christian Dior, who, most people don't know, is from my homeland."

Bull snorted laughter. Christian Dior is not Ethiopian."

"What? Oh, my friend. Christian Dior was a tribal leader and came to the United States on a work visa, working the cantaloupe fields in California before making it big in fragrance."

"You smell."

"Like Christian Dior. People in this country did not realize that he could spear a cheetah on a full run at fifty meters." Michael paused and pretended to smell his shirt. "I do love this smell. It reminds me of home."

"Yeah, the smell of camp fire and musk oxen meat drying on sticks."

"Exactly."

Bull started to lose it. "Dior is not from Ethiopia. He's from Tulsa—and you still smell. If that is Christian Dior, then I don't want any. I know, we'll ask Miguel. Miguel, go over there and smell Mr. Caris' armpits," Bull said as he pushed Miguel towards Michael, who had raised his arm. Miguel broke free from Bull's grip and ran off towards his friends screaming in playful laughter. Both hands were holding onto his pants. "Miguel, where are you going? I wasn't going to tickle you again—honest. Okay, Miguel, we'll finish this later," Bull yelled at the back of the running child. The two men stood for a moment and watched the boy run away.

"I don't smell," Michael said to Bull, not taking his eyes off the running boy.

"No, man, you really do. You got that new cologne for your birthday and ever since we have not seen one bug on this campus."

"It is Christian Dior. Not that horse piss you wear."

"Hey," Bull smirked. "Mennen Skin-Bracer is not horse piss. My father wore it and if it was good enough for him then it's good enough for me. Besides, where did you buy yours?"

"Macy's," Michael said proudly.

"See, that's the problem. It's not convenient. I buy mine at the grocery store. I can get my milk, beer, fruit, and vegetables when I actually eat them, and aftershave. You don't have that customer service at Macy's."

The two men watched the boy leave. From the side of the cafeteria, next to where they were standing, Hanna walked up from her classroom on the other side. "Was that Miguel Sanchez you were just talking to?" she said as she shaded her eyes from the afternoon sun.

"Yep, good taste and all," Michael said, grinning at Bull as he said it.

Hanna paused for a minute trying to figure what he meant before she continued. "Well, I need to talk to him."

"What's up?" Bull asked.

"He was caught cheating on his English test and since he's in my class I need to take him to PRC."

"How do you know he was cheating?" Bull said as he moved his body to cast a shadow across Hanna's face so she didn't have to look into the sun.

"Two other students saw him."

"Well, how do you know they're just not giving him up to save themselves?" he said, moving the shadow off of her face and allowing the full sun to hit it just as he finished his question.

"Officer Thornton."

"Bull."

"Bull, may I please just have my student and I'll get out of your hair."

Michael snorted. "That's funny, Hanna. My dear brother here does not have enough hair to stop the sweat from running into his socks, let alone get you out of it."

"At least what I have is mine. If I had hair as long as yours I'd have to vote Democratic."

"Gentlemen!"

The two paused and looked over their shoulders at the woman. "I'll go get him," Michael said.

"Thank you," she said to Michael as he walked off to get Miguel. There was a pause between the two of them as they watched Michael leave. Hanna felt it getting painful; especially since the last time they had spoken she had laid into him. She felt badly about it. "I think I owe you an apology for the other day."

Bull knew she was uncomfortable but wasn't quite ready to let her off the hook. He knew he would. Frankly, she was right about some in his profession. "What did you do the other day?"

She cleared her throat. Crap. He forgot. She didn't need to do this at all, she thought. "Well, at my mother's party, I was a little—pretty rude to you. I had a run in with a police officer a few years ago and I guess it left a sour taste in my mouth."

"Yeah, your husband really jammed you," Bull said as he watched Michael tap Miguel on the shoulder and point back at them.

Heat came over her face first. She pulled her hand away from over her eyebrow and placed it on her hips. Bull could see the change. He began to rewind the tape in his brain to find out where exactly he stepped on the land mine. "Excuse me—how do you know about my husband?"

He did his best to try to down play and ease the conversation into safer waters, but he would have better luck harpooning a butterfly, he thought. "I, uh, read it in the report. And you're right," he said. "I actually should be apologizing to you for the way 'Fifty-seven' Warwick handled that. You couldn't have gotten a worse draw for a police officer if you picked one." "We call him 'fifty-seven' because he's five feet seven inches tall and has such a chip on his shoulder that anyone riding with him should be drawing extra pay for the fights that idiot gets into. About the same time your case came in, he was dealing with his wife leaving him. She was always beating him up verbally about his height, especially in public. Everyone thought she was kidding, but I guess his height, or lack of it, really bugged her. He never told anyone why but one of her close girl friends worked as a dispatcher and she said that his wife was leaving because she found someone else. The guy is like six-five. He's huge." Bull stopped to take a breath and then kept going. "She's about four inches shorter than Fifty-seven when they were married." Air, he needed air again. "Together I bet they looked like they worked for the circus," he said, with a little bit of a snicker. Hanna didn't laugh.

"I don't believe it! You checked me out! You looked into my private past! Who else did you share this with? Hum? Michael?"

"No, I didn't tell him. No, why would say that?"

"Or was it just you and the boys down at the station house reading over the reports and whooping it up?" Her hands were still on her hips but her voice began to break.

"First of all, we don't have station houses, we have districts, and secondly, I thought you'd be flattered that I took the time to see who you were," he said with his hand on his chest, covering his heart as if he were promising the world. The heat from her eyes was enough to burn steel.

"Flattered? FLATTERED? I want you to know something, Officer Thornton. I am not one of your bimbo, adolescent girlfriends that can be just swept off her feet by your attempts at machismo charms."

Machismo charms? he thought to himself.

"I do not find you searching into my private affairs at all amusing. In fact, it's quite insulting. Please mind your own business from now on." She finished just as Michael got to them with Miguel. "Come along Miguel," she said throwing her arms across his shoulders and turning back the way she had come.

Bull and Michael watched her walk away. "Have you ever heard anyone use the word 'machismo' before in a sentence?" Bull said without taking his eyes off of the woman.

Michael simply shook his head. "Machismo is a word we did not use a lot of in Ethiopia."

Bull nodded then turned to his friend. "She is kind of feisty though, don't you think?"

"She is something. I do not know if I would call her 'feisty.' Did you really check her out?"

"You heard."

"Yes, my friend. I think most of the school heard."

Bull shook his head. "No. Her mother told me about it."

"You like to live dangerously." Michael turned and looked back at the kids who were still on the court. "Have you thought about asking her out?"

"Out? Like on a date?"

"Yes. In my former life, a woman with a boooo-tay like that, we would make her a queen and bow to her."

"Crap, Michael, a woman with a butt like that in your country would get speared and eaten."

Michael nodded. "Yes, but we would make her a queen first." He paused for a minute. "Truly, you should ask her out. Take her somewhere that you are comfortable in taking a fine Ethiopian queen. There are many places that you could carry her tray."

"Hey, I know how to treat a woman."

"Ah, but do you know how to treat her like a queen?"

Bull watched the woman and child walk away. "It has been a while since I've been with a queen," he said softly.

Hanna walked Miguel over to PRC and then back to her room. The day had been long and the idea that a strange man had been digging in her past was going to bother her for the rest of the day. She was temporarily flattered at the idea that a man had gone to the trouble of looking into her life. Something caused him to be interested in her. She was hoping he was truly interested. Then she switched back to the fear of what he did discover. When she was able to look at her life objectively, she could see she was a victim. Bobby did violate her and their trust relationship. But she also knew that every relationship has enough blame to go around just like her mother said. When she could look at their life together she could see she was a contributor to their problems. She wondered if Bull saw the same thing or if he saw a woman who caused her husband to leave her. She wasn't going to follow that road again. If a man was going to be interested in her and she in him, there were going to be terms, clear and understandable terms. Maybe written on a piece of paper, typed, notarized—with witnesses, she thought.

She stood next to her desk staring out the wall of windows in her classroom watching Tony standing on the corner. Some of the children were starting their way home. He would hold the red stop sign down to his side and away from his body as if to keep the kids behind it as he looked both ways for cars. Then he stepped out into the street, the sign held straight as a rail in front of him. He walked them halfway across and stopped while they continued. He waved good-bye with his off hand and smiled, then turned back to the corner. She looked at him with a pang of embarrassment and then sympathy. He still lived in that little house and she, part of her anyway, still regretted that he did.

"Mrs. Jarger—Mrs. Jarger," Abby called from the other end of the classroom, causing Hanna to come back to the world.

"Yes, Abby," Hanna said with her arms crossed.

"I said the bell rang. Can we leave?"

"Oh, I'm sorry Abby. Did it? I must have been somewhere else, thank you. Yes class, if you have everything you are free to go. Have a good weekend." The sound of chairs sliding on the carpet, bumping into their steel desks and the children pushing them back in, lasted for only a few seconds. Their voices continued outside and down the walkway then faded where they met other voices.

She gazed back out the window. She watched Tony and the kids, the occasional car driving down the street, or the mother walking her child home while holding a baby in her arms. She was lost again and didn't notice Bull standing in the door, knocking gently on the steel frame. He could tell she was daydreaming. As he walked towards her he softly cleared his throat. She turned to him. She slowly closed and re-opened her eyes while taking a long, deep breath, anticipating another conflict.

"God, you can't leave well enough alone," she said as she exhaled.

"I'm a–," he started and then stopped to try to remember exactly why he had come. "Look, I just wanted to come by and say I was sorry for what happened. You're right. I never should have checked you out and I should have thought of your feelings before blurting out my trophy of a find. I'm reasonably bad at that.

Anyway–," he looked down at his hands, one picking at the nail of the other. "I guess I was a little angry about what you said at your Mom's party and I just wanted to see what I was going to be dealing with this year. I find that as I get older, I get less patient." He looked at her. He noticed how the light lit up the side of her face. He noticed her figure. He liked what he saw. He laughed at himself. He ran the inventory, which all men do, of the likes and dislikes, and almost all the items he came up with were in one column, dislikes. She was arrogant; middle-aged; her hips were almost too big; her shoes were stupid, and she had an attitude. Then he started to re-examine his list. He was middle-aged, he had an attitude, he definitely had his moments of arrogance and frankly his hips were getting a little—bulky. He knew he didn't want to go all year bumping into this woman every day and have the temperature of a Nor'easter breeze pass him. He thought he was reading the list wrong. Maybe it was reversed. There was a strength that he saw in her, although he didn't know where it came from. He could feel it more than see it. Maybe it was one of those 'queenly' qualities that Michael would no doubt mention. Women like Farmer, fancy, beautiful, fake, women who cruised with money and things, would always be around. Something about an older man would always be attractive to some younger women. But he was not in that mind set. He was still wrapped in a world that still had his wife in it, although with each day it faded a little more. He hated and loved to see it go at the same time. His daughter, outside of work, controlled a large part of his life. How could you even entertain the idea of another? he thought to himself.

True enjoyment of every day fell off the planet that day in Mexico. The daily engagement with teachers and other officers was pure show. It made him tired. They didn't want to hear his tale, he thought to himself, although he had spent hours listening to others vomit their turmoil on him and he took it gladly. It always made him feel good to help others just by listening. But it did tire him.

They filled something in his life that was voided by the loss of his wife. He couldn't make himself do the same with anyone else, however. He thought he should be the strong one and for whatever reason he turned inward and away from any relationship that was not superficial. But this woman, whose room he was standing in, seemed different. His list was confusing now; a man of confidence was beginning to feel confused about what he thought. All this was whipping through his mind as he stood there and looked into his hands, trying to form the words after being distracted by her initial response to his presence. Then an almost panicked feeling came over him just before he spoke.

"I hurt your feelings? I can't believe that," Hanna said with her arms crossed.

"Look, you might find this hard to believe, but I've been doing this cop stuff for a lot of years now. I have seen a lot over the years and I have had to grow a pretty tough skin. I guess that's part of this job. But, when I'm around friends I let my guard down and yeah, it does still sting a little when someone smacks me. My tendency is to strike back. I wanted to let you know that I know about you and that was unfair of me. I, uh," he stopped and regained his thoughts, "that was unkind of me as well. I just want you to know that I am sorry if I hurt or embarrassed you. I just wanted you to hear that from me. I truly am sorry for the intrusion into your life."

He looked up at her and gave a partial smile, then turned to leave.

"You like working with these kids, don't you?" she said without uncrossing her arms.

He stopped and turned back to her. He could see her soften towards him. "Yeah, I guess I really do. I never thought I would when Gwen roped me into this. The school days that you and I grew up in seemed much simpler than today. We had our problems, but some of the stuff these guys are dealing with is beyond even my imagination."

Hanna nodded, and with a deep breath she seemed to cleanse herself. "Yeah, we didn't have the child abuse or drugs or abandonment or child pornography like these babies have."

Bull grinned and pulled at the collar of his shirt, tugging at the back of the neck. It was the way she spoke. There was a confidence in it. There was a quiet knowledge in her sound that emitted a level of strength that he liked. He could see she was distracted with the conversation and he eased his way across the room towards her. "Don't let us off too easy. I remember a friend of mine in early high school was killed because his step-daddy beat him to death. You got to remember who invented the drug craze. I do believe it was us, with a little help from our parents. We were just able to keep it more of a secret than today." Bull finished by sitting on a desk chair, squeezing himself in sideways.

She sat on the edge of her desk and played with a stack of spelling papers and a container of colored pencils. She turned and looked out the window and her eyes came to rest on the largest thing moving outside. "At least they have Tony," she said. A smile came to her face as she watched the old man outside. Was his limp getting worse? She hadn't noticed it before but he was dragging his right leg a little more than normal. "They will never know what a gift to each of them that old man is," she said. She could speak the words; she just had trouble believing them.

She stood up and walked back around behind to recapture her composure. "Look," she said to the large man crammed into the little desk. She paused as she looked at him stuck there "Do you want to come over here and sit in a big person's chair?" she said, gesturing with her hand to a chair next to her desk. Bull held up his open hand, "No, I'm fine."

"Like I was saying, I think we got off on the wrong foot. Why don't we start over?" She walked over to him. As he got up, the desk and chair came with him. "I'm Hanna Jarger, school teacher extraordinaire, hunter of lemmings, slayer of children's runny noses, and daughter of Mrs. Gwen Jackson, also an extraordinary teacher, although not as good with noses." She reached out and shook Bull's hand as he freed himself from the jaws of the desk.

"It is a pleasure to meet you, madam," Bull said as he shook Hanna's hand, ignoring the crash." I'm Packard Abraham Thornton, Phoenix Police Resource Officer, son of Harrison Monroe Thornton, also an extraordinary police officer. My friends call me 'Bull'."

Hanna had a full-blown smile on her face. There was a moment for her when there was no ex-husband, no baggage, at least none that she wanted to put on the train platform. It was just her, not so middle-aged, looking at an obnoxiously cute, although older man—tearing up her classroom. Bull noticed he wanted it to continue. He noticed her teeth.

"I'm sure this will be an entertaining year working with you, Officer Thor–I mean Bull. May I call you Bull?"

He smiled back at her. "Since you are a certified teacher in this district and a card carrying member of the teachers union, you are authorized, yes. And my guess is you are probably right. This will be an entertaining year." He paused and looked at her through squinted eyes. He was still holding her hand when he spoke. "I realize that this might be too early in our new-found professional relationship to ask this but— there are several teachers going to a little place up north tonight to listen to some music, grab a little something to eat and watch our blood pressure drop—maybe even dance. Would you be interested in going? I'll have you home early, if you wish. Of course, this is strictly for the purposes of détente, you understand."

Hanna looked at him sideways. She had told herself never again, but this was just a work trip, with others from work. She squinted, intrigued by him. It could be just the loneliness she hated to admit she had. "I suppose if I say no, you'll keep asking until my ears bleed," she said with a grin.

"Or fall off, yes ma'am. I'm afraid so."

She let out a heavy sigh. "Then I guess this is as good a time as any to get this over with."

Bull smiled. "That's what I like, a woman who throws herself into a public appearance with me," he said placing his hand over his heart. He turned to leave and spoke back over his shoulder as he left. "I'll come by about 6:30 to pick you up."

"Do you want my address?"

He turned and looked at her.

"Oh, that's right, you checked me out. I guess you know I live with my mommy," she said crossing her arms and smiling as a last poke at him.

He turned back to the door. "Dress casual."

"Whoa, how casual? Where are we going again?"

He turned sideways to her. "Dress like you're going to brand something."

"I suppose you'll be a perfect gentlemen when we get there. Wait, what do you mean 'brand something'?"

"Dress like you could get some splash on you," he said with a grin.

She stared out the open door. "What the hell is 'splash'?"

"Friday night I'm going nowhere, all the lights are changing green to red."

David Gray

An October evening

All the lights were on in the house. Gwen and Hanna were preparing for Hanna's "non-date," as Hanna said in response to her mother's smile-laced comment regarding this actually being a date. Hanna denied it and then felt her face flush.

There were six blouses, two shirts, three skirts, two pairs of pants, and one dress that she wore to a christening about two years back, laying on her bed. Gwen had finally convinced her that jeans and a plaid button up collared shirt was perfect. While Hanna finished putting on her make up and pulling the curlers out of her hair, Gwen said she would iron the shirt.

"I don't know why I'm doing this," Hanna said walking down the hall. Gwen just smiled as she rolled the iron over the shirt and negotiated the collar.

"You're doing this because you want to have fun. There's nothing wrong with that. I think it's great you're getting out of the house with someone other than your mother," she said with a sarcastic tone. In her mind there was no one better to venture out with than Bull.

Hanna stood in the hall in her jeans and bra. "Look, I will go out, okay, I just don't need to be pushed. I'll go when I'm ready," she held up a pair of earrings to one of her ears while her other hand finished with the curler. "Do these go with the shirt?" Then the doorbell rang. "Oh crap, I'm not ready." She said as she darted back into the bathroom. "Mother."

"Here you go, dear, all nice and pressed. You're wearing denim jeans and a flannel shirt. You could hang chicken bones from your ears and they would go. Just relax," Gwen said as Hanna brushed out her hair. "Your date's here,"

"This is not a date."

"Uh, huh." She turned from her with a smile. "You might want to put that shirt on before you come out. And please try to relax."

"Mother! I am relaxed. Why should I not be relaxed? Just because I'm going on a da– out with a strange man somewhere out in the wilderness. Remember, when they find my body I want to be cremated," she said as she threw the shirt on. "Will you please answer the door?"

Gwen was smiling when she opened the door for Bull.

"What are you smiling so big about?" he asked as he handed her a bouquet of mixed flowers with the Costco price tag still on them.

"Get in this house and hug me," Gwen said, continuing to smile. "Oh, nothing, Hanna is on the verge of a melt down about tonight and this thing you invited her to. These are pretty. Costco?"

"Mrs. Jackson, there is something about seeing you in that house coat and slippers and knowing that you are a seasoned and experienced woman that really does something for me," he said with a big grin. "Of course, I know how much you like those so I grabbed some."

"I'll go put them in some water. She'll be out in a second," she said as she walked across the living room and into the kitchen. She poked her head back around the corner at Bull. "She's a little nervous," she whispered as Hanna came into the living room from the hall. She looked good, not relaxed, but dressed to relax, Bull thought. The jeans and shirt complimented her figure and her hair hung loose just past her shoulders. She carried a light windbreaker over her arm in case it got chilly, wherever she was going.

"Hi," she said as she came out and saw Bull. He was wearing jeans and a pair of well-used Roper boots. He had on a long-sleeve brown plaid shirt and as he entered the house he took off and held in his hand a wide-brimmed Stetson that looked like it was more for work than dress. He also had on a large silver belt buckle in the center was a cowboy riding a bull. The words '1988 Jay Cees Runner-up' ran along the top.

"Bull, honey, she's my daughter. Now you take good care of her, won't you?"

"With my life, dear. What time do you want her home?" Bull said, holding his hat across his chest.

"Well, don't be too late. She can use all the sleep she can get," Gwen said, winking at Bull.

"Mother," Hanna said while nodding her head. "It is not I who needs her sleep. This man, if you haven't noticed, is significantly older than I am. Although he is not quite as old as you so it's you, who should probably go to bed about—well—now," Hanna said with an air of sophisticated snobbery.

"I understand, dear," Bull said while taking Hanna's jacket in his hand and slinging it over his arm. "Come on girl, your momma wants you out of here so she can rest," he said as he opened the front door. When the two got to his truck, Gwen walked out to the edge of the front porch and called to them.

"Son, you make sure you carry her tray for her," Gwen said with a large grin.

"That's enough, Mommy," Hanna said

Bull escorted Hanna around to her side of the almost new Ford F-150 pickup and opened the door for her. They both waved to Gwen as they pulled away. There was country music playing softly on the radio. Bull could tell Hanna was nervous. "You look nice tonight," he said while he turned down the radio.

"I'm sorry but I'm fresh out of branding clothes. They're all at the dry cleaners," she said with a smile.

"Those will do just fine. I'm sorry if I worried you about tonight. This place has a western flare and is real laid back. I like going there just to relax. There is going to be quite a group from school. This actually should be pretty fun. If you let it," he said looking at her. "Who knows, we may even get you out on the floor and do a little 'two-steppin'," he said.

Hanna was shaking her head. "I don't think 'two-stepping' would be a good thing. I don't think three-stepping would be a good thing at this point in my life. How about one-sitting or one-talking, along with a glass of white wine?"

"Naw, you'll do all right," he said.

"You want to tell me where we're going?"

"So what happened to Miguel?"

"He got two days in-school suspension. I suppose you think that was too harsh." As soon as she said it she wished she could have pulled it back. She didn't mean to sound so hard.

Bull just shook his head. If he felt the sting of her answer he didn't show it. "I'm not in your shoes. You made the call; I can support that."

She paused for a minute looking out the front window "Thanks. Sometimes it's so hard to tell if you're doing the right thing."

"What makes it so hard?" The tone in his voice made her feel like he truly wanted to know.

"These kids; I've done this for so long that the faces change but the events in their lives don't change; different upbringing, different backgrounds, different colors. It never ends, does it? There are always going to be these casualties, especially for the children from the reservation or the barrio."

"I guess that's up to someone other than you and me. Either when God comes back in a cloud of smoke and fire or when pigs fly. It's probably safer to bet on the pigs. You and your mother lived and worked on the reservation for a while. Those kids have a special meaning to you, don't they?" His voice was calm and soft. She watched him speak

The images were distant. Her mother had taught for a half a year on the Pima Reservation, filling in for a teacher who left in mid-year. It was while Elias was in Vietnam. Gwen loved it there. It was right before she got the job at Borman.

Hanna spent her first year of pre-school there. She had mixed memories. She remembered being the only white child in the classroom full of Indian children. She was sometimes picked on by some of the older children at the school, but most of the time the children treated her as if she were Indian. She thought later that it was because they knew what it was to be a stranger in a strange land. That and they really liked her mother as a teacher. Gwen loved them and they in turn loved her. "I guess that never leaves you. I didn't think about it much but sometimes it comes back." There was a pause in what she was saying. "Look, I'm really sorry for the way I treated you. No matter what happened I should not have unloaded on you," she said as she looked out the front window and over to him.

"No, don't apologize. Sometimes I can come on a little, how can I put it? Strong?

"No, I, what makes you say that? I can give a sincere apology if I want to."

"Your mother chewed on your butt, huh?" Bull said with a wider grin. "Sure you can. But your mother put you up to it, or we wouldn't even be going out tonight."

"What makes you say that?"

Bull grinned at her. He liked her eyes. He liked her hair. He saw how one tooth in front on the bottom row was just a little bit crooked and thought it was cute. "Because I'm your mom's favorite. Ever since I came to the school years ago and pulled one of the kids off her, she's loved me. She even called the Chief and told him that I would make a great SRO." He shook his head. "That was my inevitable downfall, poor bastard that I am."

"She never told me about your first meeting."

"Yeah, we got a call and I was the unlucky one who was closest. She had a child going wild and one of the teachers called it in. By the time I got to the school, the boy was up in your mom's face. She was holding her own and he hadn't touched her but it was about to happen." Gwen could see that Bull was seeing the events in his mind as he told the story. He smiled. "That, as they say, was my downfall."

"Come on, you chose this. Don't be such a 'Mary'. Big guys like you are all the same; ya talk tough but get a splinter in your hand and you cry like a strung out alley cat," Hanna challenged.

"Are you friggin' kidding me?" Bull said. "Do I look like the kind of guy that would sign up for SRO duty? I do hate splinters, though."

"Well, I don't–,"

"The correct answer is: No, I don't. The fact that I now enjoy it is another matter, but I would never have signed up for this if it was the last duty station on the planet. I quickly realized that this was my calling after the Chief called me in and personally asked me to 'volunteer' after your mother called him. You know she has the private line into his office? They went to school together or something."

Hanna smiled. "Yeah, Chief Cochran and mom go back to grade school. His nickname was 'Stumpy.' She will still call him that. He just rolls his eyes and smiles at her."

Bull smiled. "Stumpy, huh. I don't think I want to know why. I wonder what would happen if I walked up to him and called him that. I would either get promoted or sent to the worst detail the city has."

"What would that look like?"

"Probably the guy who does cavity searches on street people."

"Your lucky day."

"Yeah, I don't think I'll be calling the Chief 'Stumpy' any time soon."

"Good plan."

"Yeah, he was pretty persuasive. 'Thornton,' he said, 'You really should volunteer for this program'."

"He 'convinced' you, huh," she said with a smile.

"Let's just say he 'inspired' me to choose well," he said as she began to laugh and relax. "It wasn't funny. Here I was with years on with the department. I was able to retire in one or two years and this wedgy dropped. I'm sorry for the graphics, but come on," he said gesturing with his hand.

"So, what did you do?"

"I went to talk to your mother. I went to explain to her that I had just a couple of years to a real nice retirement. I just wanted to finish with the department, stay as an NRO and die happy. That's not too much to ask is it?"

"What did she say?"

"There's a little Scottish in your mother, huh?"

"Her father was from Glasgow, yeah."

"I thought so. My grandfather was from a small village outside of Edinburgh. She just smiled and took my face in the palms of her hands and in a really bad Scottish brogue said, 'Aye laddy, yer destiny lies here guarding–,"

"—the hearts of our future," Hanna finished. "God, I've heard that line from her ever since I told her I wanted to become a teacher, or doctor, or whatever I wanted to."

"Hold that thought," Bull said, holding up his hand to her and then pointing out the front window.

Hanna hadn't really noticed that they had gone from two lanes to one and it seemed that they were moving out of the city. Up ahead of them were lights illuminating a small western town. Cars were parked just off the road next to the shops and restaurant under an old water tower. A 'Welcome to Reata Pass' sign was along the road. "Is this it? This is Reata Pass. I've been here," she said with a voice of familiar confidence.

"No, our turn off is just on the other side," he said as he pointed to a sign on the side of the road, about one hundred yards beyond Reata Pass. It needed paint. The words *Greasewood Flats* were faint and the arrow that pointed off towards the dark desert was barely visible. Down below the sign was another in equal disrepair and it merely said 'eat' with an arrow pointing in the same direction. They pulled onto a dirt road. Bull flipped on his high beams and eased their way parallel to a barbed wire fence. To the right were three horses standing together eating the short grass in the dark. About fifty yards ahead, Hanna could see the reflection of taillights as the high beams hit them. There were dozens and dozens of them. There were more horses in another corral just on the other side of a row of cars and there was the smell of fire.

Bull turned a corner and found a single space between two SUV's. Just beyond them was a row of motorcycles. Hanna saw them as Bull pulled into the space. "We're at a biker bar?"

Bull just looked at her. Then he smiled. "Not just a biker bar, THE biker bar, and cowboy bar, and home to the best country dancing in the state. It's also the home to the best burger around and the coldest beer on the planet." He looked at her with serious eyes. "You, my dear, are on hallowed ground. Come on," he said with a wink.

The two got out and walked across the dirt path to the front gate. There must have been thirty motorcycles parked in front of the gate. All of them, with the exception of about five, were Harley-Davidson. The other five were Indians. Bull knew that each bike was worth a minimum of twenty grand. The bikes were driven by doctors and lawyers and architects and professionals who wanted to think they were still a little wild. They were parked alongside an old Chevy pick up with a rusted bed and two bales of hay sitting in it. As they came to the front gate, which opened to the patio area, two men greeted them. They were the gatekeepers and kept out the un-welcomed. One of them, the shorter of the two in a sweat stained Stetson, called Bull by name and shook his hand. Bull introduced him to Hanna before the two walked in.

Greasewood Flats looked like a large patio with picnic tables lined up in rows. At either end of the rows were fifty-five gallon drums lying on their sides with one quarter of them cut away lengthwise. This allowed them to be used as fire pots. Construction wood was stored in a large pile at the far end of the patio, on the other side of the dance floor. The center of the dance floor had a metal pole sticking out of it to about eight feet high, which held an old wagon wheel that was circled with mini-white lights. From the wagon wheel, radiating out in all directions, came another set of white lights.

You found your place, got some wood and lit a fire in the drum. The tables were old and splintered. Someone had painted them with a redwood stain, but had been darkened over the years with spilled drinks, spilled food, and the weather. There was a huge Tamarack tree that reached out and shaded the concrete dance floor, right in the middle of the patio. It was between the outdoor bar, the stage, and the restaurant-bar-bathrooms. The restaurant was an old wooden house, lined on the eaves with Christmas lights tastelessly placed inside styro-foam cups hanging on the edge of the walkway out front of the building. There was a walk-up bar inside next to the walk-up window for ordering food. The food menu was sparse You had your choice of a burger, burger with chili, hot dog, hot dog with chili, chicken sandwich, or a grilled cheese. All of them came with a generic ribbed potato chip side and a pickle. If one didn't like it, one didn't have to eat it. But Bull knew the burger and chili made the beer taste better. On the west side of the dance floor, opposite the bar and food order station, was an outdoor bar. There were rusting wagons and farm equipment everywhere. In most of the old, falling apart Conestoga wagons were empty, broken beer bottles.

Bull and Hanna walked in and saw the group from school near the dance floor. "They must have gotten here in the middle of the afternoon to get a table that close to the floor," Bull said, putting his coat on. Even though it was still early in the fall, the restaurant was higher in elevation and in the desert. The temperature was at least ten degrees cooler, if not more, than in the city. They walked over and said hi to the eight or nine people there with their spouses or dates. Bull asked Hanna what she might like to eat and drink and after reciting the menu to her, he excused himself to get them both a drink and place their food order.

"You came with Bull?" Gayle Sonet asked with a wide-eyed look that wrote volumes of dialogue. Gayle was a fairly robust woman, which was even more pronounced when she stood next to her live-in boyfriend of three years, Calvin. He was thin and pale, even at night. His skin was almost translucent.

"He asked me to ride along with him, that's all," Hanna said, trying to decide whether to leave her jacket on or take it off.

"Hey, you brought my man," Hanna heard over her shoulder. She turned to see Jessica Farmer, standing next to a man with a bad Chinese mustache and dread-locks. He was kissing her neck as she spoke.

"Hi Jessica," Hanna said. Jessica's black long-sleeved shirt was unbuttoned too far to be an accident. The man with the bad mustache also had a ring on with a diamond, or something that looked like a diamond, the size of a wad of gum.

"Who else is here?" Hanna asked Gayle.

"The Tripolis, Jack and his wife, Tom, Judge, Samantha, Carol and her fiancé," Gayle said as she looked around and spotted who had come from the school. "I just got here myself." She turned back to Hanna and asked the question with her eyes as her brows raised.

"He just asked me to ride with him and he was going to bug me until I said I'd go. I didn't feel like fighting about it. Besides, I think Mom wanted to be alone tonight, you know, just for a little while."

Hanna could tell that Gayle was looking past her at someone, then she heard the familiar voice coming up behind her.

"Did Hanna tell you that I threatened to beat her to death if she didn't come to this thing tonight?" Bull said as he walked up and held out the Fat Tire that Hanna wanted. "I hope you like extra hot chili on your sandwich. It makes the beer worthwhile—Skoal," he said as he clinked the neck of the bottles. He was drinking a Glenlivet neat. Hanna seemed surprised. Hanna took a sip of the beer and it truly was the coldest liquid she thought she had ever had. It drained down her throat and chilled her. Bull was right.

The bar started as a cowboy hang out for real cowboys that took care of the ranches in this part of the county. As the city grew, the bar became an ever-increasing hang-out for city people who wanted to pretend they were cowboys. They brought their Beemers and their Benz's and those that wanted others to think they were real "wild" road their Harleys. The people even called them their 'hogs' as if acting like a serial killer or a member of the Hell's Angels gave them that edge to their lives. The real cowboys and their wives or girlfriends only sporadically showed up on a Friday or Saturday night. They retreated to times during the week when the wanna-bes would be too busy and too tired from their business day. The owner, an old crusted range rider with bloodshot eyes, named Doc, still held his table by the stage and next to the dance floor. He and whatever guest he had that night would have front row seats. Bull had known Doc for years and was able to walk over when he arrived and shake his hand and say hello. He knew one time what his last name was but they never used it so Bull had mentally thrown that information out as useless. He also borrowed Doc's 'fire starter,' an old short-handled shovel, so he could start the fire pit by their table. The others who arrived early didn't know the routine and Doc was never inclined to advise people one way or the other. He was happy to take their money and serve them cold beer, but he wasn't going to coddle them.

He handed Bull the short shovel. Bull walked over to Doc's fire, took a shovel full of coals, and walked back to his own pit. The wood was already placed along with paper and the coals only took a minute to erupt into flame. Hanna watched Bull as he moved comfortably between the centuries. While he petted Duke, the bar dog, he talked to Doc about something they seemed interested in. He then excused himself and walked over to the group where Hanna was standing and talked and laughed just as easily.

The western "band" showed up just after they arrived. It was one man. 'Big Bad Bob' had played there for years. His real name was Bruce but 'Big Bad Bob' made much better sense for the location. He was in his early forties, was full-faced and had a high receding hairline. He played a good acoustic guitar, but also was good at mixing the sound from the soundboard that made him a band. He played mostly country but a lot of Jimmy Buffet, which, to Hanna, seemed pretty appropriate if you ignored the fact that it was in the desert. The sound was good, even though the words didn't always match what Buffet had originally written. Bob made them up, depending on how many beers he had. Maybe it was the beer and the coolness in her throat; maybe, it was the burger with the big green chilies on it; maybe, it was the relaxed air and the friends and the sound of Buffet. It actually could have been the man who brought her, looking out from under his stained Stetson with silver in his hair and one eyebrow; she needed to remember to ask him about that. Maybe it was any one of these things that allowed her to feel, for the first time in months, she was relaxing and finding herself smiling while just standing there. She was going to hate to admit it when he asked and she knew he was going to ask, but she was having the best time she'd had in a long time, maybe even before the divorce.

People were on the dance floor and doing everything from a plant and sway to a two-step. Bull caught her eye and nodded in the direction of the dance floor. She shook her head 'no' but he shook his head 'yes' and walked over to her. "You're probably wondering if I'll ever ask you to dance. Come on, I'll show you how to two-step."

"You know, I have gone my whole life never knowing how to two-step and I think I can go the distance without knowing, thank you very much." she said with no firmness what-so-ever.

He took her beer out of her hand and placed it on the table next to them and walked her to the floor in the center of the patio. As they walked past the pile of people from school he said, "Don't watch." They walked to the center of the floor, next to the big steel pole that held up the lights that fanned from its center like a May Pole. "Okay, real simple, I'm driving,"

"Of course," she cut in with a little edge of sarcasm.

"Hey, pay attention. I'm driving because you are going backwards and you can't see the little old lady behind you, so I have to steer." She could smell the Glenlivet and chili on his breath. That, with the slight odor of his aftershave, added to the painting of the night in her mind. She cautiously allowed herself to like it. He took her right hand in his left and placed her left hand on his shoulder. His right hand found her left side at the waist. "This is simple, you take two slide steps back and one forward, then two back and one forward." As he spoke he gently pushed her backwards. She could feel the beat of his steps and the motion of his body and she fell into the same rhythm.

She wanted to look at her feet and he told her to keep her head up. The floor was empty enough not to bump into people and yet had enough people on it to let her feel safe. After one spin around the floor, she could feel herself relax her grip and actually look at the others from the school and smile as they danced past in their orbit of the floor.

"You never danced before?"

"Well, no, I was more of a classical fan,"

"Well honey, tie yourself down and hold on, 'cause it's time to put the spurs to it."

Right at the end of the song, he spun her. She squealed. They both laughed.

He led her back to the sporadic applause of those at the table.

They danced and ate and drank. They danced with each other and of course, Bull took Jessica on the floor and they danced like they were professionals. But it was funny, Hanna thought, every time he moved away to dance or get a drink or another plate of nachos with the jalapeños and sour cream, he always found his way back to her side or somewhere near it.

They sat for a while and talked to the others, as if the other was not there, yet, they almost sat back to back on the same side of the picnic table. They both would reach for a nacho and continue with their independent conversations. The people shuffled again and Bull and Hanna found themselves staring into the same fire at the same time. She could see the side of his face and the lines in it were highlighted by the orange glow of the campfire. He wasn't old, she thought. She searched the fire for the word that described him; 'charred', that was it. Maybe it was the beer, but that was the word that described him.

He took her back out on the floor to a slower song. The floor was crowded and so the dancing was contained in one area. "You did pretty well tonight," he said.

"You've done this before, haven't you?" she said looking into the eyes.

"Once or twice," he said as he looked around at the others on the floor.

"When you were married?"

"How did you know? Oh, that's right. Your mother is United Press International. My wife thought it would be fun to take country swing lessons."

"Did you go dancing a lot?"

"No, only a few times. I'm sure Gwen told you about Beth."

"Only that you were married once and that your wife died trying to save your daughter." She said it so fast she didn't realize it until it was already said.

"Yep, that's the story," he said as he navigated around the pole.

"I'm sorry. I didn't mean to—,"

"No, that's fine. It's fine. It was a while ago and you'd have found out anyway. Let me see if I can answer all of your questions in one rotation of the floor. I was married to Beth. We had one daughter, Cheri, yes, she did survive, and no–she doesn't live with me. She didn't survive very well, I'm afraid. She's in a special home for kids. I spend as much time as I can with her. She stayed at home for as long as she could. There were services I couldn't provide for her. The round the clock nurse, the feeding tubes the, God the list goes on and on. I eventually petitioned the court to make her a ward of the state. Now she can get everything she needs. She's twelve now. Yes, I did love my wife and yes, on occasion, I do miss her very much."

"I'm sorry, I didn't mean for all that–are you okay?"

"Yeah, you needed to know and I really don't mind talking about it," he lied.

They walked off the floor towards the back side of an old storage shed. When they rounded the corner, away from the music and dance floor, it got significantly quieter. They walked with their hands in their pockets while they talked and looked at the old tractors and the three donkeys in a smaller barn.

"The visions are still there; thanks for checking, though," he said with a smile. "You know, its funny," he said as he leaned against the railing of the donkey stall. "I can still taste the salt water when I swam out to get them. I remember there was a set of waves I had to cross. I swallowed about half the Gulf as I tried to make my way out to them." He looked at her over his shoulder as she stood next to him. "That's just the way life is." He stood up and turned back towards the sound of the music. "Besides, how are you ever going to be able to separate legend from fiction? How are you ever going to find out things about me?"

"Such as?" she said with a gentle smile.

"Well, such as, where I got all these great dance moves. You've had to realize that I spent a pretty penny to be able to dance so well, so-professionally."

"Professionally?" She snorted.

"Now, don't try to cover it up. It's a fairly common issue among people who see me out here. Or, the alternative," he said, baiting her as he gently guided her back to the dance floor.

"Oh, and what might be this alternative?"

"It's fairly obvious, my dear, that my dancing skills are a natural gift from God. All this," he said gesturing to the length of his body "is Fred Astaire in hiding."

"Fred?"

"AAAstaire, yes ma'am."

"Does that mean that I'm your 'Ginger' tonight?" Hanna said with a dripping pile of sarcasm.

"Well, I think you're going to have to arm wrestle Jessica for that title. Now that would be something I'd like to watch."

"I bet you would."

Bull ignored the comment. "Hey, you think I'm good at this, you should see my Waltz or better yet–my Foxtrot."

"Did you pay for that, too?" she said, glancing over to him for only a moment.

"Absolutely."

"I thought so."

It had seemed to her it had been less than an hour when he said it was time to go, five hours after they'd gotten there. The ride home was a little quiet but it didn't seem awkward. This was a different man then the one she was introduced to. She had never been to a place like the one they were at that night. She liked it but she didn't know if that was his life. She was definitely a city girl and even though she liked the evening she thought that maybe he might ask her next to the tractor pull competitions.

He pulled up in front of the house. Her mind sprang to the realization that this was the end of their informal date. Who was she kidding? They were on a date. She could say all she wanted about them not being on a date but the facts are clear. He picked her up;

he danced with her; he bought her drinks and food; he brought her home. Now it was the end of the date and she remembered from her dating years that the boy will walk her to the door and want to kiss her good night or even come in for a 'nightcap,' what ever that entailed.

Before she knew it, he had unfastened his seat belt and had walked quickly around to her door and opened it. As they walked up the sidewalk she watched the door, hoping her mother would open it. Then again, why shouldn't there be any events at the door? She was a free woman. He was a free man. They were free people. The words 'never again' ran through her mind. A shiver rose up her back. She was instantly cold.

"I had a good time tonight," she said as she reached the porch and stood under the one-hundred watt bulb her mother had her put in about a week before.

"You didn't think you would, did you?" Bull said as he took his hat off.

"No, actually, I thought I would have a terrible time. But it was–really good. Thanks for inviting me." She looked up at him. It was the look she would use to let the man know she was interested. Women use it sparingly or else it wouldn't be 'the look.' It's the one that men can read as a look of promise—promise of love, romance, butter-rum cake off the naked tummy look. The one women use to lure men to their deaths. Hanna pulled it but unfortunately or fortunately for the two of them, she didn't know she did. She quickly erased it when she became aware that she was smiling bigger than when she did eat butter-rum cake. The chill of fear became even more intense with a fear of repeating something she had done before. However, she was finding him something more than the big guy in the uniform. There was a wave in her mind that quickly thought of the two of them going inside and tying each other in a twisted knot of human flesh. Then, as quickly as it came, it leaped from her brain like someone jumping from a run a way train.

He watched this process in the expression of her face. She looked at him; she smiled, placing her hand momentarily on his chest; she retracted the smile and the hand like she had burned herself on a hot stove. Good, he thought to himself. I'm not the only one. "Shucks missy, that's just yer whiskey talkin'," he said.

There was a pause. That's what she was waiting for. Does she move? Does she wait for him? Why does that bulb have to be so damn bright?

"Do you want to come in–," she started.

Bull cut her off. "Not tonight. I am working a patrol shift tomorrow–actually today–in about four hours," he said looking at his watch. "And frankly, teaching you how to dance wore me out. I'll see you later, Miss Hanna," he said as he turned to leave, placing his hat back on his head.

She reached out and placed her hand on his chest just before he turned. The open palm rested on the center of his shirt. This, to any man, was a sign that there was hope, maybe not right then, but hope that a barrier had fallen, like a crack in the Berlin Wall. There was hope. "Good night," she said stumbling over those two words "You're at school on Monday?" she asked to his back.

He stopped halfway down the sidewalk and took his hat off and stretched his arms out to the side and looked to the sky. "Do ya hear that Father?" he said in his best Scottish brogue. "She misses me already." He turned to her and smiled. It was a smile she wanted to see every day, she decided right then and there. She couldn't explain the feeling that smile gave her. He placed his hat back on his head, rubbed the edge with one finger as a salute and without answering her question, turned back to his truck and drove off.

She was happy with her brief, shallow, wading step into dating foreplay. Gwen heard the door open and shut and came out of her room. She had been up reading and wanted to see how her daughter did.

"Well, did you have a good time?" she said as she tied her bathrobe closed.

Hanna leaned with her forehead resting on the door; her eyes were closed. "Mother, you raised such a ditz," she said without lifting her head from the door.

"Yes, dear."

The one thing worse than a quitter is the person who is afraid to begin.

AUTHOR UNKNOWN

"Good morning, Ms. Sonet, can we come in?" Hanna said as she held the door open to Gayle's classroom and her class streamed in for the science show that Gayle had invited them to watch.

"Oh yes, Mrs. Jarger, we were just getting ready for you. Okay class, please, everyone stand up and let's push our desks against the walls. We'll sit in the middle of the room during the presentations. Mrs. Jarger, I have a chair back here for you. Regina—watch that honey, your chair is caught. There you go. Mrs. Jarger's class is going to be joining us to watch our presentations. Just have your students can find a spot on the floor anywhere and my class, you can join them after you finish moving your desks."

"We want to thank you for the invitation to come and watch your science show. We've been looking forward to this all morning," Hanna said to Gayle.

It was Oscar, a little Hispanic boy about twice the weight he should be, who told the truth. "Yeah, none of us wanted to take the spelling test today. Hanna smiled. "Oscar, because of your love for spelling, I'll make sure that we get it in first thing tomorrow morning."

Just before everyone settled in, the door opened and Tony walked in carrying a student's chair. "Here you go, Ms. Sonet. I was able fix the leg so it doesn't wobble anymore. It's as new as a two-dollar pocket watch. Where do you want it?"

"That's good right there, Tony, thanks," Gayle said as she gestured with her hand.

"Oh, hello Ms. Jarger. I didn't see you there," he said, seeing Hanna behind him.

"Hi Tony, how is your day going?"

"My day is going just fine," he said as he pulled a rag out of his back pocket and wiped off a small spot on the seat. He got a little close to her so he could whisper something. Hanna noticed so she leaned in.

"I hear you had a pretty good weekend yourself with you dating Mr. Bull and all," he whispered with a little grin.

"Wow, stories travel fast around here," she whispered back.

He nodded, "Very fast." He then turned and waved at a couple of the children as he left.

"Bye, Tony," a couple of the children were heard saying.

"Bye, my charges," he said going out the door.

Hanna walked over to the seat that Gayle had for her. "Actually, I owe you one," she said.

"For what?"

"Your invitation came just in time. I'm with Oscar. I didn't feel like grading thirty-two spelling papers."

The two women began their own nesting. As the students crumpled on the floor, jockeying for the best positions, the two women settled into their seats. "Class, before we get started, I have a short video on Thomas Edison, the man we talked about last week, as a kind of lead in for these demonstrations. Let's pay attention to it and then we will jump right into the group presentations." Gayle started the video with a remote on her desk. She aimed at the large TV hanging from the ceiling at the opposite side of the room. The children watched while the two women continued their conversation in low whispers.

Gayle leaned over to Hanna. "So, how was Friday night?"

"Geez, not you too? It was fine. I'm telling you, I just got a ride with him out there. That's all," she said not very convincingly. She wasn't so sure she was convinced herself. "You and your guy seemed to have a pretty good time. He's cute."

"Oh, he was all right I guess, in an anemic Elmer's Glue sort of way. He's a CPA with his own firm here and one in Dallas. A girlfriend set us up some time ago and he hasn't left. He has terrible morning breath though—yuck," she said as she grimaced. "It wasn't nearly as much fun as I bet you had."

Hanna thought for a moment. "You dated him, didn't you?"

"Who? Bull? Oh, you bet I did. He's a dreamscape. I think everyone under retirement age dated or wanted to date him, including a few of the male teachers," she said with a grin.

"How come you don't go out with him anymore?"

"Oh, I probably still could. He is too blue collar for me. If he was a lieutenant or a captain or something up in the ranks like that then maybe. I know that sounds shallow, but I know what I want and he can't provide that for me on a police officer's salary. It's too bad, too," she said shaking her head.

"Why? How many times did you go out with him?"

"Twice. I could tell he was probably falling for me so I broke it off with him. He is just so—so," Gayle searched for the same word that Hanna couldn't find either.

"So, what?" Hanna asked hoping she could come up with a better word than 'charred.'

Gayle had a look on her face like she was searching for something that was right there and yet a thousand yards away. "I want to say handsome, but that's not it.

"No, that's not it," Hanna whispered, interrupting her train of thought. "Did you ever, you know? You and him ever?"

"Bull and I ever spend the night together? Is that what you're trying to say? No, we didn't. Not that he didn't want to; but it was going to be tough enough on him so I didn't want to make it any harder," she said as she busied her hands and averted her eyes.

"Who are those guys?"

BUTCH CASSIDY AND THE SUNDANCE KID

Mid-October

Bull's pager went off indicating another call to another one of a thousand needs for stepped up assistance from the street units. Nine out of ten calls are in response to a domestic. Bull's response was always the same—calm, quiet anxiety. His look was the same whether he was going to a hot call or for hot coffee. He could even carry on a conversation about just about anything while driving Code-3, over the scream of the siren, and still hear the radio traffic. Inside his skull there was a different game going on. It was the ultimate multi-tasker. In his brainpan, he was pulling up the vision of the location he was going to. He looked out the window and saw the Seven-Eleven with the Purple Cow Ice Cream store next to it. He knew he was getting close. He recognized the corner.

Many calls he could recognize the general location. Sometimes the exact location, like the house that the NRU team had gone in before, but usually it was just the neighborhood. He was plotting his approach, calculating his speed and traffic and figuring out what time he would arrive. Even the time of day and where the sun was came into play. Just like in the old west or in an aerial dogfight, the good guys always wanted the sun at their back.

Stan Garrison was already there and was giving approach directions to responding units, bringing them in from the west, down streets that were out of the field of fire. Bull determined by the radio traffic that there was a man holding a woman hostage in the front yard of a house. There was a call for any unit with a bean-bag gun to respond shortly after Bull got the page and responded. He hadn't heard anything for some time while he was driving. He pulled his car down the street and turned off his siren.

"4-32 Adam, I'm coming twenty-three," Bull said as if he was coming in for a soda and fries. He was focused. There were a lot of cars and news vans. He had parked down the street and used his trunk release, got out of the car, grabbed his gear from the car and ran to where Stan was crouching behind his own unit. Bull figured by the close proximity of Stan's car to the house, he was one if not the first one on scene. "What did you have to pay to get these good seats, my friend?" he said as he came up and crouched down next to Stan, who was on the radio.

"You should have been here when I rolled up. This bastard made me age to where I almost look like you. I didn't see him until he came up behind me with the woman and the gun. The guy is every bit of six-five or six. I gave him a palm strike right to the snot locker and ran like a skinhead in Harlem. I think I just pissed him off."

Bull looked over the roof of the Sergeant's car. "Wow, he does look like he's corn fed. I heard the call for the bean bag."

"Yeah, he wiped his ass with that. This guy is so high we tasered him and bagged him and he is still standing out there. He couldn't make up his mind whether to use his gun or his knife. He actually dropped the gun when I hit him. I picked it up when I ran so all he has is the knife. There's an officer in the house. That's why he's not going back inside. I'm thinking the more this guy gets ramped up the more he's likely to do a suicide by cop thing."

"Let us do his dirty work."

"Exactly. SAU is on the way but they're coming from the other side of town and they might not make it in time."

"We have any long guns?"

"Just the M-16, and that is too long a shot to try to get a head shot on him and miss hers."

Bull looked down the street behind him for about a block. The ground press was well back and they couldn't see much unless they used their long lens, but there were four news helicopters that maintained a perimeter outside of the police helicopter that maintained a respectful distance in a right hand orbit over the house. The media choppers didn't need to be close. They were all equipped with their 'Zoom Action Lens' that could focus in from far away. Whatever happened in the next few minutes was going to make the five, six, and ten news.

"Anyone else with us from NRU?"

"Just you and me and about fifty-thousand street units."

"What does the buffalo want? Looks like he's not starving, so he must have enough food stamps and beer."

"We can't get a clear answer," he said, as the man screamed something, but it was too slurred to be understood. "We think he's three-ninety. The neighbors say he's been drinking all day."

Bull looked over the car again at the man holding a Hispanic woman around the throat with his arm the size of Bull's thigh. He was mumbling something and holding what looked to be a carving knife to the woman's throat. There were an easy sixty yards of open ground between Stan and Bull and the two standing in the yard. The officers in the house and on the side were within ten to fifteen yards, but that was still too much ground to cover. She'd be dead before they got to him.

"There's too much distance between us and him. Even if we ran and coordinated it with the guys in the house we'd never get there in time. We got to get to him and buy some time for the others to rush him," Bull said as he slid back behind the protection of the car. He thought for a moment. "Remember that course on task force management we took in San Diego about six years ago?"

"Yeah, parts of it," Stan said "We got hammered at the Boll Weevil that one night-remember?"

"Bull, get to the point, fer Kriz sake, I remember nothing from that trip except that I threw up in my shoes that night, and wore 'em the next day for two hours before I realized where the smell was coming from," Stan said as he pulled his shirt and the underlying Kevlar vest forward and blew air down inside to cool himself.

"Remember when that waitress and I were balancing limes on our chins?"

"Vaguely."

Bull smiled. "Remember what I had to do when I lost?"

Stan frowned, picturing an obscure image that didn't make any sense. "How is that going to help anything here?"

Bull began to unbutton his shirt. "Have the team from behind the house get ready just in case this goes south." He unbuckled his tool belt and handed it to Stan. Pointing to the can of pepper spray on the belt, he said, "Pull that out and hand it to me when I get these shoes off."

"What are you going to do with that?"

Bull continued getting undressed and ignored the question. "Have the others go to the side of the house. When I use this," he said holding up the can Stan gave him, "and get's the girl loose from him, have them move in." He pulled off his shirt and Kevlar and stripped down to his underwear. "Don't have them wait. As soon as this spray goes they need to be stepping it." Bull pulled a roll of duct tape from his bag and tore a piece about six inches long and taped the can to the inner part of his thigh, high up in the groin.

"Be careful with that stuff. It's riding right next to your Johnson. If that goes off you'll wish you had it sprayed in your face," Stan said as he crawled around Bull, opened the passenger door to his car and tossed Bull's gun belt on the front seat, then locked the door again.

"I will. What's this guy's name?" Bull said as he looked up over the hood of his car.

"Jeremy Gillis."

"Jeremy Gillis, all right. As soon as I go out you get on the radio and tell the perimeter what we're doing."

"Got it." Stan smiled.

Bull looked at him. "What are you smiling at?"

Stan shook his head. "It's nothing."

"Listen you ol'bastardsombitch," he took a deep breath and looked around to see if anyone was watching before he continued. "I'm going out here in my underwear, by the way—I do not want any comments from anyone about what they look like, and I expect you to make sure THAT happens unless, of course, this guy kills me—in which case I'm going to come back and haunt your 'No-Plan-Got-to-Make-Shit-Up-as-I-Go-Because-They-Sucked-My-Brains-Out-When-I-Became-a-Sergeant'. All I have to save my stinking life is a lousy four-ounce can of pepper spray shoved up my tail pipe. Now tell me what you were laughing at you bastard?"

"I just thought that it, uh, well I thought you might wish you were–you know–bigger. Down there–I mean."

"You're a piece of shit."

"I know," Stan said.

"I never liked you," Bull said as he pulled off socks, thought about it for a minute, then put them back on.

"I know that, too." Stan looked out of the corner of his eye to see what kind of underwear his old friend was wearing. "Oh, thank God," he breathed out with a sigh of relief.

"What?"

"I was scared you were wearing a thong. Of course, those couldn't be much better."

"Yeah, I got your thong right here," Bull said as he flipped off his friend.

"You ready?" Stan said, locking eyes. The smile was gone. They both knew that this time was just one of thousands of times that one of them, or their kind, stepped into the gap. There are no words shared between people like these. After the preparation and the nervous relief, there was just a moment that those in the gap had. Most never stopped to think that this could be the end. That they might not see the sun set, hear the laughter of their family, or feel the warmth of a friend's hand. If they thought of it they would never step out. They did it for the girl that was held captive but they also did it for the man. If there was a chance to end this peacefully with everyone still alive at the end of the day they had to take the chance.

"Here we go," Bull said as he stood up. "Hey, Mr. Gillis," he called as he walked around the front of the car and out into the open area between the couple and the police line. His hands were head high. He had on his white undershirt and his pants but the belt was undone and he didn't have on any shoes, just socks. He walked towards the couple, but not too fast, just a steady, clean pace with no overt movements, closing the gap and getting in close.

"Mr. Gillis, I'm Officer Bull Thornton. Look, we just need to talk. I'm leaving all my stuff back at the car, okay? Look, the pants, I'm leaving them right here," he said as he stripped off the pants, exposing his white boxers with big yellow smiley faces all over them.

"Stay back," the man said, and tightened his grip on the woman.

"Look man, I got nothing on me except a smile. We just want to end this thing and no one can hear what you have to say from over there. I'm here to help you help us."

In just a few seconds he had cut the distance in half and continued to approach. "I don't want to talk to you," the man slurred and blinked hard.

"Look Jeremy, I left all my stuff back there. If I didn't think you wanted to resolve this and if we wanted to hurt you do you think I'd be standing out here like this? Huh? Look, my Sergeant knows that you got judged badly by the first units here. We're trying to make up for that." He was within ten yards. Bull knew a person with a knife could cover twenty-one feet in one and a half seconds and fatally stab a cop before he could draw and shoot if he wasn't prepared. Bull didn't have a gun and the gas would be an even tougher item to get into play. But he had an idea. Surprise and treachery were his allies as well as his mantra. "Look, Jeremy, can I call you Jeremy? I just want you to see I'm serious. I want to talk," he said. He stepped within five yards.

"Stop right there," the man said. Spit came out of his mouth and fell onto the woman's shoulder. "I don't care what you did with–,"

"Look, we know you don't want to hurt anyone. Tell me what you want and maybe I can get it for you."

"You can't get me jack, man," he said as he gestured towards Bull with the knife before he returned it to the woman's throat.

Bull sneaked another yard closer.

"Maybe I can, man. Look, you got to believe me, what person in their right mind would do this?" he said as he held his arms out and took another step. He could smell them. Stale whiskey breath, cigarettes, sweat, and dirt.

"You're a liar. You don't want to help. You're a liar, just like this bitch here," he said with clenched teeth as he tugged on the woman's head and looked at her, tipping the knife closer to her throat. Bull took another half a step. He moved a little to his left so the man looked directly into the sun, right over Bull's shoulder.

"I ain't goin' to take this crap no more. I'm going to end it right here."

Bull looked up into the man's face. Bull was a big man, but this guy was bigger; big, drunk, and no reason to live. A lousy tri-fecta, Bull thought.

"Tell me, Big Man," Bull said holding his hand to his chest. "At least tell me what she did?"

"You don't care," the man said as he shuffled to stabilize his stance.

"Jeremy, can I call you Jeremy? Jeremy, focus on me," Bull said as the man's eyes wandered, "look what I'm doing. I'm standing in the middle of the damn city wearing my boxers and a smile and you have the juice to tell me that I don't care. If I didn't care I would have shot you from that car over there and spent the next seven hours doing paperwork on it. Don't you tell me I don't care. You hurt my damn feelings," he said as he shook his finger at him in mock discipline.

Gillis clenched his teeth again. "She told the court I was a lousy father. She said–she said I beat her and the kids. She said I drank too much and beat her."

"Well, did ya?" Bull said while shrugging his shoulders.

The man thought for a minute, staring at Bull. "I might have swung at her a few times."

Bull shrugged again and in a calm, understanding tone said, "She probably deserved it. What was it? Dinner cold or late or something like that?"

The man shook his head. "No, she didn't like my friends comin' over. She said we drank too much so I got tired of her mouth and you know..."

"She didn't like your friends over?" Bull said "Your friends, in your house? What right does she have to tell you that? What about the kids?"

"They get mouthy when she and I go at it."

"No respect for you, huh?"

"None man, they're just like her," he said, looking at the woman.

"So you popped them too, huh? Sounds like they needed it as well,"

The man hesitated, then nodded as he watched Bull nod. Bull looked at the woman with a look of disdain. "Jeremy, my friend, it sounds to me like they asked for it. It really does. I think once you tell that same story to my boss, he'll understand and have the same opinion of you that I do. But if you stick her now there's nothing I can do for you. Look at yourself," Bull gestured as if he was painting a wall. "You let this bitch get to you? Come on, you're too smart for this. You know, I'm thinking that if you let her go, I'll tell the courts everything you said here. I know they'll understand what you're thinking. And, more importantly, what kind of real man you are."

"Jeremy, let me—," the woman started while pulling on his arm before he jerked her back.

"Shut up," the two men said to her at the same time.

"Look, man," Bull said leaning in close, talking in secrets. "I feel for you, I really do."

Jeremy's eyes wandered in the direction of Stan who was on the radio getting the perimeter set. They were ready when they saw Bull do whatever Bull was going to do.

"Jeremy, look at me, Jeremy! Look at me—look at me!" Bull snapped his fingers in front of his face and directed his gaze back. "Why are you even bothering with her? If you let her go now we can do this. You get another chance. You screw up now you're done. Look, I mean it. I wouldn't be out here in my shorts if I didn't believe it. I got to tell you something," Bull said quietly. He leaned way in. "Big men like you, strong as you are in your beliefs, 'King of your Castle', I have to tell you something, you, you, you make me hot!"

Jeremy's eyes almost crossed

"Look Jeremy, can I call you Jeremy? I can tell you're special. You are really doing something to me and I'm at a point in my life that I don't care who knows, I want to show you something, something that you've done to me." Bull's eyes locked onto Jeremy's as he reached into the front flap of his boxer shorts. He winked at Jeremy just before he pulled the can free from the duct tape and his inner thigh.

Bull pulled the can of ten-percent capsicum fogger in his left hand and gassed Jeremy's face at about six inches. His response time was so delayed that Bull was able to cut loose a full blast with Jeremy's eyes still open. Jeremy reeled backwards while at the same time coming up with his arm that held the knife in a defensive reaction. Bull's right hand was curled in a fist and was already on its way to Jeremy's throat, hitting the soft tissue as hard as the short jab could muster. As Jeremy's head lurched back, Bull let go of the can, tossing it over to his left and then came back and, grabbing Jeremy's right arm just above the wrist, controlling the hand with the knife. As Bull's hand came back from the throat he hooked the woman's head with it and pulled her towards him. There was slight tension on the pull but then she broke loose, surprising him and almost causing Bull to fall backwards.

Behind Jeremy, Bull could see five officers at about three yards and coming fast. He didn't want to let go of the knife and felt the woman tugging on his other arm. Stan was pulling her and there were another four officers that he could see already at his side. Jeremy, Bull, and about six officers all went to the ground, wrestling the knife from Jeremy. The fight was out of him. The fog of the spray was injected up his nose and into his sinuses. He had trouble breathing and even more trouble with six men on him. Bull rolled off after the knife was secured and rolled away on the dirt yard. He realized that a lot of the spray bounced off of the man and fell back on him. His eyes were burning and his face felt like it was on fire. "Holy Crap," he said as he instinctively grabbed his face and his eyes, shoving more of it in. From the time he went for the gas to the handcuffing was no more than seven seconds. Jeremy was picked up by both arms and dragged off to be searched before being placed into a car. He was screaming and moaning and screaming again. Snot and mucus was draining uncontrollably from his mouth and nose.

"You okay, buddy?" came Stan's friendly, if not concerned, voice toward him.

Bull was able to open his eyes to a squint. The air caused them to burn but he could look up at his friend. "You move pretty quickly for an old man," Bull said to him.

"Yeah, well make sure you keep your day job. Ralph Lauren will never want you to be an underwear model."

Bull was sitting in the dirt wearing a tee shirt and his boxers, a little worse for wear. He pulled the shirt up and blew his nose into it. "What about Victoria's Secrets?"

Stan smiled a bit and pondered the image. "Maybe Sears."

Bull just nodded and blew his nose again. "I can live with that." He reached up and Stan grabbed his hand and helped him to his feet.

"Come on, Fire is over here and they'll wash your eyes out." Stan took Bull's forearm to guide him.

It took about fifteen minutes of a steady stream of cool water from the engine company that was there to get Bull to a point where he could carry on a conversation with his eyes open. The paramedic helping him gave him a towel to wrap around his waist and another to dry his face. Stan walked up with his clothes. He left the gun belt still secured in the front seat so Bull could get it after he was dressed. "You okay?" he said as he sat the clothes on the gurney just inside the ambulance. Bull sat on the first step. He stood up and turned around, picking up his pants and sliding the legs in, then the vest and shirt.

"Yeah. I was just in the wake of that stuff. I hate it when I get that in my face," he said. Stan smiled. "Brother, you have redefined the term 'hot pants' for me. Boxers with smiley faces? Please tell me that someone bought them for you as a birthday gift. Please tell me that you didn't spend money out of your own pocket to buy those? God, do you know how much fun the entire department is going to have with this? I bet Macy's is going to be having a run on these shorts in a few weeks after they see you on the news tonight."

Bull looked over at his friend. "Those news guys were too far back to see anything."

"We put them a full block back, but you know those guys, with their long lenses, especially on their helicopters. Oh hell, I'm sure they didn't see anything," he said teasingly. "You're going to be a star! Well, at least some parts of you are."

"Very funny. You're just jealous because you wish you had a pair," Bull said as he finished pulling his shoes on over his dusty socks.

"No, seriously buddy, good job," Stan said, patting Bull on the shoulder. "I got your belt and gun along with your bag in my car."

The two walked over to Stan's car and Bull finished getting dressed. He looked around and he could see the press at least a block away, but there were still two helicopters orbiting the site. As the officers broke down their equipment and returned to their units, Bull received one wolf whistle and two "hey good lookin'" calls from the other officers. He responded with smiles and hand gestures.

Across the street, he heard Jeremy calling to him. "Cop! Hey cop." The sound was muffled because he was calling out of the back seat of a patrol car. "Come here."

Bull finished buckling his belt keepers and then pulled his Glock from its holster, sliding the magazine out, checking it instinctively, and then pressing it back in before placing it back in the holster. He walked across the street towards the car.

"Hey, Colin," Bull said to the officer in the front seat writing in his field notebook.

"Hey, Bull," Colin Evers said. He was a medium size Hawaiian who had been on the department for about four years. A good guy and one of the few that Bull thought had the potential to go the distance and make a good commander. "Good job on this thing."

"Thanks. You got transport duty on this guy, huh?"

"Yeah, good job, cop," came the mocking slur from the back seat.

Colin looked up at Bull. "Yeah, should be fun at booking."

"Hey! You, hey cop, you said you'd tell them! You promised me man. You better not be jerking me around."

Bull looked through the window at the man in the back seat. "Colin, unlock his door for a minute, will you?"

"Sure, Bull," he said as he tripped the automatic door lock for the car. "I'm going to go check out some times for my log with the Sergeant. Can you watch him for a minute?" Colin asked as an excuse to leave the two men alone for a minute.

"Sure Colin, I'd be happy to." Bull moved to the side and let Colin out of the car and watched him walk away before he turned back to the man in the back seat. He opened the back door and took off his sunglasses. The sun was setting and the area filled with shadow. As he opened the door the smell of the man hit him again, along with a trace of the pepper spray.

"You know, I did promise. I'm always a man of my word. That you can count on. I will tell them exactly what you said. That you thought she deserved a hit every now and then because you and your drunken friends didn't like her mouth. I'll even tell them that the children had her mouth and you beat them too," he said resting his arm on the door.

"You're jamming me, you're going to shove it in and break it off! You lying pig!"

"Pig? Boy you are behind the times. I haven't heard anyone call me that for I think eight years now. Is that the best you can do?" Bull said with a smile.

"What?"

"Is that the best bad name you can think of? You are pretty thin in the old brain bucket. You could have called me a thousand things. You could have insulted my mother, my father, and my children. You could have insinuated that I have descended from the mating of dogs, or that some of my orifices, that are considered private in this society, are used as a sexual receptacle. You could have questioned my sexuality, or whether I had sex with my mother. You could have come up with all these things, and the best you could do is to call me the other white meat," Bull leaned in, bending in half, talking in a low, soft tone and wanting the man to see his eyes as he spoke. "Listen to me you open wound. The world is about to cave in on that vacuum you call a brain. I am going to fulfill the promise I gave you and tell the prosecutor everything. I will not lie. I promised you I would tell them about you and you can count on that fact to take place. I'm going to follow you through the court system and see to it that you go away, away to a cell block filled with residents that love wife-beating, child-hating pukes like you. And if by some chance you get out in this lifetime and even think about coming back and seeing this woman or her children, or her grandchildren, or her great grandchildren, I will be there. I will personally see to it that you dine in Hell before the sun sets on that day. You think you're having a bad day now, brother, try coming back here. I will rip your head off and piss down the hole it leaves." Bull stood back up and grew a big smile on his face. "Have a nice day."

Stan was standing by his car and saw Bull wave Colin back to his car. As the two men passed, Bull shook Colin's hand and kept walking towards the woman at another ambulance, now surrounded by family. Stan watched as Bull talked to her. He couldn't hear what he was saying but he didn't need to. He knew his friend. He was apologizing for what happened as if it was his fault. In a moment he would give her a business card with his name on it. If she or her family needed anything they could call him. Stan was pretty sure what the conversation was like between Bull and the man in the car and some form of that information would be passed to the woman. Packard Thornton himself was going to watch this one and maybe for the first time in years she could sleep tonight.

Hanna and Gwen were curled up on the couch watching the first part of the six o'clock news and finishing the mushroom and olive pizza they got at Pat's Pizza down the street when they saw it. They both stopped chewing in mid-bite.

Darrel Horton was also sitting on his couch rubbing his wife's feet while she was balancing the check book, looking for two ATM withdrawals that somehow didn't make it into the register, when they saw it. Darrel stopped rubbing, which caused his wife to look up over her reading glasses at him and then turn her head to what he was looking at on the television. "Isn't that your SRO?" she said.

Little Miguel was channeling through to find if Homer was on, but stopped on the news when he saw the face he knew. "Mommy," he called out in Spanish as his eyes stared at the television. "It's Officer Bull, he's on T.V."

Bull was sitting in his recliner in a clean Tee and boxers with his legs pulled up cross-legged, holding a bowl of strawberry ice cream topped with butterscotch when he saw it.

"We're sure down here at Channel 3 that Officer Thornton didn't think that this was how his day was going to play out in his successful apprehension....." the voice on the television said as an up close and clear shot of Bull standing in front of the man in his underwear with large yellow smiley faces took up the whole screen. It was the helicopter's view but then switched to the ground camera, which had almost as good a view.

Bull stopped chewing and dropped his head to his chest. It had been a long day.

There is always some madness in love. But there is always some reason in madness.

FRIEDRICH NIETZSCHE- 1844-1900

Gwen always said that elementary school was a funny place. She told Hanna before Hanna, herself, became a teacher that when children start to get up into seventh and eighth grades, they start to lose their innocence and grow hair and develop a need for deodorant. They punctuate their responses to adults with a "ya", "naw", "I don't know", "whatever", "like", and Gwen's favorite "cuz", which, depending on the part of the country one was from, could be "cause" because it was used in place of "because" or actually be short for "cousin." It just depended on the part of the country people were from. They began to develop attitudes of resistance and their cuteness begins to wane and develop into that of a young adult. Gwen gave an example of this by saying they will lose their interest in Easter egg hunting, kissing their parents or grandparents' goodbye, especially in front of the school when those adults drop them off. Backpacks of Sponge Bob Square Pants are exchanged for Jansport, and apples packed in lunches for the one piece of good eating that parents relied on for their child are often traded for chips or thrown away after only a bite or two. But here at Borman, most of the students hadn't reached that nightmare age yet. Gwen loved it.

Hanna knew what her mother said was true from her own teaching. But here, she was rediscovering the love and seeing it in its true form. Inner city kids, she thought, needed what she had to give more than others. They were still soft and supple for the most part. Many were from low-income homes and had artificially had to grow up quickly with only one parent or in some cases no parent. But even these children were able to be looked at and loved. They were still able to receive love from teachers and staff and not turn away from it as it happens to those who have lived long enough for it to develop into rejection. Hanna knew one could only love to the level and extent that they were willing to let others love them. If they allowed themselves to be loved by staff, there was hope that they would be able to love, purely. It was something that many of them did not get at home. Later, when they began to smell and grow hair, marking them as adults, they would seek comfort in the arms of others of their kind and call that 'love.' Unless they could see what love was in its pure form, a selfless giving, at the giver's expense.

Tony, in his own way, loved each child who came on foot, crossing the neighborhood intersection nearest the school. When you watched him, he greeted each child, excited to see them, each one of them. He patted them on the head or shook their hand, or messed up their hair. He would play with them in an adult humor kind of way. Occasionally, he would grab one of the smaller ones and carry them under his arm across the street while holding his stop sign. Or, with some of the bigger boys, who were starting to feel their antlers, he would take his large hand and fill it with the collar of their shirt, right behind their necks, and pick them up to where their feet were just barely taking the weight on their tiptoes and then walk them across the street as if he was carrying a laundry bag full of wet towels; the child laughed and tried, in vain, to remove the hand from their oversized shirt.

From there or from the buses, they entered a world of halls and staff that said 'good morning' on a routine basis to all the children as they walked down the sidewalks to their homerooms. Darrel was always out in the morning greeting the buses. He tried to call them by 'Mr.' or 'Ms.' if he could remember their last name or, if he didn't, he used the first name. As the first bell rang, signaling children to begin heading for their classrooms, he turned and headed back to his office, clapping his hands, as if he were herding sheep, to the children running late. Other teachers found themselves doing the same nearer their classrooms. Even Bull would find himself herding the kids to their classes. He added his own twist to the ritual by hollering. "Yup doggies, git along 'lil doggies, yup now," as he clapped his hands. Sometimes, a child came up to him; they were always the littlest ones with the biggest eyes, look up at him with a big grin which usually included a missing front tooth and say, "Officer Bull, I'm not a doggy." He took their face in his two hands and look into their eyes. "You're not? Then you must be a wolverine! Or a Muskrat! Or a Democrat!" and squeeze their face with each exclamation and then tickle them as he shipped them to their class. This was the atmosphere of love that surrounded these children. It happened here. It was happening at a thousand other schools across the country. The teachers and staff knew it was a battle for their scarred souls. Sometimes, there were victories and sometimes there were losses. But Hanna and Gwen both knew that seeds were sown daily. When they would sprout was anyone's guess.

After the herding ritual, Bull wound his way to the office to check his mail and wish the staff good morning. He could always get a pulse on the office by how Barbara was. If she was feisty then the day was going to be a good one. If she was quiet, misery would follow. "Good morning Mrs. Gaven. How is my 'Lil Lilac of the Southwest doing this morning?" Somewhere in Bull's walks through life, he had picked up a calendar of 'The Flower of the Month.'

Barbara looked over her glasses at him without a smile.

'Crap, misery', he thought.

"Come here," she said to him in a low tone. Bull moved in and leaned over the counter. "I had a test done yesterday," she looked around. "It's official, I'm carrying your love child," she said with a wink and an air blown hint of a kiss.

Bull smiled, "Good, but how do I know it's mine, you vixen!"

"You don't."

"Mrs. Gaven!" Bull said, standing straight.

"Officer Thornton!" she said, standing up straight.

Darrel and Gayle came out of his office. "I thought I heard

you out here. I saw you on television last night," Darrel said with a smile.

"I saw a lot of you on television last night," Gayle said without breaking stride as she walked by the three of them on her way to the mailroom.

"Okay, people, let me have your quick attention," Darrel said loud enough for the five or six staffers in the room to hear. They stopped to listen. "People, people, please! Officer Thornton, I'm sure, would appreciate a little sensitivity for his situation. We're supposed to show kindness to our children and to our peers, please people a little decorum," Darrel finished with his hand on Bull's shoulder as he scanned the room for understanding.

"Thanks, Darrel–,"

"I told Cindy that all that smiley face stuff would come back one day and she would be sorry if she threw my shorts away. You, my friend, are my hero for wearing those. It gave me the guts to go pull my old ones out of the back of my sock drawer and put them on last night," he said with the face of a middle aged boy getting a new toy.

"Darrel, I–,"

"I was back in the seventies again. I felt twenty years younger. It was cool. It was bitchin', it was boss, it was–,"

"I get the idea. I'm glad my nakedness made you a happy man."

"Cin' liked them too, if you get my meaning," Darrel said with a wink.

"Darrel, you need to get out a little more, maybe take in a movie. Take Cindy to that little cafeteria she likes, buy her a happy meal." he said as he walked away.

You da Boss, Big Guy," Darrel said as Bull walked away. "Just you and Springsteen."

Bull walked into the mailroom shaking his head, but there was a grin on his face. He didn't see Hanna standing in the corner looking at some papers. She had been listening. She was developing anger at herself. She was intrigued with him. She had to admit it and it angered her. She didn't want to go down this road again with any man let alone a man that Bull appeared to be, whatever that was. He was treacherous, she figured. She didn't trust him. He was too dependable, too nice, too perfect, and too pompous. He dated everything in a skirt at the school, according to the skirts, and if he liked those women she wasn't sure she wanted him to take an interest in her. If those were his 'type' then she definitely wasn't his type. She thought, if he liked those women, she didn't want to be lumped in with them.

Still, she considered as she stared at his back, the outline of the Kevlar under his shirt, there was something she thought to be safe about him. Something, under the veneer, that kept her from thinking about him in fear. The fact that the man actually had a pair of boxers like that meant something. She didn't know what it meant but it meant something.

"Smiley faces, huh? I figured you were a whitey-tightey kind of guy," she said to his back.

Bull turned around and saw her. He looked over the top of his reading glasses. She noticed his face changed in expression as he turned to see who was going to ride him now about what happened. It got soft when he recognized her. She saw a small smile. The corner of his eyes softened. That look, she thought, she could get used to that look. "Okay—you too, huh; it was the end of the wash cycle. They were in the back of the drawer next to the sock garters.

"Hmm, sock garters."

"I can take you down to John's Uniforms and show you. They're regulation. Any motor officer would tell you."

"A little sensitive about the news last night?"

Bull paused. He knew this was going to be a long day, "They didn't even get my good side. I photograph so much better from the other side."

"Oh, I don't know, the world seems to think you shake out pretty good from the side they got. It sound like you've given Darrel and his wife some Fantasy Island stuff and I'm sure they're not the only ones."

"Oh, I know," he turned back to his mailbox and pushed his glasses back up on his nose.

She paused for a minute. "I want to thank you for the other night. I had a good time."

"So did I," he said without turning around.

"I was wondering," she paused and took a breath, "if you would be interested in going with me to an engagement party. It's at the Phoenician," she said as she crossed her arms. She immediately felt she'd made a mistake and wished, again, she could pull the words back. The idea that she was asking a man on a date was fearful.

Bull took off his glasses. "The Phoenician, a clean tee-shirt and bring your own sack lunch kind of night, huh? What shall I wear? What- shall- I -wear?"

"I assume you have something a little more formal than smiley face underwear," she said

Bull leaned against the counter and watched her squirm. He saw her struggle with the invitation. "You mean like a suit or more dressy underwear with cupid hearts? I'm okay with the underwear. I did a wash last night and I can probably borrow a leisure suit from my Uncle Ned. I think he still has that powder blue one that he likes. I might have to have it tailored a little, but it should work," he said in a cold business-like answer. He didn't have an Uncle Ned.

Oh, God, what did I do? He has to be joking—I pray he's joking, she thought to herself. "Look, its okay if–,"

"Oh no, I would really enjoy it. You and me, Ned's blue suit, you in something polyester, we'll 'trip the light fantastic'," he said, snapping his fingers and pointing to the ceiling like the album cover to 'Saturday Night Fever'. "When is it again?"

Hanna choked out an answer. "This Saturday." Why did I do this? Why—never again I said, never again she thought.

"Great, I'll pick you up at—?"

"Five," she said almost in a whisper. "Five would be fine."

"Six forty five it is then," he said and put his glasses back on.

"No, five–, oh, you're joking. Of course, joking on the time, yes," she struggled to leave. "Great then, I think."

Hanna was kicking herself for the rest of the day. This was a bad choice and she even thought about going and telling Bull that it was a bad idea. It was only after she told her mother what transpired and seeing Gwen break into full-blown laughter that she began to feel better, although how dare he play with her like that. She was quiet that night as the two women sat on the couch. Gwen went out for her nightly walk and Hanna, as she did every night, asked her if she wanted company, already knowing the answer. She sat on the couch with a paperback by John Connelly that she had tried to get into but the thoughts of that day kept jumping in the way.

She toyed with emotions of anger, stupidity, and fear that she was, again, dealing with a man on a personal level outside of work. Finally she got up and went to bed and tried reading after propping the pillows under her head, pulling the covers up and folding them back. She pulled her knees up and used them as a book rest. She heard her mother come home, as she had ten thousand times before from her walk, shut the front door and lock it. Her mother called to her that she was home and that she was going to bed. Hanna heard her go into her room and turn on her little nineteen-inch that sat on top of the dresser.

Often, Hanna would get up in the middle of the night and go in and turn off her mother's television that she had fallen asleep in front of. Hanna read for a while and then rolled over and put the book down on her nightstand, after marking the page by cropping the corner of the page. She flipped off the light and rolled to her side, hugging two pillows with another under her head. It wasn't long before she floated off into sleep. The dream came some time during the night.

Hanna was about ten. The dress was really nondescript but her hair was longer. She recognized herself. She saw something and began to walk towards it, just like she did when she was the girl of about four. There was a gentle smile on her face. As she moved, it was as if she was in slow motion. Hanna always woke up at the same time in the dream. She saw herself walking towards something; something that she saw that she did not fear but that she recognized. When Hanna awoke, the sun was bleeding through the weave of the Roman shades. It was another day.

Discipline is a love word.

Bill Thrall

The sun was just up and warm already. Before school, Bull went to daily see his daughter. The Conright Building was one storey in the shape of a 'T' with the administration office at the junction of the two lines. Bull had researched places for his daughter when it was time to move her to a full-time care facility. It was named after a family that had set it up as a rehabilitation facility for their own daughter twenty years earlier and developed a trust fund to keep it running. It now was a regionally recognized care center for children like Cheri. Rooms went down the center and off to one side with the administration and nursing area at the opposite end of the top of the 'T'. Bull walked in and said hello to Katie, the older Hispanic nurse he knew years ago when she worked at County as an ER nurse. He then walked down the hall into his daughter's room as he did almost every day for the last few years. "She awake yet?" he asked as he passed Katie.

"She just had her breakfast and bath," came her reply.

Bull walked with a clip of a man who had walked this hall many, many times. Still, even though he was aware of the room and could walk the course blindfolded, he still entered on tiptoes, sliding around the large door after knocking on it lightly. The curtains were open and bathed the room in the morning light of burnt orange and clean crystal. Cheri was sitting up in bed. Her eyes were open and her mouth was set in a partial smile. Her hands had pulled up and curled on her chest, a clear sign of extensive brain damage. There was a small pink braid holding her hair back on her right side. He went over and kissed her forehead. Her hair smelled like fresh strawberries, with a cool dampness. He had bought that shampoo for her a couple weeks prior. He loved the staff but it was also a way that he could check to make sure they were doing what they needed to do. He pulled a chair up next to her bed and, after asking her how she felt and combing her hair with his fingers, he sat down and opened the newspaper that he brought in and began to read it out loud to her. He made sure he could see her face over the tops of his reading glasses. He put the side rail of the bed down so it to did not block his view of his daughter. He read the headlines and articles that he found interesting.

"Here you go, Bull. Just like you like it." Katie came in and brought him a cup of coffee, set it on the table next to the bed and left.

"Thank you, dear," he said as she turned to leave.

"Cardinals won again last night," she said as she went out the door.

"Yeah," he said as he scanned the front page of the sports section. "I wouldn't be banking on them for the playoffs," he said in Katie's direction, even though she had left.

"What do you think, Cheri? Cardinals in the playoffs? Nope, you're right, girl. Not a snowball's chance."

She was there; she was included in their life discussions. When he finished his paper and coffee he kissed her again, straightened the covers, checked to make sure her tracheal tube was clear and then quickly scanned her for bedsores. He finished by pulling the covers up under his daughter's arms and stuffed the pillows under her side. He kissed her again and pushed her hair out of her eyes and left the room. He walked back the way he came and out to his car. He would be at work in fifteen minutes.

Hanna's classroom was an example of the world's elementary classroom. On the walls were works of art from her students, some in crayon, and some in watercolor. She loved children and each picture was a work of one of her children. Hanna made it a practice to not only know her own student's names but those of their sisters and brothers and all those that were significant in their lives. That was a custom she brought with her from the Estrella. She would try to make all the concerts, games, and the dreaded Christmas Band concert where wood recorders were known for playing Jingle Bells in several different keys at the same time. Whenever her students asked her to attend, she would try to do so. To most of the kids, she was as close to a mother as they ever had. She was starting over at Borman but it would only take a couple of years and the relationship would be the same. At the end of the year, she would pass these children to the next grade and then the next before they would leave the school to go to the neighboring Osborn Middle School, as seventh graders. The two years after being in her fourth grade class allowed her to wean herself slowly from their company before they left her sight.

Her room was filled with hand drawings and maps with blue and pink pins in it that showed the birthplace of each child that she ever had, hundreds of pins. The corner by her desk, where the two walls came together, was covered in school pictures of hundreds of students, some with students and teachers. There was even one with Tony in the middle of a cluster of kids crossing the street. Sometimes, next to a picture, would be another picture of an older student or in some cases a young adult, standing with his arm around her pointing off to the side where they were pictured as a child. Hanna would pin the picture of her kids from Estrella next to the school picture so the finger of the older would point to the younger. On her desk was a heavily used coffee cup from Disneyland-Orlando. One of her students bought it for her when she went there years before. Shamu was stained from years of coffee or tea and never being washed. She was creative and loved to teach. She was mother to many of the kids who came through her classroom just like all the other teachers. Parents had relinquished their duties or were just too tired to care. So early in the morning, just like hundreds of other mornings, she stood in front of her class of young minds, sipping from her cup—today it was tea—and looking into their young faces. She waited until Sammy, on her left, finished picking his nose and Angel finished talking before she began the lesson for the day.

Bull was walking by the open classroom door on his way to the office when he heard her voice. He stopped and leaned against the wall just outside the room and listened. He found himself doing it more and more often. She often had her door open and he found himself wanting to walk by under some pretext of teaching something or moving something or, well, something, he thought. He would stop and listen just outside her door, like he was doing now. She never knew he was there and he always stood like he was reading something in his hand in case someone was watching. His mind was allowing her to enter. Slowly, cautiously, he allowed an idea of a woman other than his wife and daughter to be in his mind for more than just a moment.

Her voice was different. She always had a confident flare but there was a mask she sometimes wore that he swore he would penetrate. He was sure he wore one as well—he knew he wore one, sometimes several, depending on the moment. There was something in her voice, a confidence that bathed the room. He found himself loving to listen to her teach. He smiled and turned and continued to the office. Michael was standing there with a grin, showing his large, lightning white teeth of his.

"You are hanging around Hanna's room?" he whispered.

"I just was reading an old report," Bull said as he continued to walk and act like nothing was up, but really trying to put distance between his conversation and the open door.

"You are drawn to her."

"What? No, come on," he said not wanting to look at his friend.

"Ah, it is just as I thought. I remember when I was young. My father and mother took me out into the plains one early morning. It was where the lions and the leopards roamed and hunted. We crouched down and watched them, both the male and the female. I remember my father turning to me and saying 'When the gazelle and the beast wander, you will hear the softness of the morning cry for the song of the grass."

Bull stopped in mid stride and looked at his friend who had

also stopped and was smiling at him. "What crap are you making up now?"

Michael held his gaze for a moment and then laughed. "I know, it sounded good, did it not? Almost like I knew what I was talking about."

"You are so full of—,"

"Yes, I know. I have learned that from you, my friend.

"'Poo poo?' You are a twisted man."

"From you, that is a compliment. You do like her. I have watched you, Bull Thornton. You are smitten by her Bootay."

"You don't do street black very well."

"I will work on that. You, my friend, need to work on her."

"You think?" Bull said with a look back down the hall at the open door. "I don't think she likes me."

"Of course she does not like you. That should not stop you. Where is the heart of the lion?" Michael said as he placed his hand on Bull's shoulder. "In my country, if we saw someone like Miss Hanna we would sweep her off her feet, throw her on the back of our horse and take her back to our village and make her our—,"

"Queen, yeah, we've been down this road before. Then tell the rest of the story. You don't have horses in your country unless they're on a stick over a fire and you and I both know she would lose half her body weight and die of dysentery."

"That is also true—but she would be a—"

"QUEEN! I got it. I'll think about it."

"You really need to work on her."

"Okay, okay, I said I'll think about it."

"Someday, you will tell me about being a queen?"

Bull smiled as he opened the door. "I'll do you one better. Some time, after school, maybe on a Friday, I'll take you to a place where all the queens in the city get together."

"Really?" Michael said.

"Promise," Bull said with a grin.

"This week we're going to talk about emotions and if we could smell them, what they might smell like. We'll talk about a different emotion every day this week and at the end of the week and the beginning of next week, I'll make something to eat that smells like that and we'll eat it for a treat. How does that sound?" Hanna panned the room and most of the children reacted to the word 'eat' and lost their interest in 'emotion'.

"Miguel, let's start with you today. If you had to describe 'kindness' what might that smell like? How would you describe it? What would kindness smell like to you?" She took another sip from her Shamu coffee cup and waited.

Miguel shrugged his shoulders and after some prodding and great thought, "I think it smells like honey."

"Honey? Oh, I can see that. That sounds like it would describe 'kindnesses." She nodded at another child. "Megan, what do you think?"

Hanna knew Megan was the thinker of the group. She had two parents and she wore pretty dresses on Mondays. She was always clean and smelled like lavender. Most of the kids, on a good day, smelled like soap. She smelled like lavender. "I think kindness smells like rain."

She turned to another. "Tolisha, what do you think?"

Tolisha was at the other end from Megan on the hygiene scale but Hanna didn't care. Her hair always came in tangled and sometimes the shirt she wore was the same one she had worn for the last two days. Her shoes had holes in them until Hanna bought her a pair. Tolisha's mother was tepid about the gift and when Hanna asked if she could give them to Tolisha, she was almost acting as if Hanna was saying that she couldn't take care of her child, which everyone knew she couldn't, even Child Protective Service. CPS had been out to the house at least twice since she came to the district the prior year. Hanna quickly changed the conversation to make it sound as if the mother were doing her a favor. "You see," she started, "I bought these shoes for my niece and they didn't fit. But the receipt was lost and my niece had worn them for a day or so before telling me about them. I can't take them back and Tolisha tried them on and they fit. You would really be doing me a favor if she took them."

The mother bought it and allowed the gift. Tolisha wore them every day but kept her old shoes in her desk. Hanna wondered why until she saw her take the new ones off and put the old ones on when they went to P.E. Hanna just smiled.

"I think it smells like powdered sugar."

Hanna loved that answer. "Ooh yes, what can we make with powdered sugar?" In unison the answer came back "Cookies!" Hanna knew she would have to research recipes for a cookie that has honey and powdered sugar in it.

Hanna's morning passed and rolled into the lunch hour. She marched her class to lunch and after she got them seated she went and got her own tray. She usually ate her lunch in her room, not wanting to deal with lunch duty unless she had lunch duty. Gwen was over at a table by herself and busy pushing the food around her plate. Hanna got a turkey sandwich and walked over to the table. Gwen didn't notice her until she was standing by her side. "This is one of the things that are so nice about this job, I get to have lunch with my Mom every day," she said as she placed the tray on the table next to her.

Gwen looked up as if waking from a dream. "Oh, hello dear, I didn't see you walk up."

"Boy, you were somewhere else," she said taking a bite from her apple and sliding into the bench seat. "Do you mind if I join you or did you want to go back to whatever you were thinking about?"

"Oh, I wasn't that far off," Gwen said with a half smile.

"The medicine again?"

"This new stuff the doctor has me on is really taking a toll on my stomach," Gwen said, finally putting her fork down on the tray.

"Did you call him like we talked about?" Hanna said, looking at the side of her mother's face and taking another bite of apple.

"No, it's only for three weeks, then I'm off for three. I'll just wait it out."

"Mother, we talked about this–."

Gwen cut her off. "I know."

"–and you said that–."

Gwen was getting short. "I know what I said."

Hanna didn't hear her mother's voice and just kept rolling. "You said you were going to call him and tell him about this."

Gwen turned to face her daughter. "Hanna, I said I know. I changed my mind." She got up from the bench table. "You need to be careful about getting our roles reversed," she said as she picked up her tray and walked it over to the tray return. Hanna watched her leave. She, at first, was angry that her mother would take the tone that she had with her. After all, she was concerned and they did talk about it. She thought that she did agree to call.

She fought through her lunch, finishing her sandwich and barely tasting it. After a couple of minutes she toyed with the thought that she had overstepped herself. She remembered her mother trying to ask about her and her husband. She didn't want her mother's interjection then unless she asked for it. The problem wasn't that her mother didn't have good advice. She always did. The trouble was control. When the world around her started to spin out of control the scariest part was that Hanna was not in control. Gwen had to be saying the same thing.

Late that night, she could hear her mother retching in the bathroom. She had heard it before, but late at night, lying in bed in a dark room, it sounded much louder than normal. She pictured her mother standing on her tiptoes holding onto the back of the toilet. She then heard the toilet flush and then the sink run. Soon, Gwen would shuffle down the hall and open the front door. Whenever she got this way, Gwen would go for a walk, just up and down the street, for about forty-five minutes, allowing the fresh air to clear her mind and calm her stomach. "Going for a walk?" Hanna called to her.

"Just a short one. I'll be right back," she said as she opened the front door.

"Want me to go with you?" she asked, already knowing the answer.

"No, I won't be long," she said as she closed the door. Hanna got worried when her mother went out after just turning her guts inside out especially when it was two or three or four o'clock in the morning. But after a while, Hanna realized it was exactly what Gwen needed.

After almost an hour, Hanna heard the door open and Gwen come back in, walk down the hall and shut her bedroom door.

The next morning, Hanna woke to the smell of bacon frying. "What are you doing?" she said as she tied her robe in a loose knot. She had to squint. Her mother had the lights on as well as the kitchen blinds open to the full morning sun pushing through the east windows in the kitchen. "You were just heaving your lungs out a couple of hours ago."

Gwen looked up from the stove and into her daughter's eyes with a smile. "Good morning to you too, dear. To answer your question, I'm making you some oatmeal, and bacon and eggs for me," she said as she crushed a piece of bacon in her teeth and chewed, smiling again at her daughter.

"You were throwing up just–,"

"Yes, thank you for reminding me dear. I was just about through remembering how wonderful last night was until you reminded me," she said, wincing and holding her side from a shot of pain.

"What's wrong?" Hanna said as she saw her mother flinch.

"Nothing. I just pulled a muscle last night, that's all."

Hanna moved over to the stove and looked into the saucepan as her mother stirred. Hanna opened a white spice container that was one of four of staggered height that sat next to the stove. She spooned out some brown sugar and put it in the cooking oatmeal. "You always wait too long to put in the sweet stuff. You pulled a muscle last night? You going to stay home today and recover?" she said as she put the container back and snatched one of the eight pieces of bacon on the paper towel.

"Why should I stay home?" she said.

Hanna just shook her head as she went over to get a bowl down for her oatmeal and a plate for her mother. "Never mind."

Gwen heard the frustration as she dished up the oatmeal and plated her eggs and bacon and the two of them went out to the porch. The air was cool but not too cool and the sun warmed them. There was freshness to the day. Fall was here and colder mornings were on their way. They didn't talk until they sat down. It was Gwen who broke the silence. "Look sweetheart, this is either going to kill me or I'm going to get well, or God knows, somewhere in between. If I can work, I'll work, if not, then I won't. If I stop moving, it will run me over." There was a pause in her voice. She pulled the fatty end of the bacon off and placed it on her plate. "Sometimes, all I have is the momentum of the days to carry me from one to the next. If I stop before I need to stop then I'll have time to think about just how sick I really am and what the outcome might be. God will keep me moving as long as I need to move. Then he'll take me home. Until then, I work." She took a bite of bacon. "I have to keep moving. I have to keep thinking." Hanna knew her mother was right. She also knew that her mother would lie down when she needed to. She was one of the smartest people Hanna knew.

Gwen looked over at the small flower garden just outside the edge of the porch. Her green bathrobe with white trim puckered at the neck but she didn't seem to mind. The air felt good on her skin. "This year, I think we'll plant tulips and daffodils right there so they bloom in the early spring."

Life is a series of surprises and would not be worth taking, or keeping, if it were not.

Ralph Waldo Emerson

A cold November day

Friday afternoon was always a torrent of activity around Borman. There was always a basketball game or some type of game that Darrel or one or more of the teachers were involved in. The kids were either talking about those games, or what they were going to do the following weekend. There was always a discussion about who was going to go and with whom and how they were going to get there. No one wanted to pull up anywhere and be seen by their friends with their mom driving, or worse, the city bus.

Tony went to watch some of the basketball game between the Borman sixth graders and the Longview Trojans, which was a rare double-header so it started before school ended. He stood alone along the sidelines, next to his supply closet, where he kept the mops and buckets and the self-propelled floor polisher. The score was close, which always made Tony nervous. When the score was tied in the early few minutes of the first period he forced himself to leave and empty the trash containers in the library and the fifth grade wing.

Hanna found herself checking the clock at the end of the day. "Okay children, don't forget to take those permission slips home, get them signed, and don't forget to bring them back on Monday," she said as the paper found its way to their backpacks on their way out the door. "All right, be careful this weekend and I'll see you on Monday." Her smile softened when Bull filled the door. "Bye, Officer Bull," several said as they passed the rock and found open water.

"Bye, my little squirts of phlegm," Bull said as he entered.

"Oh my gosh, what did you just say to them?" Hanna rasped.

"What?" Bull said with his arms outstretched in mock misunderstanding. "I was speaking scientific truth. Hey, you might have let them go but I was still teachin'. Phlegm is a science word. A word that someday they'll understand and then they'll remember where they heard it first and then, you'll see, they'll come back and thank me for teaching them the foundation for such an important word."

"Forget I asked," she said as she dropped her head.

"Okay, it's forgotten. Well?"

"Well what?" She just didn't want to be reminded.

"Well–it's the weeeeek-------end."

"Well, yes, yes it is."

"Well, what time do you want me to pick you up tomorrow? I know we talked about it, I just wanted to confirm."

"Look," Hanna sighed. She couldn't deal with this anymore. She couldn't see this being anything but an embarrassing moment, and she didn't want to be a part of it. She remembered what her mother said about Bull but she couldn't see it. She just didn't trust that it was going to do anything but blow up all over her reborn dignity since her recovery from her divorce. "We don't have to do this. Why don't we just not. I don't think I really want to go anyway." A fear of embarrassment came over her. If she did this, she would be seeing 'a man.' She wasn't sure she wanted to take that step. She knew she feared that step.

By the time she finished, Bull was standing at her desk and had picked up the picture.

"Who's this?" he said almost interrupting her, oblivious to her speech.

She sighed again. She didn't want to talk to him, let alone talk to him about the picture. "That's Mom, Daddy, and me."

"Humph, you were cute back then. What are you, about three here? At least three, but not any older than four," he said as he looked into her eyes. "Your mother is still good looking. What happened to your Dad? You can't even really make out his face."

"Gwen never told you?" Hanna said, finding it odd that they were close but never shared a key element like that. She reached out and took the picture back and looked at it herself.

"You know, she might have, but I don't think so. I knew he was in Vietnam and died there but we didn't go much beyond that," he said as he adjusted his belt and sat on the edge of the desk next to Hanna's desk.

"He died in Vietnam in the sixties," she said as she stroked the picture and placed it back on the desk.

"Army?"

"Marines," she said with a smile, not taking her eyes off the picture.

"I was Marine Air in my former life," Bull said, crossing his arms.

Tony walked in and emptied the two wastebaskets without saying anything. He nodded to the two of them with a smile to Hanna. He took the baskets out to the larger bin on wheels outside the door.

"Oh, really? Did you load 'em or drive 'em?" she said with a distracted smile.

"I was a first lieutenant driver. I flew A-4's out of God knows where to God knows where." Bull looked down at the picture. "I was in that show," he said quietly.

"You went to Vietnam?" she said with a surprise. "You're not old enough."

"Twice. Right when the war was ending."

She took a breath. It wasn't a deep one and barely discernible, but Bull noticed it. "Dad was on the ground. Mother said that planes made him sick." She looked up at Bull. "She said that his commanding officer, a Captain, personally called her to tell her about his death." She looked again at the picture for a long time without saying anything before she continued. "It was night and his company was overrun. Men were dropping everywhere, explosions, rockets screaming, men screaming. Their back was to the Mekong by some place called Fire Base Six. They were waiting for patrol boats to come in and get them but the Captain said they were having their own problems getting up river." She took a breath. The Captain told Mom they fought all night. Finally the sun began to come up and they could see the boats and helicopters. The problem was there were only a few of them who could still walk. Daddy was shot in the foot," she paused as she touched the picture frame.

"What happened?" Bull asked.

She smiled as she looked at the picture as if she was seeing it. "He walked."

Bull frowned trying to understand. "I thought you said he was–."

"I did. But he did. He grabbed the first marine he could find alive or dead and put him on his back. He would drag another in one hand and his rifle in the other and pull them to the boat. He made that trip four times. The Captain was one of them. Just as he got the last two to the boat he was shot in the head. The Captain told Mom that he went quickly." She looked up at Bull. Her eyes were dry but she had told that story before when they weren't. He could tell. "That's my Daddy. The father I never got to know. I'm sure you've heard stories like that." She didn't notice Tony at the door returning the empty trash can. He seemed to be lingering, as if listening to the story himself. He then turned and left.

Bull looked at her. He locked her eyes in his and gave her a smile. "None like that."

"Look, if you don't feel like going to this thing, I can understand," she said breaking the moment.

Bull stood up and unfolded his arms. "Are you kidding? I just got Uncle Ned's suit back from the cleaners. I went out and got "The Best of the Bee Gees" and have been practicing all week."

"Did your mother drop you on your head when you were born?" Hanna said, cocking her head to one side.

"What time?

She stared at him for a beat or two. "What time what?"

"What time do you want me to pick you up?"

She sighed.

"I told you five. Five-thirty would probably be better." She paused for a minute. "Look, I know you're kidding, but if you show up in your grandfather's leisure suit I'm going to cut your nuts off with a rusty knife. I swear. I'll make soup out of them if you do that to me." She held her hand up. "No, you know what? I just won't go. I'll cut them off and just won't go. And you know what?"

"No, what?" Bull said. He took a step back as she stepped towards him, exclaiming her point with her finger in his chest.

"There won't be a court in the world that would convict me for it. I'd just show them a picture of you in your bloodied leisure suit and they would make you pay the court cost." The finger hit his Kevlar with the word 'cost'.

"I understand."

"You b-e-t-t-e-r," she spelled out, giving each letter a jab. From what she had heard he very well could show up dressed like her prom date, junior year, Ted Redmond. Ted had on a powder blue leisure suit with sequins. She hadn't thought of Ted until that morning when she woke up to realize the party, and possibly the suit, were upon her. She found out ten years later he had his own burlesque show in San Francisco down in the Tenderloin, 'Teddi in a Teddy,' which really explained a lot.

"I do, I do understand." Bull said.

"Soup," she said to him as he moved away. "Carrots and a creamy base with those two. I swear it."

"Five-thirty it is," he said as he turned to leave, then stopped halfway across the room and turned back to her. "Hey, this is a tie affair isn't it?"

"Yes," she said with her hands on her hips, her shoulders square and her brow furrowed as if they had already talked about it and she wasn't quite sure why he would ask about it again.

"Good," he said. "I meant to ask you, what's your favorite tie? Bow or Bola?" he said with a true look of someone seeking an answer. "You look like you might be a Bola lover. Never mind, let me surprise you," he said and he turned to leave. "I'll see you tomorrow night," he said over his shoulder as he went out the door.

She thought for a minute and let what he said register. Then her eyes grew wide and she was almost in a panic. She called after him, "You can't wear a tie with a leisure suit! I swear I'm going to cook them," she called out to him as he moved down the corridor. "Oh God, what did I do?"

It is wise to apply the oil of refined politeness to the mechanisms of friendship.

Colette (1873-1954)

'Date Night' were two words that Hanna thought she would never hear again. She was fine with that idea. It meant the great possibility of loneliness but more importantly, the opportunity to never deal with relationships with the opposite sex ever again. The idea of risking her heart again only to have it come anywhere close to the pain she felt from the divorce of her husband was nauseating to her.

Gwen sat on the couch reading her copy of NEA Today while Hanna changed her dress for the third time.

"Then he wanted to know what my favorite tie was–bola or bow," she said from the back part of the house.

"Well, what you're wearing doesn't go with either one of those ties, dear," Gwen said, never taking her eyes off the magazine and producing a small grin. "You're not going to match."

"Mother, I am serious," Hanna said as she stuck her head around the corner from the hall. She was balancing on one foot trying to put her other foot into her panty hose.

"Well, so am I. Those pearls do not go with a bola and they would only match a bow tie if it were black and accompanied by a black or charcoal tuxedo. I don't think he'll wear a tuxedo to this thing tonight. Do you, dear?"

Hanna growled as she stumbled back to her room. "Mother, he said he is wearing a leisure suit."

"You know, dear," Gwen started by folding the magazine in her lap. "All the styles are coming back. It wouldn't surprise me that he would wear one. Bull can be a handsome man when he gets cleaned up." She paused for a moment. "Honey, seriously, you have got to relax. I told you he was kidding. He will joke with you and joke with you until you tell him to stop."

The doorbell rang. "Crap," came a distant voice down the hall.

Gwen opened the door to Bull, who was standing in a Dior charcoal grey four-buttoned suit with a white Arrow shirt and a Jerry Garcia silk tie of grays and blues. He was holding a dozen roses. The two looked at each other and Gwen, without turning around, yelled, "Hanna, your date's here." The two grinned heavily at each other.

"Is she still as nervous as when you called this morning?"

"Oh my gosh, Bull, she is off the charts. Those for her?" she said, nodding at the flowers.

"No dear, they're for you. You have a vase we can put them in?"

"Oh, I sure do," she said as she took them. "I'm glad you wore the grey one. You took my advice on the tie, I see," she said as she let Bull in.

"Yeah, I did. I like this tie anyway. It goes better with the charcoal grey than the navys or the lighter grey suits I have. Is she about ready?" he said as he came in and followed Gwen casually about halfway across the room as she disappeared into the kitchen.

"Hanna, your date wants to know if you're ready, or do you want him to come back later?" She stuck her head out of the kitchen from around the corner and winked at Bull, who shook his head and smiled.

"Yeah, I'm ready," she said as she came around the corner from the hall. She wore a soft pink sweater top with a dished neckline and a black, fairly short skirt. Her neck held a single strand of pearls with matching earrings. Her hair was back behind her ears and swept to one side. She was beautiful, he thought. Her eyes fell on him as she rounded the corner; her mouth open with surprise. She recovered her expression quickly, hoping that no one noticed. Everyone did.

"What happened to the leisure suit?"

"I'm sorry. I figured you would be disappointed. Uncle Ned had a Bris in Omaha he had to go to and so he needed his 'prayin' n' trimmin' clothes' as he called them. So I just had to wear whatever I had available," he said.

Gwen walked back in from the kitchen and over to Bull. She brushed off some unseen lint from his shoulder. "This one is my favorite of all your suits," she said brushing the shoulder.

"Are you ready?" he said to Hanna.

"Yeah, yeah, I'm ready," she said. She had never thought of Bull as a handsome man. She had never contemplated that this man was, how could she place it in her own mind, handsome? But he was. She fought for a moment all the thoughts in her, but things were spinning too fast in her mind to get a handle on any of it. She turned and walked to the front door. "Good night Mother, don't wait up."

"Good night dear, have a good time. Drive safe." She winked at Bull as the two of them walked out the door.

Hanna walked to the edge of the porch and her eyes were drawn not to the truck she took to Greasewood, but a cream colored Honda Accord that sat in the driveway.

"What happened to the truck?" she said as he opened the door for her to get in. She sat down without him answering before he shut the door.

As he sat down in the driver's seat he said "This one is mine too," and pulled his seat belt across to buckle it. He reached up to open the moon roof with the push of a button after he started the car. "What? We can't go to the Phoenician in my truck. Well, actually we could, but this one is much nicer," he said as he gave Hanna a small smile. He slipped a CD in and the Bee Gees began to play. They smiled at each other.

Hanna looked at the side of the man's face. She smiled, although it was almost hidden by the shadows of the car. He looked good. There was something about this man, something that didn't match what she had heard and what she herself had thought. He was something other than what his name implied. The fear that crept over her earlier in the evening was diluting itself with the walk to the car and the drive. She felt, for the first time, maybe in years, comfortable around a man. Maybe comfortable was too strong a term but at least she was in a form of easiness that she hadn't felt in a very long time.

Bull commented about the Bee Gees and other musicians he liked. It ran the spectrum from Joe Cocker to Andrea Bocelli. She admitted that she liked the guy at Greasewood, even though she couldn't remember his name, causing them both to laugh and relax even more. Bull couldn't remember the man's name either and he had been to his house. "You have to admit it," Bull started with a sideways look at her. "You really thought I was going to show up in a leisure suit didn't you?"

"No, I–,"

"Come on, your mother already gave you up."

"My mother is in such trouble," she said trying to look out the window without smiling too widely.

"You don't know how close I came to showing up in one just to watch your face. But Gwen and I agreed you needed a break. I do have the ability to run a joke, even a good one, into the ground and then plow it over with the largest tractor I can find." He looked at her for a moment. "Plus, there was the whole soup issue."

"That is good to know."

Within what seemed just a few minutes they were pulling onto the waterfall-lined driveway of the Phoenician Resort. This was the grand lady of resorts in Phoenix. It sat on the rising slope of the south side of Camelback Mountain overlooking the massive city. The lights from the buildings lit up the side of the mountain, climbing clear to the top, casting shadows that moved across the side of the rocks. There were two lanes up and back. In between was a manicured lawn outlined with flowers and shrubs that were backlit with ground lighting that made them look as if the plants glowed.

Bull was signaled to stop about two hundred yards in. A young man exited a guard house and after Bull told him where they were going, the man asked for Bull's name and then thanked him and wished him a good evening. The two continued up the hill until they reached the lobby drive. A huge fountain highlighted the circular drive. The sound of pounding water filled the area. Two valets came to the car, one for Hanna and the other for Bull. The young man opened Hanna's door and helped her out while his partner opened Bull's door. Hanna looked back at Bull as she waited for him to come around the car. He spoke to the valet like they were friends. Then she figured the man at the lower guard gate must have called ahead. The large glass doors opened behind her. Without noticing, Bull was at her side and lightly held the underside of her arm just below the elbow, escorting her. They entered the large lobby filled with glass and gleam and the sound of water falling from another fountain just inside the door. The far wall was glass and the city's lights were spotted on a black canvas. Bull guided Hanna to the left as they entered and Bull walked them past the concierge and the front desk and made his way to a waiting elevator.

The restaurant was at the top of the resort on the fifth floor. Bull found the elevator and the two of them road it up with a Japanese couple who looked like they had come from the pool restaurant two floors down.

"We don't have to stay very long," Hanna said, almost with a voice of apology.

"Bull frowned. "I thought Cathy was one of your long-time friends?"

"Well, she is, but we just don't have to stay. I haven't seen half these people in years."

"Hanna, I'm a big boy in case you haven't noticed. I'll be just fine," he said "Just point me towards the jukebox and the beer keg and I'll be fine." The other couple said something in Japanese and nodded at their backs.

The doors to the elevator opened to a short paneled hall covered in a soft butter cream wallpaper and painted wood paneling halfway up to a chair rail. At the end was the Maitre 'D. Behind him was the bar and seating area that was at one end of the dining room with walls of glass overlooking the thousands of city lights. To the right of the Maitre 'D was a wide hall and at the other end was a private dining room and to its left, completing the circle, was the main dining room. The Maitre 'D was behind his stand facing the elevator, but looking down at the stand and appearing to be writing something. He then gave the note to a waiting female hostess. She was not in the same uniform as the man she stood next to but a black conservative dress and waistcoat. The Maitre'D was in his fifties, with silver hair and a full moustache neatly trimmed and dressed in a standard tuxedo. He looked up at the two as they approached him and then he smiled—a big toothy smile. Hanna first thought that this man was truly excited to see them. 'What a friendly man,' she thought. It truly surprised her when he spoke to Bull—in French, or what she thought was French. She turned to her date who was responding—in French. Bull walked around the platform and the two hugged while shaking hands. She physically caught herself closing her open mouth as she watched and listened as the two spoke in fluid French about nothing that she could understand.

"Monsieur Bull Thornton, how is my dear, dear friend tonight?"

"Jen'ot, it is good to see you again. What has it been, about three months since I was here last?"

"At least that. I was surprised when you called yesterday. The reception is not a friend of yours? They're in the side room," gesturing down the hall.

"How is your beautiful wife?"

"She is going to have another baby," he said.

"Oh Jen'ot, you old stallion. How many does that make now, sixty-three?"

"No, that is only going to be number four. Samantha wants to name this one something special–'Gerald Packard'."

"Tell your beautiful wife that my heart sings, but that she shouldn't be drinking so much of that crappy French wine when she dreams these names up. No one can spell that last one she came up with," Bull said. Then he realized his manners and that he had forgotten about Hanna.

"Hanna, this is a very old and very dear friend of mine. Jen'ot, this is Hanna. It is her friend we are here for."

"Ah, good evening Mademoiselle," Jen'ot said as he took her hand and kissed it. "Your party is in the Gold Room right around the corner. Would you like for me to show you the—,"

"No, no, Jen'ot, I can find it," Bull. "So, what do you think of this one?" he said nodding towards Hanna and speaking in soft French.

Jen'ot looked at her, still holding her hand, and squeezed it. "This one has light in her eyes."

"Oui," Bull said with a smile. I will catch up with you later, my friend," Bull said, this time in English and the two walked down the hall.

"Samantha will be happy to hear that you came by. Call us and we can have you over again for dinner. And my friend, make sure you tell your daughter that her Uncle Jen'ot says 'hello.'"

They walk to the side down another short hall. "You speak French?" Hanna said without looking at Bull.

"A little."

"That was a whole lot more than 'a little'," Hanna said. That was a lot.

"You look confused."

"No—I-just–,"

"In Vietnam, during my second tour, I was shot down. It was a fairly tense time of my life but I was able to come out of it all right. The Corps thought that it might be a good idea to transfer me out to another air wing, so a couple of us with some other pilots from different branches were shipped to Europe to help teach the NATO pilots air tactics in the different planes they had. Lieutenant Jen'ot L'Cyuer was one of them. We became friends. He taught me French and wines and I taught him how to stay alive in the woods in winter if ever he got shot down flying photo missions over Soviet-owned Czechoslovakia. He has stayed my friend. I've had opportunities to use what he taught me and fortunately he never had the opportunity to use what I taught him."

They got to the door of the Gold Room. Bull put his hand on the door and looked at Hanna. "Look," he said with a deep breath and a smile. "You can relax, at least for tonight. I wanted to come with you and I wanted you to go with me the other night." He looked at his hand resting on the door. He looked at his hand for a minute then back at her before he spoke. "I promise I won't embarrass you in front of your friends; as a matter of fact, I think you'll be pleased with this evening. Hanna," he paused again and the smile melted as his eyes locked onto hers. "We have both had life experiences. I'm too old and tired to play head or heart games," he said with all seriousness. He looked into her eyes and talked softly with just a hint of a smile as he moved close to her, her back almost against the wood paneled wall. "I will make you a promise. I'll always be truthful with you. You ask me a question and I will give you the best answer I have. I'll never lie to you, unless it's your birthday. I can't promise I'll never hurt you but I can promise that I will never do it intentionally. I don't smoke, except for the occasional cigar. I like an occasional beer, mango margaritas, or Glenlivet 18, not necessarily at the same time. I eat meat, but mostly chicken. I don't like late nights or wet socks and my favorite time of the week is Sunday morning reading the paper before church. Yes, I go to church. If that is a problem with you then we do have a problem on that point. I make great blueberry biscuits and I love dogs and tolerate cats. I try to exercise every day and to read a page or two of something fun at night. I'll open your car door but I might forget sometimes and I expect the same from you if I'm carrying something in both hands. I'm right handed and contrary to all the stories that you have heard or seen, I have not really dated. I know there are stories floating out there and I would be happy to address them when the time is right. I don't care who you vote for as long as you vote. You have a right to your own opinion. I don't mind talking on long trips but don't worry if I don't say a word for hours. Maybe it's because I'm too long in the tooth and too tired most of the time. I don't believe in 'men's roles or women's roles' most of the time. I believe in getting the job done. I can watch television or listen to the radio while giving a wonderful foot rub but I don't necessarily like my feet rubbed. I'm at a time in my life when I would like to get to know you. I'm not seeing nor do I plan on seeing anyone else while you and I are dating if that's what we're doing. I would like to think so but that requires two votes and you have one of them. There's more, but you will have to decide to spend more time with me after tonight to find out. There are things about you that I want to know as well. I'm willing to hang in there and learn about them if you want to tell me. Now, before we go through these doors and into another phase of this apparent journey we're on, do you have any questions?" He was inches from her face, speaking almost in a whisper.

"Ah—yes," she stuttered with eyes that were like salad plates looking up into his face. "Good, save it for later," he said as he kissed her forehead. "First—We Dance!" he said as he opened the door and snapped his fingers as if he was starting the Flamingo. Then he snapped them again and pointed at her. "Big Bad Bob."

"Wha–," she said with an inquisitive look, then one of realization. "That's right, Big Bad Bob!" It caused her to smile. The two stepped into the room and time stopped.

Love is not blind-it sees more, not less.
But because it sees more, it is willing to see less.

Julius Gordon

The party was underway in the Gold Room, off the main dining room. A large section of the main dining room had also been reserved for the guests. After mingling and trying the four different types of caviar, cheeses, and canapés, one would go and order the dinner of one's choosing and enjoy the evening. If this was the engagement announcement dinner, there was no idea in Hanna and Bull's mind what the wedding would look like. Hanna was watching Bull as they started. She was struggling with the vastness of the cost and the extravagance of it and she thought he must be overwhelmed. If he was, he didn't show it. He was as cool and confident as he was in his Ropers and hat at Greasewood.

The two walked in and Hanna was approached almost immediately by Kathy Cryer. She was wearing a low cut sequined blouse that changed from slate blue to a steel grey as she moved and the light changed its color. Her pants were black, probably silk, Hanna guessed.

"Hanna, Bull, I'm so glad you could make it," she said as she kissed and hugged each of them. She turned and looked Bull up and down before she spoke. "Bull that is my favorite suit. It's your best color," she said with a smile and wink at Hanna. "Look guys, just make yourselves comfortable; the bar is over there. The Tripolis and Darrel are around here somewhere. They might already be sitting down to dinner in the dining room or out on the patio. I'm going to go find my future." She sent an air kiss towards Bull and squeezed Hanna's arm before she turned and left. Bull stood with his hands folded in front of him and watched her walk away. "Her future? She reads Cosmo, doesn't she?" he said as if he just solved the riddle of the ages. "What do you want to do first?"

"I want to know if I'm the only one who really thought you were coming to this party in your uncle's leisure suit," she said with a playful frown.

"Yes ma'am, you were pretty much the only one that bit that hook."

She nodded and panned the audience. "In that case, how about a mango margarita?"

Bull's eyebrow rose. "Now you're talking the language of my heart," he said.

Bull made eye contact with one of the waiters standing in the corner, who immediately came to attention at Bull's side. He gave him her order along with his request for an Oban 14 neat. "What was that you ordered?" Hanna asked.

"Scotch—a single malt scotch; they don't have Glenfiddich 15 so I went with the Oban 14 because the Glenlivet 18 is a little too strong for right now, maybe later," he said looking at her with a smile.

"I didn't know that ordering a drink required so much math."

"You would be surprised," he said.

The two made the rounds and Hanna introduced Bull to friends she knew and others she didn't know. After a while Bull excused himself and wandered over to sit with Darrel and his wife at a table off to the side in the main dining room. The room was walled with thick, floor-to-ceiling glass so every guest could see the lights of the city. The walls were covered in the same painted wood paneling with fabric wallpaper. Jen'ot came over and asked Bull if he was ready for his table. Jen'ot and Bull walked to a table on the balcony, in the corner, slightly away from the other tables, the best seat on the patio. There was a gas driven-fire in a concrete basin fire pot that added an amber glow all around them. Bull and Jen'ot swapped a few quiet words between them and then Bull walked back inside and into the room where the guests were and found Hanna. Bull told the waiter they would be taking their drinks at the table. "Of course, Mr. Thornton," the waiter said within earshot of Hanna. She took Bull's arm as he offered it and they followed behind the waiter.

"The waiter knew you," she said as they walked.

"No," he said in a matter of fact tone. "He must have heard someone call my name." The two went to their table and a waiter stood behind each of the two chairs. After they were seated, a third waiter came over with a short stool and placed it next to the chair for Hanna's purse. Their waiter, Robert, acted as if he were there to serve only them.

After he explained the menu and the options available, the two talked and laughed. Hanna was surprised by Bull who seemed right at home. Each phase of the meal was its own experience. Bull offered to order for her. She liked the small artichoke salad but really didn't care for the lobster bisque cappuccino soup. She rolled her eyes in delight at the tenderness of the venison that Bull ordered for her and laughed when he made her switch with his empty soup cup so he could finish hers. His scallops were enough for him and when Robert asked if he wished for another scotch he had to think about it before he declined.

They listened to the salesman with his wife and daughter at the table next to them who was trying to impress the Wine Captain with his knowledge of wine. Hanna noticed the air was cooling and a slight breeze dusted them lightly on the patio. Before she knew it, Bull had signaled Robert, who was at his side.

"Robert, Ms. Jarger is a little chilled. Is there something you can do for that?" he asked as if he knew the answer.

"Absolutely, Mr. Thornton. Robert turned and in a quick snap of his fingers a younger waiter assistant was next to him in a flash of time. Robert gave instructions in a low voice and the young man was off.

"It will be just a moment, Mr. Thornton."

"Thank you, Robert."

Hanna picked up that she was the focus of some attention. "Oh, no, I'm fine. I don't—,"

"It's no problem," Bull said, reaching out and touching her arm.

"Trust me, it will be fine." The young man returned with a black shawl and presented it to Robert, who came up behind Hanna and prepared to apply it to her shoulders. He looked at Bull when he was in position. Bull looked at him and nodded. "Thank you Robert," Bull said as Robert gently placed the wrap on Hanna's shoulders.

"We can't have the lady chilled. It's too beautiful a night for that," Robert said as he finished with the wrap. He turned to Bull and nodded, then asked if there would be anything else he could get for them. Bull asked for a French press coffee and asked Hanna if she would like some coffee as well. She nodded and smiled at him.

After a few minutes, the music for the party began. The two of them went inside and Bull found a corner chair while Hanna walked over to Kathy. When the small band started up, Hanna saw Bull watching her. He smiled and waved and then with his hand he drew a circle in the air at the dance floor to signal that he wanted to dance. She shook her head no with a face of slight fear. He nodded yes and started to get up. She knew she was going to dance, whether she really wanted to or not. She feared that he really could dance and that she wasn't going to be able to keep up.

The musicians were playing a Christopher Cross song. The lyrics were about two people meeting in a grocery store and the man asking the woman out for coffee. Hanna put her drink down and he took her hand and walked her out to the center of the floor. They were the only ones dancing. "Relax," she heard the word in her ear spoken so softly she delicately said "Huh?"

"Relax, I won't drop you," he said as he took her hand and wrapped his arm around her waist.

"It's not you dropping me that I'm worried about. It's me tripping that I really worry about," she said as she looked back around.

"You won't trip. I won't let you," he said in her ear again. She felt the arm around her waist pull her tighter to him. Her back grew warm and she felt her face flush. She hoped he didn't notice. She was self conscious about others in the room watching her dance but then she noticed, as she looked around, that they weren't paying any attention to the two of them. After a minute, there were other couples on the dance floor and they were just one pair out of about a dozen. She felt him move and turn and she moved with him. She stole a glance at the side of his face and could see him smile. Before she was ready, the song had ended and another slow one picked up where that other left off. They danced three dances straight and then moved off the floor and toward the open French doors overlooking the city. They found their way back to their open table next to the rail and he held the chair for her as she sat down. The table was covered with the amber light of the fire next to them as well as the candle on the table in a short crystal luminary.

"I'm going to get another cup of coffee. Do you want something?" he said, resting his hand on her shoulder just before he sat down. Robert was by his side in an instant.

She thought for a minute and then told him she would like something sweet with a straw

"Very good, Miss," Robert said.

The two sat quietly and looked out over the city. She felt relaxed. As if there had been a load on her shoulders and it had been removed. She then began to think that this might lead somewhere. Then she was thinking that he might want more than she could give him. That led her to think that he might not be able to give her everything she needed. Then she was thinking that the drink might make her too cold sitting outside in the night air and they might need to move inside. Then she thought she was thinking too much.

Robert came back with Bull's coffee and a White Russian for Hanna. They could hear the music in the background and occasionally the French doors would open and close, lending the muffled sound of the music some clarity before they were muffled again.

Bull opened a packet of sweetener and poured a little cream into his coffee. Neither said anything for a time while he tended to his drink. She watched him stir the cup with the spoon from the table. Slow figure eights she noticed.

Bull sat sideways in the chair. His back was to the rail so

when he crossed his legs he had room. "So how is living with your mother?" he said as he took a sip.

A safe question, she thought to herself. "Oh, she's a Mom. But she's my best friend. I was worried about us working at the same school, but it's working out," she said as she sipped her drink after stirring it. "Umm, this is good."

"I'll tell you a secret. The other teachers think you're pretty good," he said as he looked at her. They aren't just saying that because you're your mother's daughter but because they really believe it."

"How do you know what they say?"

"Hey," he said placing his open hand on his chest. "It's my job to know all and to see all. Besides, I've watched you, too."

"Is that like when you checked me out on the computer at work?" She knew that was a mistake as soon as she said it. "I'm sorry, that was uncalled for."

Bull never changed his expression, except the smile got a little wider as he looked into his coffee cup. "No, I lied to you. Your Mom gave up most of the information and I did kind of sniff out the rest. I should have respected your privacy. Old habits are hard to break and I never should have done that. I was willing to stalk you to find out more about you." He paused for a minute before he continued. "I've seen teachers just going through the motions and teachers who really care. It's in the eyes. It's always in the eyes. You care about these kids. I never really gave a damn about students before your mother roped me into this gig. Now, they are mine. I'm probably too old to have any more and the one I have," he paused again, "is just enough for right now."

Hanna looked at him as he spoke. "Really?"

"The teachers love your mother. Hell, the whole district loves your mother and they see a lot of her in you. But they also know that you are different from Gwen. Given time, they'll love you just as much for yourself."

"What do you think of my mother?"

The question brought a smile to Bull's face. "I'll tell you what she told me the first week I started at the school and she has repeated every year since then. 'Honey,' she said, 'Honey, if I was only a couple of years older, you and I would be a thing'."

Hanna's mouth was open. "My mother said that? Not my mother! Oh, I'm so sorry," she said as she covered her mouth in laughter.

Bull laughed. "She is only about fifteen years older than me and a couple years on top of that would be just about right. I do love your mother; she is truly one of the great women still left around."

Both of them got quiet before Hanna spoke. "She is my best friend. I don't know what I'll do if she dies."

Bull leaned forward on the table with both elbows resting on it. "Everyone dies Hanna, everyone. It isn't the dying that is so traumatic; it's the separation. Once she gets to where she's going, I guarantee she won't want to come back." Bull smiled at her before he finished. "Even if you begged her."

She stirred her drink with the straw. "Do you still miss Beth?" she said, not looking up until the last word moved out from her lips.

Bull smiled and sat back in the chair. "Seems like someone's been checking out my past." He paused and looked down at his hands wrapped around the mug of half drunk coffee that rested in his lap. "It used to be every day, all day. Now, with work and my daughter, it is less. The ache has been gone for quite a while. Some time ago, I came to the realization that it was not going to change. Sometime, I hope not for a long time, Cheri will go. I feel guilty sometimes when I dare to think that she should go—now. Then I see her, and all that goes away." He sat for a moment, then he finished. "She's my daughter, my only child. It took a long time to deal with the guilt of what happened. Someday if you want to see her I'll take you."

"I would like that. What about tonight?"

"Tonight?"

"Yeah," Hanna said, leaning forward on the table. She smiled at him. "Let's go tonight."

"Oh, I don't know."

"I guess it is kind of late."

"Well that's not the problem. I have a key," he smirked. "Part of the perks that came with the job. You got your friends and this party—."

"Screw the party!"

"Madam?" Her exuberance caught him off balance.

"You heard me," Hanna said, sitting back in her chair. She was making a statement, a declaration of something. Maybe it was the drink, the night air, the fact that the man she was with was not the man she had thought of before. He was not a repeat of her husband, maybe he was. She didn't know yet. There was a fundamental difference between the two. She could see it. She also could see that this topic of his daughter, this was the soft gooey center of the chocolate in the box if she could put it into words. She could see it on his face. He had this persona to the world, this mask. She saw, for just a moment that this was the man under the mask. If she wanted to get to know the heart of the man, which she still wasn't sure that she wanted to do, this was the way in. "These aren't my dear friends except for the ones from school. Besides, we've made a showing and it's so large they'll never miss us."

As if on cue, Darrel stuck his head out the door and called to the two. There was a sense of glee in his voice. His face displayed a large grin, one that caused wrinkles in his forehead. "Hey guys, come on in. They're going to line dance." Then Darrel disappeared back into the room.

The two looked at each other for a few seconds before Hanna spoke. "Now is definitely as good a time as any to leave. You with me?"

"But they're line dancing. You know I can line dance," Bull said, as he turned to signal Robert they were leaving.

"Why does that not surprise me?" She got up, grabbed his hand, and pulled him to his feet. "Robert, we are going to leave. Is there anything we need to do for our delicious meal?" Hanna asked.

"No, Miss, your evening has been taken care of by the host of the party."

Bull paused for a moment to thank Robert again and to shake his hand. Hanna noticed that Bull passed him something.

"What did you just do? I thought the evening was covered?"

"It was. I just wanted to make sure that Robert was," Bull said, as he walked with her. They walked the edge of the patio in hopes of finding another way out without crossing through the main room where the party was. The balcony patio wrapped around and joined the patio extension of the main bar. Bull opened the door and the two walked in and across the open bar at the far end of the dining room. As they crossed the front Jen'ot spotted them and stopped in the middle of seating a middle aged couple to say goodbye. "You are leaving so soon?"

"Hanna said she wanted to see Cheri. We're going over there now."

Jen'ot looked at Hanna and then back at Bull. "She is special, this one."

"Oui."

"My friend, please give that beautiful girl of yours a kiss from her Jen'ot." Bull raised his hand as he walked away and said over his shoulder that he would do so.

When they arrived at the Conright Building, the doors were still unlocked and the two walked past two couples walking out. Bull recognized them from other visits but couldn't remember which children were theirs. He took Hanna's hand as they walked down the hall. He didn't look at her and she only glanced at him. Then she smiled. As they approached the door to Cheri's room, Bull eased the door open. The room was dark except for a soft lamp in the corner.

Cheri slept better when there was some light so Bull had brought in a small lamp and put in a low-watt bulb with instructions for the nurses to turn it on when the sun went down. He was glad to see they listened to him. It was these small, seemingly insignificant things that made him feel that he did the right thing by having her here. Bull went to one side of the bed and Hanna followed him. He lowered the bed rail and quietly pulled up the chair next to her. He lowered his head to her face and kissed her forehead after first brushing the brown hair out of her face. Her eyes were half open and Hanna couldn't tell if Cheri was awake or asleep. Hanna watched the two of them. His open hand was so large it could cover the whole side of her face and yet it brushed the hair aside as if it was the wind from the flap of a butterfly wing.

He spoke softly to her in both English and French. She heard the word 'Jen'ot' and she knew he was telling her what Jen'ot told him to tell her. What amazed her was how, out of such tragedy, such love could still not only grow but flourish. She heard him whisper to Cheri three or four times softly in her ear, "Daddy is here." He continued to stroke her hair and then he talked to her. "Cheri, baby, I brought a friend. Her name is Hanna and she wanted to meet you. We went to a party at Mary Elaine's tonight. Like I told you, Jen'ot said to say hello to you and give you a big kiss for him." He kissed her forehead. "He and his wife are going to have another baby." He stopped and looked up at Hanna and then back at Cheri. "The doctors said that they think she can hear me talking to her and maybe even know what I'm saying to her. I always thought she could."

Hanna moved closer to Bull. She rested her left hand on his shoulder and patted it. Cheri was still curled in a fetal position. Her eyes were a little wider, as if her father's voice woke her, or maybe it was the stroking of the hair.

"She knows her Daddy is here. That's all that's important tonight." Hanna put her purse down on the foot of the bed to her right and then sat on the edge of the bed in an empty spot. She gently leaned to her right over Cheri's ear, supporting her weight with her right arm behind Cheri's head, almost laying on her, getting close enough to whisper in her ear. "Cheri, this is Hanna. I danced with your Father tonight. He said that your mother and he took lessons. I bet you helped him. He's not bad. He made me laugh. I bet he makes you laugh too, huh?" She finished by stroking her hair and pulling it behind her ears.

Bull watched as Hanna spoke to his daughter as if she were a real, hearing person, just like he did. He watched the face of his daughter and he could swear it began to soften with the conversation. She seemed to almost smile. Her breathing got easier. He couldn't swear to it but she seemed to take a deep breath, slight and almost imperceptible but still there. He watched Hanna tell the story of Greasewood and the truck as opposed to the car and of course the leisure suit. They were there for an hour. The nurses came in twice to check on Cheri and then retreated after they saw the two with her. The two of them laughed and whispered to her some more and told other stories from school and about boys and girls and really nothing at all. Just like three adults would do.

After visiting Cheri, Bull drove to the Dairy Queen on Central just north of Camelback Road. It was a small, fairly old, borderline clean Dairy Queen. But it had a few benches out front and after they ordered a couple of Blizzards with extra chocolate, they sat and watched the cars drive by while the eased through their ice cream. "She knows you're there, you know," Hanna said as she began to lip her spoon and dig in for another scoop.

"Yeah, I think so, too. That was good of you to sit there and talk to her like that. No one ever has."

Hanna stopped and looked at him. "You've had other people there? You have had other people there, haven't you?" she said. Bull kept the ice cream moving while he shook his head. "No one ever wanted to go before. Oh, her grandparents come by whenever they're in town, but they haven't been here in a year. You're the first non-family person, ever. I really haven't been knocking down doors to get people to go see her." He paused. "I don't know why exactly. Maybe there was a little embarrassment or protectionism or something, I don't know." He dug out another scoop and turned the spoon over in his mouth as he looked at her. Then as he withdrew the cleaned spoon he pointed it at her before he put it back in the ice cream. "You madam, scored some heavy points with my daughter tonight."

"You think so?" She said as she scooped another puddle of ice cream from her cup. She looked deep inside of it as she spoke. "I hope I get to go see her again."

It was as subtle as a freight train carrying plate glass and having the load shift on a mountain turn. Bull saw it and from the outside he was calm. Not that he really needed to respond any other way. This woman was looking for a reason to see him again. "You think so, huh?" he said without looking up.

"Well, only if you want me to go. I, ah, thought that if we do go out again we could go by and see Cheri either before or after and let her know what we were doing. You know, I think she would like to know that her Daddy might have a life again." She was looking at him. He turned and looked at her. There was a smile on his face. She saw his eyes travel from her eyes down to her lips then back up to her eyes. "I think, I think I want her Daddy to have a life again," she said as she looked at him and then out at the traffic.

The drive from the Dairy Queen was only four blocks from her home. There were three Gecko lizards around the warmth of the front porch light waiting for any stray moth to enter their reach for a quick snack. Hanna was going to have a word with her mother about leaving the porch light on. Bull moved closer to her. He was looking down at her and she looked up at him. "Did you have a good time tonight?"

"Oh, I did have a good time. I don't know what the best part of the night was, the dancing, the Mango margaritas, Cheri, or the mint chocolate chip."

"Well, I can understand if it was anything other than the dancing, I was a little bit off my game tonight." He slid his left hand around her waist. He pulled her slightly and she responded without hesitation.

"Oh, I don't know. I don't think you were off your game one bit."

"You don't?" Bull said.

"No, I don't," Hanna.

There was a pause. "Do you want to come in?" She said, glancing into his eyes then sweeping away.

He reached down and put the palm of his hand on the side of her face. She closed her eyes for a brief moment and leaned into it. It had been years since she had been touched by a man. It had been even longer since she had been touched by a man that she felt safe with. He leaned down to kiss her lips. It was barely a touch, so soft and sensitive, the two hardly touched. She felt her legs begin to buckle.

He wanted to go into the house. He looked at her in the light from the porch light. All night he had watched her, looked at her, and analyzed her from top to bottom. That's what men do; they analyze, he thought. During the night, he remembered being young again and his bones weren't brittle. When he was young, he looked at the young women and saw a body of beauty or ruin. He remembered seeing the eyes and hips and teeth and breasts and wondered if it was at all possible to have all of it before the night was over. As he watched over the years, his thoughts about the woman did not change. His life with his wife developed and he lost the newness of their earlier days. But as he aged, especially now, things were different. He looked at Hanna and he wanted her, physically. But there was a draw to her that, with age, meant more. He knew if he went inside the home, he would find himself in a situation that, later, would have to be dealt with by the two of them. The fact that Gwen was probably on the couch helped make up his mind.

"No, I'm going to go home and you are going in and going to bed. I had a wonderful time tonight. Good night, dear woman," he said as he kissed her one more time on the forehead before he turned to leave. "Oh, by the way," he said, stopping halfway down the steps and turning back to her. "Want to go see her tomorrow morning, actually-," he looked at his watch, "later on this morning?"

Hanna looked at him with a smile as she leaned up against the door jam. "Yeah, yeah, I can do that. Oh, and one more thing." She walked up to him and grabbed his face with both hands and pulled him down to her lips. She kissed him. She kissed him like she had wanted to all night. "Take that with you."

He turned and walked out to his car and she watched him get in and drive away.

What is most beautiful in virile men is something feminine; what is most beautiful in feminine women is something masculine.

SUSAN SONTAG

Early November

Her eyes opened like blinds in a window, quickly and with a purpose. She could smell coffee and bacon. She lay there for a minute, thinking that her mother had gotten up and started the usual Sunday routine. Then she remembered that Bull was going to come over and she really should get up and shower before he got there to take her to see Cheri. She cupped her hand in front of her mouth and exhaled. She rolled over and slid her feet into her slippers that she still hadn't named and as she walked out to the hall bathroom she slid her bathrobe on.

When she came out and walked past her mother's room she noticed the bed was made. Mother only did that when she was going out for the day. She sometimes would start early and go for a walk in the mountain preserve and then meet some friends for breakfast. There was noise in the kitchen, a lot more noise than usual, as well as the sound of pots. She couldn't figure out what her mother was doing.

Bull was outside, through the French doors of the kitchen. She saw him as she crossed the living room. He had placed a linen tablecloth on the patio table and had some fresh flowers in a small vase in the center of it. He must have stopped at the grocery store to buy them. In the kitchen he, or maybe her mother, had made a large pot of coffee. Fresh biscuits were on the stove cooling, a pitcher of orange juice was on the counter next to them and a plate of crisp bacon next to that.

Bull was in shorts and a sweatshirt. He hadn't shaved and had an 'NYPD' ball cap on. A dish towel was tossed over his shoulder. He didn't see her come out. He was busy setting the table and sipping a cup of coffee with his free hand. She reached around and was able to pour herself a cup of coffee without him seeing her. She stood for a moment and watched him. The cap was down and not back on his head like many men wore them when they are relaxed. He looked comfortable in this element.

As he walked around the far side of the table, he looked back into the kitchen and saw her standing there and he smiled. His whole face moved. His eyebrows raised and his cheeks perked up. "Your mother said you wouldn't be up this early. I thought I had more time," he said as he came back into the house. He walked over towards her and poured another cup of coffee. She was a little disappointed that he didn't kiss her good morning but then she remembered her breath. She quickly took another large gulp of coffee. Before she realized it, he was done pouring the coffee and he had taken her jaw gently in his left hand and turned her face to him. He kissed her tenderly but with more pressure than the night before. He pulled away and looked in her eyes with a smile. "Good morning," he said from under the ball cap. His breath smelled like Crest and coffee.

"Good morning. Did you do all of this?"

He looked at her standing in front of him in her robe. Through his eyes she looked good, even with bed head and no makeup. She smelled like morning. "Well, actually, your mother helped. I called her on her cell phone. She said she had to go out for a little bit but would leave the door open. She had the coffee and bacon done. I did the biscuits," he said with a little pride. He could cook; she had heard that about him.

"I told you I was coming over. I thought we could eat outside; it's so pretty. It's a little cool this early so I brought out the blanket from the couch. Here, come here and sit down," he said to her as he walked to the patio. She followed him and sat in the chair he held out for her. They were in the shade and even though she had her bathrobe on and a warm cup of coffee, she felt a little chilled.

He walked over and picked up the blanket that was resting on the third chair and wrapped it around her. He then went in and brought out the food and placed it on the table. They ate and drank coffee and juice and talked about everything, from Gwen to Toby, the fourth grader with the clubbed foot and one ear lower than the other. They laughed and ate apricot jelly on their biscuits. She noticed he took his coffee with cream and two sweeteners. He liked it when she pulled her feet up on the chair with her and when she put her hair up in a clip. As the morning warmed, Hanna was able to shed the blanket. Eventually, the two came in and did the dishes and threw suds at each other.

They returned to the patio and they laughed some more. Then they stopped and looked at each other. His face turned to a soft smile. She wanted him. The fear was there but so was the desire, the emotional and physical desire that she hadn't felt for years, even while she was married. He made her feel safe. She unfolded herself in her chair and came over and sat in his lap, catching him by surprise. She took his face in both of her hands. She held him there for just a moment and she lost her fear in his eyes. She knew, at that moment, that he would not let her fear be validated. She knew, at that moment, he would protect her; she could and would want to protect him. She couldn't remember ever thinking of doing that with her husband. Then she kissed him. Her hands moved from his face to his back and she pulled him to her. She allowed herself to be kissed the way she did not ever remember being kissed.

"Hi kids, Momma's home," came the voice around the corner. They smiled and Bull pushed her hair back off her forehead and gently reached across and closed her blousing robe. He would protect her from both of them.

"We're on the patio," Bull announced over the top of Hanna's head. He kissed her again on the forehead as Hanna move back to her seat on the other side of the table.

Remember this- that there is proper dignity and proportion to be observed in the performance in every act of life.

MARCUS AURELIUS ANTONINUS (121 AD--180 AD)

After Gwen came home, Bull went home and showered. Later that morning he came back and picked Hanna up and they went to see Cheri and told her about what they ate and that they were going to go to the mall to shop for a wedding present for Kathy. In the two weeks to come, usually at night or on weekends, Bull and Hanna went to see Cheri regularly. Hanna brushed her hair and talked to her almost as much as Bull did. He listened as she talked to Cheri about something Lord Fauntleroy wrote. Bull couldn't figure it out.

They became set in a routine; one they both felt comfortable in. Bull didn't make Hanna feel pushed and Hanna didn't feel pushed. She knew that Bull cared much for her and it wasn't conditional on her loving Cheri. She was falling for the child as well. There were parts of Hanna that were waking to the songs of their relationship. On some days, however, the fear would seep in. Between the two of them, it was Bull who felt it more. But it was also Bull that talked about it.

"You're quiet again, Hanna said.

"I know."

"What's wrong?"

"Nothing."

"Liar."

"See? That's why I just say 'nothing's wrong'."

"So."

"It makes me nervous going where we're going. I want to go.

I really do. But I hate the pain that it might and probably will bring."

"Yep, me too. Know what else I'm scared of?"

"What?"

"That you'll love your wife more than me. I can't even compete with her, like bowling or a game of darts."

"I can see where you would come up with that. I can only tell you that I think that's behind me. I'll always love her just like I bet you'll always have a place for your ex. You'd fight for me? Like with darts or bowling?"

"Yep," she said.

"You any good?"

"They don't call me 'Nine Ten Hanna' for nothing."

"What the hell does that mean?"

"No idea. We just need to keep talking, okay? Don't go quiet on me or I'm going to think the worst."

"What if I'm taking a nap? I'm quiet then?"

"Stop."

"Okay."

Two weeks after the breakfast was the 'Parade of Pilgrims'. It was the Friday before Thanksgiving break and the school had its annual concert and Thanksgiving play for the parents. All the teachers and staff were encouraged to come dressed as Pilgrims and Indians to support the students. Hanna and Gwen actually had costumes of Indian maidens. The play had all the flavor of Thanksgiving, complete with paper trees and a backdrop of a small town. The sixth grade was the group that headed up the event. They sang in the chorus, they danced on the stage; Amir Elinisovich, from Bosnia, was a six foot one inch sixth grader who spoke little English. He couldn't sing and dancing was out of the question. So, Amir Elinisovich was Tolga, the Magic Tree of the Outer Forest. He had tree branches for arms and moved them and pointed when the Indians wondered where the feast was.

Tony laughed out loud as he stood along the wall and watched. He was wearing what looked like a pilgrim costume with two florescent sashes crossing his chest. Gwen helped him with it. The 'first crossing guard' he was later heard to tell Amir Elinisovich's mother when she asked him who he was. Hanna and Gwen stood with the other teachers in the back corner of the cafeteria.

Darrel was walking around with a huge Indian headdress, a long-sleeve deerskin shirt, and long pants along with leather moccasins. He thought he really looked like an Indian, at least according to his wife, except he was white and the headdress was of a native Indian from the plains and two hundred years later. Bull told him that many of the natives of the time ran naked or with minimal clothes on, but that was something a grade school principal couldn't do unless he was craving an end to his career. Darrel agreed.

In the back of the cafeteria, the doors opened and the positive air fan automatically came on, making a loud sound of wind. Hanna turned to see who it was coming in halfway through the play and dropped her jaw when she saw Bull enter in a full pilgrim outfit, complete with hat, gun belt, and a silver star pinned to his vest. Hanna went with him to see Cheri and then he went home and changed after dropping Hanna off at home. He never mentioned to her that he was going to go in costume to the concert. He saw Hanna busy nudging her mother standing next to her. Gwen was trying to keep the fluorescent orange feather out of her eyes that was hanging from her paper headdress. He stood next to Hanna who was looking at him up and down with a toothy smirk on her face. "Oh, my, gosh!" she said out of the side of her mouth.

"What?"

"Oh, my, gosh," she repeated.

"You said that already. What? You've never seen John Proctor before?"

"Mom, what did you do with the camera?" Hanna said.

"I think you look cute, dear," Gwen said as she looked at him.

"I'm not supposed to look 'cute.' I'm John Proctor, the baddest boy in the new Puritan world," Bull said as he stood with his back to the wall and his hands behind his back. He pretended to watch the play but was really just waiting for another comment from the Indians.

Hanna moved close so she could whisper. "Puritan, huh? Want to test that resolve later?"

"Shush, you're going to get us hung or have a big scarlet 'A' stamped into our heads."

"You've been drinking some more of that scotch with the math equation haven't you? Let me smell your breath." She started to reach for his head and he pulled back.

"Funny. I bet you don't even know who John Proctor is."

"I do so," she said.

"Oh, yeah?"

"Oh yeah!"

"Then why did you ask if I had any scotch before I came? You know those guys didn't drink. See, you didn't know who I was," Bull said as if he had rehearsed this stretch of the conversation.

"I know he dies at the end of the play," she said with a smile.

"What? No he doesn't."

"I think you look just like Mr. Proctor, dear. I didn't know he wore a gun belt," Gwen said around Hanna and then turned back to the play.

"Thank you, Gwen. I can always count on you."

"You're welcome, dear."

"Mother," Hanna said with a smile.

"Honey, if the boy wants to look like John Proctor with a gun belt, just let him. It'll make him happy.

"See, your mother wants me to be happy. Humor me."

Jessica Farmer came up behind him and goosed him, making him jump.

"Oh, hello Jessica."

"Hello Mr. Pilgrim man," Jessica said to Bull, then Hanna and Gwen on the other side of him. "Oh, hi girls, isn't this a great night for a play?" She spoke but no one heard her because they were looking at the man in the suit behind her who was holding her hand, a deeply tanned man. He was in his mid-to-late fifties with a sand colored suit, a gold watch on one wrist and a old bracelet on the other to match it. The gold bands for each were the same. His hair was slicked back with some hair gel. Bull thought this guy was a lawyer; defense—no, personal injury, he thought. Bull thought he had a look that he was serving a penance by being here and Bull, Hanna, and Gwen all said later that he made Jessica promise certain things for him to follow her to the school cafeteria in the inner city, especially the way she looked. She was dressed like a pilgrim woman. However, her blouse was unbuttoned a little too far for a puritan woman in the early sixteen hundreds.

"Who are you suppose to be?" Hanna asked her around Bull's shoulders with Gwen looking on, smiling.

"Well, Antonio here, oh, by the way everybody, this is Antonio. Antonio, this is everybody." Antonio nodded his head as the other three in unison said, "Hi, Antonio."

"Anyway, Antonio said I should go as 'Abigail' from the play 'The Crucible.' Have you guys heard of it?"

The three just froze for a moment. Their lack of motion was picked up by Antonio, who appeared used to watching body language; it was a professional 'skill' that he had acquired, which supported Bull's hypothesis of his being a lawyer. Jessica, however, did not have this ability and just kept talking.

"Well, it's a famous play by a guy named Arty Miller. He said I would be the perfect Abigail. She was the star of the play." She was so proud that no one wanted to let this end. They just wanted to freeze this moment and store in the folders in their brains, labeled 'precious moments.'

The play finished with a whirling flourish of singing turkeys, geese, cows, Indians, pilgrims and, of course, Amir Elinisovich as Tolga, the Magic Tree of the Outer Forest. Antonio took his pilgrim out the door as soon as Chief Darrel got up on stage and thanked all the parents for their support of the children. Hanna and Gwen helped with the clean up and Bull got side-tracked with students coming up to him and wanting to know who he was. He got tired quickly of telling them who John Proctor was and he withdrew to the label of 'pilgrim' after Darrel questioned why he would pick someone who was put to death by hanging.

Within fifteen minutes, Gwen, Hanna, and Bull walked the few blocks home. When they got to corner of Borman Avenue,

Gwen told Hanna that she wanted to go for a short walk before she went in for the night. "Mother, you're in an Indian costume."

"I know. That's why I want to go for a walk, its warm. I'll be home in a while." Bull and Hanna finished the walk another half a block to the house. They held hands as they walked alone down the sidewalk and turned up the walkway to the house. He took off his hat as he walked up the steps and she removed her one Indian feather and headband.

"Did you have fun tonight?" he asked her.

She leaned against the door and looked at him. "I had an amazing time, John Proctor."

He leaned one hand on the doorframe over her head. "He really gets hanged, huh?" I must have slept through that part of the play." Bull's pager went off.

"Crap," Bull said as he looked at the number.

"What is it? Work?"

Bull looked at Hanna. "Cheri." He turned to leave without saying another word. His mind was racing. It was as if the world just evaporated. Hanna knew something terrible just happened.

"Something's wrong, isn't it?" she said. It stopped Bull halfway down the sidewalk and he turned back to her. "May I come?"

After a moment's hesitation he stuck out his hand. "Sure, come on." Bull hustled to Hanna's car door and opened it for her and trotted around to his side of the car and jumped in. Hanna thought something was wrong, very wrong.

When God's will is fulfilled through us, he pulls us home to him; where suffering and tears are only a distant memory.

JOHN LYNCH

The two drove about a block before Bull spoke. He was reaching for his cell phone to call. "There is something wrong with Cheri."

"How do you know?" Hanna asked as they took the turn off the street at a steadily increasing speed.

"Cheri's care team has instructions to call me if anything seriously goes wrong. They're to call me with the home's number, then 911." Hanna watched as he pushed two numbers on his cell phone.

"Has this happened before?"

"More times than I can count," he said as he turned out onto Indian School Road and headed for St. Joseph's Hospital. She knew he was anxious. But you couldn't tell by looking at him. He was calmly driving as if they were going to church and not to meet his invalid daughter being transported to the emergency room with some unknown health issue. He hung up after a minute. "She just got there."

They turned right down Third Avenue and after passing Osborn Road they handled two "S" turns and then made a final turn into the emergency parking lot.

"You go in. I'll park the car, hurry!" Hanna said as Bull pulled up to the circle drive, seeing all the parking places were full.

He looked at her for a long second and nodded. "I think you can take it–," he began to say, trying to give direction before she interrupted him.

"I can park this car. You forgot I know this hospital pretty well, too. I'll take care of it. Go to your daughter," she said as she put her hand on his forearm and squeezed it. Bull smiled and took a deep breath then leaned over and kissed Hanna on the cheek. "Thanks. It's probably nothing. It never really is." He trotted to the double sliding glass doors marked 'Emergency Entrance'.

Hanna drove across Third Avenue and up into the parking garage. That time of night it was surprisingly busy. This was a normal Phoenix night with drunks and gunfire and the occasional baby being born that brought people to the hospital. She stuffed the parking stub into her purse. She called Gwen at home, who had just gotten back. She told her mother what was going on as she stepped quickly down the ramp and crossed the street to the same glass doors that Bull walked through. The reception area was full with people of all ages sitting or laying in the blue chairs waiting for their turn to see the triage nurse on duty. Bull was not there, so Hanna anticipated that he was able to go back to Cheri. She checked with the receptionist, who confirmed it and then buzzed Hanna through the steel door after giving her instructions where Cheri had been taken in the back.

The back area was a labyrinth. After numerous re-models, the area seemed pieced together with no real logic to its layout. She found the bay with the individual beds and the wrap-around curtains that guarded each bed. Noises, smells, and sights met her as she checked each one and looking at the ceiling for the bed number that she was given by the receptionist. She turned into a long hall and off to her right was an alcove area that had two bed bays that were separate from the rest of the main hall. One bed was empty but through the partially closed curtain she could see Bull sitting up in the bed holding his daughter. He looked like he was rocking her and talking, saying something softly in her ear. Her head lay across his chest and he stroked her hair. Her eyes were closed and her breathing labored through the oxygen mask. There was an I.V. of saline in one arm and a heart and blood pressure monitor on the other. The heart monitor showed erratic heart rhythms and weak, very weak beats.

From here she heard him whisper "…And when you appear, all the rivers sound in my body, bells shake the sky and a hymn fills the world. Only you and I only you and I, my love, listen to it."

"You know Pablo Neruda?"

"He was my wife's favorite poet. She would recite this poem to Cheri when she was in the crib. I use to stand in the doorway and listen to her repeat it every night when Cheri was young."

Hanna parted the curtains and quietly stepped into the space. Bull looked into her eyes. Hanna saw the eyes of the big man fill and his chin began to quiver.

"She had heart issues. Some of the problems before, it was her heart. I told the home that if her heart began to fail, to let her go. I told them that I wanted to be here if I could, you know, to see her off. That's what a father is supposed to do, isn't it?" He looked at Hanna and then turned and kissed his daughter's forehead. "A father is supposed to watch over his children, his wife, and the family dog. When the fish die it's the father that takes care of it right? He is the protector of the family. Nothing of harm—," his voice began to break, "—no harm is supposed to fall on the family without having to pass by the father."

Hanna moved to his side and rested her hand on his shoulder. The tone of the monitor was turned down but she could still hear the cadence of the tone. The beats were getting weaker. "You are a great father."

There was a pause. Bull blinked and a stream of tears slid down his cheeks. Then he spoke almost in a whisper into her hair. "I couldn't get through the waves. They were one after the other. Every stroke I took I got knocked back three. I heard you both calling for me. I can still here you calling my name." He was shaking his head and holding her close to his chest. "Baby, I'm so sorry, Daddy couldn't get there fast enough. Oh, God Oh God, you gave me one job to do and I screwed it up. Oh God, I'm so sorry, baby." He pulled his daughter to him as he began to sob. The tone on the monitor continued to slow and fade.

Hanna leaned her head against the side of his as he buried his face in Cheri's hair as a nurse entered and stood near the monitor.

She looked at the display and disarmed the alarm on the monitor so when it reached zero it wouldn't go off. She then stood silently by. A doctor followed and stood next to the nurse. The rhythm and beats were falling quickly.

After another five minutes, Cheri's postured hand and arm slid down from her chest and across his as it went limp. The line on the heart monitor went straight. The doctor turned to the nurse and made eye contact that said everything. He looked at his watch but said nothing, just marking the time. The two then left the space to Bull, Hanna, and Cheri.

"I did, I did, two people are dead because of me."

Hanna wrapped her arms around both Bull and Cheri. Her face was next to his as she stood behind him, whispering in his ear. "No, she lived because of you. No one could have predicted what happened. It would have been something different if you had known it was so dangerous and you let them go anyway, but you didn't. Whoever was there would have had this same thing happen to them. How many people would have done over the years what you have done? You guarded your daughter—and Beth. If it hadn't been for you, Cheri would have died, too. If it hadn't been for your shepherding this beautiful girl over the last few years she would have died lonely and unloved. Look at where you are." She squeezed tighter as if to strike home her point. He leaned his head into hers. It struck her what he had done. "You're holding your precious daughter while she goes home. Her last thoughts of this life are of her father, loving her so much. A love not found but in the heart of a father." She moved around to where he could see her. "Cheri is home. I can only tell you what I feel. I never knew my father. I never felt his touch that I can remember. Your daughter," she reached over and stroked her hair. "Cheri gets to be carried home in the arms of an angel."

"Mr. Thornton?" Bull looked up over Hanna's shoulder "This is Mr. Thornton," Hanna said.

It was Chauneese Richards. Bull recognized her from Cheri's home. She was an older black woman, one of the night nurse supervisors. Bull always liked her because she took a liking to Cheri and her gentleness towards the patients was only matched by her Marine-type discipline with the night staff. She made sure that the clients were "loved by design," Bull later told Hanna. Chauneese made sure that her patients were treated with respect and that her team served them. She would often be found reading some of the Old Testament stories to a comatose patient. He never really had any long conversations with Chauneese but recognized her as soon as Hanna moved out of the way. "Oh, hello, Chauneese," Bull said as he freed one hand and wiped the tears in his eyes. He looked back at his daughter, still cradled in his arms.

"I don't know if you remember me. I work nights at Con-right."

He nodded his head without taking his eyes off of his daughter.

"I brought Cheri in. I just wanted you to know that it was an honor taking care of her. I also thought you'd like to know something." Chauneese was a big woman but she gently moved to the far side of the bed and reached over the rail and stroked Cheri's hair and took her limp hand and held it. The hand was no longer curled up but loose and free. She looked at Bull as she spoke. "Just after you left tonight, I went in to check on Cheri. I know you tuck her in her bed every time you come but it's just a habit of mine, being a mother myself, and wanting all my chicks tucked in tight. Anyway, I went over to her bed and–," She paused and looked at Bull and then to Hanna. She began to smile.

"What happened?" Hanna said.

"Mr. Thornton, your daughter smiled."

"It's an involuntary reflex," Bull said after looking up and then back to Cheri.

"That's what I first thought, but I've worked with these patients for thirty-five years and I've seen that; this wasn't it. Mr. Thornton, after you left she was, I believe, truly happy." Chauneese looked over at Cheri and stroked her cheek with the back of her own hand. "I've tucked your daughter in every night I was on since she's come to stay with us. She's always had a smile or some sort of response to some of the things that we do or that you have done.

This was different. I don't want to be too forward, Mr. Bull, but you came in with a lady friend. From looking at you two, she seems to care about you and your child," Chauneese said smiling peacefully.

"You think we caused her death?" Bull said as he looked up at the woman.

"No sir, not at all. I think your daughter could tell that you had someone," she paused for a minute. "Maybe she didn't have to fight so hard to stay around anymore. I think there was still something in her that found peace in knowing there was someone else. I also think she knew where she was going."

"You mean Heaven," Bull said.

"Yes, sir. She and I, well, you know. She and I, we've talked a lot about heaven. She didn't say much but I could tell. She knew."

Bull nodded. "That would be a good thought for me."

She let go of Cheri's hand and stood up straight. "Anyway sir, if there is anything I can do, please feel free to call. I just thought you should know."

Bull looked up as Chauneese finished. The words worked their way through the fog that filled Bull's brain. "Thank you, Chauneese. Thank you very much."

"You're welcome, Mr. Thornton. It was my privilege to know her." Chauneese turned and parted the curtain as she left the same way she came in.

Bull watched the curtain for a few seconds and then slowly looked at Hanna. She was looking down at him. Tears in her own eyes spilled down her cheeks. She bent over and ever so softly, kissed him. Their foreheads rested against each other as they cried together.

Bull had decided to have the service at the small chapel at Conright the following Wednesday. After all, the people that counted most in his daughter's life were all right here, he thought. Some of the night shift, including Chauneese, was there. Cheri's grandparents, a few of Bull's friends from his squad, Jen'ot, Gwen, and Hanna were also present.

"Father, we submit this child of yours and give her back. She was not ours to keep Father, she is yours. We thank you for the time that we were able to spend with her," the minister said. The words rang dully in Bull's brain.

The service was short. People lingered for about fifteen minutes, and then began to fade off. Hanna asked Bull if he wanted her to stay and he simply kissed her forehead and shook his head. Cheri was going to be cremated and it was going to be his last act as a father. He followed the hearse over to Greenwood Memorial and their crematorium. He stayed in the car while the casket, carrying the remains of his daughter, was unloaded. He had told the driver that as soon as she was set and inside to come out and let him know. The hearse pulled into the circle drive in front of the building and Bull parked about twenty yards behind him in the shade of a palm tree. After about fifteen minutes, the driver came out and gave Bull a thumb's up. Bull waved back. Tears began as he watched the tail lights of the vehicle drive off. Then he cried fully as he gripped the steering wheel. He laid his head on the back of his hands and wept. There was nothing left. The story of his family was over.

Hanna woke up the next morning dreaming of the girl again. She was in her late teens or early twenties this time and Hanna could clearly recognize the girl as herself when she was younger. She is walking with a smile on her face. She again sees something or someone that makes her smile. Hanna still could not identify what is making her so happy. Again, she wakes up before she finds out.

If you haven't forgiven yourself something, how can you forgive others?

Dolores Huerta

January

One week ran into the next. Hanna noticed while standing in her classroom that it was raining outside. "Class," she said interrupting their writing. "While you write, remember the other day when we were talking about what kindness might smell like and we agreed that one of the things it smelled like was rain. What do you say we go outside and breathe the rain and get a good sniff of kindness?"

Bull spent his mornings running on the street around the school. He liked to run but in the last few years it had gotten hard on his knees. The doctor told him that he had osteoarthritis and he needed to take up a different exercise program. Bull thanked him, paid the bill on his way out and that afternoon went out for a five miler. But since Cheri's funeral he had put more effort into it. He pushed it. His brain was working on the equation. He didn't take his radio as he normally did. They got in the way with his processing. He ran up and down every street in the neighborhood before school started and when he got to the end of the block he turned around and ran the same streets going the other direction. He rounded the last turn and came to a stop on the side of the campus. His University of Chicago sweatshirt was soaked with sweat. He walked through the empty halls of the campus, his hands on his hips. He walked from one end of the campus to the other and came to a stop at Hanna's open classroom door. He knocked gently to get her attention so he wouldn't startle her. Hanna was at her desk reading and looked up, pulled off her reading glasses and gave the man a soft smile. "Hi."

Bull nodded and continued to breath heavier than normal. "Tell me again," he said with a puff.

"What?" Hanna said while frowning, and began to chew on the end of her eyeglasses trying to figure out what he meant.

"The night at the hospital. Tell me again."

She still was drawing a blank and began to get up to walk over to him. "What?"

"No, you don't have to get up," he said holding his hand up for her to keep her seat. "Just tell me again."

Then it clicked with her. She looked at him, into his eyes. She realized then that she had missed him the week of the funeral. She realized that this was a man she could fall in love with. She stumbled at the next thought; she could trust him with her heart. She looked into the eyes that had been a source of strength and now only called for someone to hold their owner. He wasn't broken by Cheri's death. He knew it was coming. He was wounded, by the nagging of his mind that he alone lived and he alone was responsible. He needed her. She could see that. He loved her. She could see that also. She walked up to him and stood close. She could smell him and feel the heat coming from his body and his breath exhaled from his nostrils. There was a quiver in his chin as he tried to hold it together when she reached up gently and touched his face with her open palm. He leaned into it and closed his eyes. "You did everything you could. Your daughter and your wife knew you loved them."

"I—uh, I might need to hear that every now and then if you don't mind?" he said, giving a deep, clearing breath.

She smiled. "Anytime."

He closed his eyes again and she pulled his head down gently to hers and softly, almost as if she was reaching for smoke, she kissed him lightly on his upper lip. As they touched, her eyes closed and she held her lips to his. She could feel a tear trace down his cheek and touch her upper lip. "Thanks," he said as he pulled back and looked at her with a smile and thin eyes just as he turned to leave. "Hanna?" he said as he got to the door.

"Yes, Bull," she said without having moved. She was screaming inside. The fear she had felt was tearing at her. The desire she also felt was pulling in the opposite direction. The grief she had for his heart and the loss of Cheri, even though she didn't know her long, pulled in another direction.

"Uh, nothing." He was nodding his head. "It's raining outside. Smells great. I'm going to go get dressed now." He turned and walked towards the small faculty locker room and showers.

Hanna stood in the same position and hadn't moved. She took a deep breath and her eyes were still soft looking at the empty door way.

All the beautiful sentiments in the world weigh less than a single lovely action

James Russell Lowell

February

Gwen didn't feel good when she woke up. She routinely didn't feel good and hadn't felt good for as long as she could remember. She hadn't felt good for so long that on those days when she felt bad, she actually felt pretty good. It was on those days, when she actually felt bad, that she truly felt bad. This was one of those days. Still, she got up and dressed her self, made coffee, ate, and walked the few hundred steps to the school.

She shared playground duty with Kathy Cryer on Thursdays. There was a mulberry tree that had lost its leaves to winter but still provided some shade from the warm sun. It felt good in the cool air and its shade simply allowed the ladies to stand and talk without the need for sunglasses. Gwen didn't eat a lot for lunch. The chicken lasagna the cafeteria offered just didn't do it for her so she settled for three packages of Saltines. Maybe they would help quiet her stomach. She hoped. She finished the last of the three packages as she spoke with Kathy.

"Are you getting excited about the wedding?" Gwen asked in between bites.

"It's still so far away," Kathy answered, looking at the three four-square courts and seeing that the kids were waiting in line patiently without cutting. "Hanna said she had a great time the other night at your engagement party. When was the date again?" Gwen said. She wiped some sweat from her forehead, starting to feel worse.

"Next October," Kathy said looking away again.

"Kathy, that's almost ten months away."

"I know, I know, but these Pre Cana last six months and that puts us right at summer. I don't want to get married and have people pass out from the heat. It doesn't start to cool until late October." Kathy stopped talking when she looked at Gwen. She was turning pale. "Honey, are you all right?" she said resting her hand on Gwen's arm.

"This sun, even in the winter, with all the meds I'm taking, it starts to get to me." She closed her eyes for a minute and sat down on the small seat that made up the tree planter.

"Let's go stand under the eaves, okay? There's more shade over there," she said as she pointed to the side of the gym. Tony was there sweeping the walkway that led from the side of the gym door to the restroom and scooping up wrappers, tossing them in the neighboring trash can.

"That's a good idea," Gwen said as she got up. She was following about a step behind and to the side of Kathy when the images she was seeing began to fade to a kind of salt and pepper image. She couldn't see or feel anything, including the fall to the asphalt.

Hanna was one of the last ones to hear. Gwen had been transported to the hospital almost twenty minutes before Hanna was told by Darrel. He and Barbara came into her room and pulled her out to the walkway.

He told her that Gwen had fainted at lunch and had been transported to St. Joe's. Her face was calmer than Darrel had thought it would be. She had been down this road before and it wasn't new to her. Still, she looked away from Darrel's eyes for a moment and then calmly said she would need someone to cover her class for the rest of the day. Without waiting for an answer, she turned and walked back in the room and over to her desk for her purse. She told her class that she had to leave for the rest of the day, but that she would see them in the morning. She gave them a smile and slung her purse over her shoulder and walked out of the room. Barbara offered to drive her to the hospital but Hanna opted to have her drive her home so she could get the car. She was on her way to the emergency room within five minutes.

The thoughts spun on their axis in her brain. She had run all the scenarios a thousand times. She knew there was nothing she could do and her mother was only minutes away. What she really needed was to keep her brain clear. She had no idea what she was going to be facing when she got to her mother's room. She would need a clear head to make those decisions that a child has to make when her parents get old. She couldn't have emotion blocking her mind. If there were decisions, hard decisions that needed to be made, she would have to make them.

As she found the room, off of the main emergency room, she heard laughing. She pushed open the door and saw her mother sitting up in bed with an I.V. in her arm. On one side was Tony. He was holding his hat in one hand and Gwen's hand the other. When Hanna entered and Tony saw her, he let go of the hand and moved it to the side rail. On the other side was a man in a white lab coat.

"Oh, there's my beautiful daughter. Come over here and hug me," she said as she lifted her free hand. "Let me introduce you two. Hanna, this is my doctor, one of my doctors," she smiled. "Dr. Jacardi, this is my daughter, Hanna." Hanna approached and shook his hand. She looked over at Tony and nodded at him with a puzzled look Gwen knew she needed to explain. "Tony was nearby and rode to the hospital with me so I wouldn't be alone," Gwen volunteered before the doctor spoke.

"It appears I had a little bit of a reaction to the new dose of meds I was on. One of the concerns that I needed to look for was to stay out of the sun and not get overheated, at least for a while. I'll be fine."

Hanna looked over at the doctor, waiting for him to confirm what her mother had said.

"I was explaining to your mother that she had an adverse reaction to the chemo therapy. In order for the treatment to work we have to give her fairly high doses of this stuff. It might have—it will have some severe side effects. The medication has an ability to dehydrate the patient so anything that promoted that, like being out in the sun, working, or exercise, we really want to monitor closely. She was a little dehydrated when she came in so we're giving her some fluids. We'll hang onto her this afternoon and then if everything goes the way we expect it will, we'll kick her loose in a couple of hours. I would suggest no more playground duty for awhile, though."

"I need to carry my own turn doing that. I can't let someone else pick up an extra duty just because I—,"

"Absolutely doctor. We'll do exactly that," Hanna said.

"Well, I leave the three of you alone. Gwen, I'll be around all day so I'll check back with you in about an hour or so," he said, laying his hand on her shoulder just before he turned to leave. "It was nice meeting you, Hanna," he said as he reached out and shook her hand. He nodded to Tony just before he left the room.

"Mother, you never told me about these side effects."

"I did so."

"You did not." She glanced at Tony. He had already found a chair and was pretending to look at a magazine left on the table next to it.

"I thought throwing up all over the vanity in my bathroom was a tell tale sign."

"Mother—,"

There was a knocking at the door and Tony opened it. "Knock, knock. There's a middle aged yet very handsome man who wants to see the world famous break dancing teacher," Bull said as he entered the room.

"There is the face I wanted to see. Come over here and let me hug your neck." Gwen said. Bull came in with a smile for the group. He watched Hanna as she stepped back a couple of feet to allow Bull to press close. Tony saw Bull wink at Hanna and squeeze her arm. It made him smile just a little.

He was carrying flowers. "You going to be all right? You're not planning on leaving us in mid-term are you?" he said with a grin.

She reached up with her hand toward Tony and he came straight to her bedside and grabbed the outstretched hand. She was holding Bull's other hand.

"This group is all I need."

"You had everyone worried, hon'," Bull said.

"I'll be all right. It's just the medicine." She looked at the two men and then at Hanna. "Bull, dear, will you take my dear daughter to get something to eat?"

"I'm not hungry."

"Honey, I know you didn't eat any lunch and breakfast was a long time ago. Bull, please."

"Yes, ma'am." He looked at her. "We can go downstairs and come right back," he said reassuringly to Hanna.

"Mother, I don't want to leave you."

"Honey, I'm in a hospital. If something happens I think this is where I need to be, don't you? Besides, Tony will stay with me. Won't you, dear?"

Tony gave her a smile and a nod. "Hanna, it will be all right. I'll stay right here until you get back. I'll take good care of her."

Hanna looked at her mother and back to Bull, who nodded as well, and the two left the room. They walked quietly down the hall and to the elevator, taking it down to the bottom floor and into the throat of the cafeteria entrance. Bull asked her what she wanted. She settled on a slice of lemon meringue pie and a cup of coffee. He got a salad and a soda and placed it on the same tray. He paid for the items at the check out counter and the two made their way to an open booth next to a large window that went from the floor to the raised ceiling about fifteen feet up in a virtually empty dining area. The room was bathed with indirect afternoon light.

"Trust me, a cup of fresh coffee and this slice of pie will make you all better. Your mother's going to be fine," Bull said as he unrolled his utensil set from the paper.

Hanna just sat and watched him. Her mind was not in the room, so Bull reached across and unrolled her silverware and laid them out in front of her. He took the pie and coffee along with his own food from the tray and placed the tray on the empty table next to them.

After a minute he bent over his plate so his head was low and staring at Hanna. He reached across and waved his fingers to get her attention at the same time he spoke to her.

"Hanna, look at me." He waited until her eyes met his. "I have seen people die. I held them when they went—more times then I care to remember. I have also seen many, many, people make it. Your mother is eventually going to die but it's not going to happen today—or tomorrow, or this month but she is alive today.

"She's all I have, Bull. I try to talk to her and we can talk about a lot of things but there are some things that we just can't get close to. Like this thing she has or like my Dad, for example. She always just skims the surface of who he was, of their life together. I'm tired of this." She looked at Bull and the ledges of her eyes began to fill with tears.

"What was his name?" he said as he picked up a fork and held it until she took it and cut a bite of pie. Bull did the same with his salad but after three bites he pushed it aside and started to eyeball the pie. As she talked he eased his fork across and cut a corner of the crust and meringue.

"Elias."

"You lose someone like that, that's tough. Sometimes you just don't want to deal with the memories again, even if they're good ones," he said with a mouthful of pie. Hanna adjusted the pie by moving it closer so he could cut it without reaching so far.

"It's not just that. There is so much I want to talk to her about and sometimes we can but sometimes it's like a room I can't go into. And I know time is running out. I don't know what to do. It's been just the two of us my whole life. She's always been there for me. She kept me clothed and fed and was always there to kiss my tears away. When we had nothing, she found a way to give me everything." Hanna played with her pie for a minute and took a long pull on her coffee.

"And now you feel it's your turn to take care of things?"

"She's dying, Bull. I can't watch her die."

Bull waited for a minute as he stabbed at the remnants of the pie with the tip of his fork.

"First, I am not convinced that she is dying. You have some time. Maybe years, maybe not. A wise, wise person was heard to say that in death one of the greatest honors we have is to escort our loved ones to the angels and send them home." Her eyes came up to meet his. "That wise person, a man no doubt," a smile came to both their faces, "probably very tall, with big feet and a hook nose, and smelling like Mentholatum, also said that it is a wonderful gift to be the last thought in a loved one's mind, the thought of being so dearly loved. You have that chance. I never had it with my parents, but you do. Everyone dies, Hanna. You have warning. Use this time you have wisely."

She smiled and came at the pie from the opposite side from Bull. "Big feet, huh?"

"And a hook nose."

She looked at the empty plate and frowned. "Was it any good?"

"I'm a cop. I have pie. Life doesn't get any better than this," he said as he plunged the empty fork in his mouth and pulled it out clean.

"Can I have some?"

"You did. That's why I got two forks."

"She nodded. Did I enjoy it?"

"It wasn't bad for hospital food. I spare no expense to show my woman a good time. I'll even carry your tray."

"Yeah, you've told me that before."

"You're welcome."

You're a piece of monkey crap; you know that?"

"Why?" he said with a frown.

"Because now I really want a piece of pie."

There was a pause in the conversation. "How are you feeling about us?" she asked.

"Us? As in you and me? Aren't you a little distracted with you mother to get into this right now?"

"You're right, I'm sorry, I've kind of put you on the spot. But please–distract me."

He sat back against the booth and wiped his mouth. "No, no, I don't mind. Actually, I was going to talk to you about this— this relationship we have."

"Ooh, I bet I don't want to hear the answer to this question right now. I'm sorry I asked. Bull, please I really–," She began to fidget as if trying to find a place to hide. All of a sudden, the fear was back. There was a wave of panic that she was vulnerable again and now history was going to repeat itself. If she could have run she would have.

"No, probably not, but I figure that since you brought it up you're ready for the answer."

"No, really, you don't need to rush this. I'm sorry I asked—,"

"I love you, Hanna."

"-because we really need to—what did you say?" She stopped and stared at him.

"I love you, Hanna. I have since Greasewood." He wiped his mouth again and took a sip of the soda. "Look, I'm a simple guy, really. I kind of pride myself on being shallow. I'm not a real deep person. What you see is what you get. I will never try to hide anything from you. Sure there are some things from my past that will raise their heads every once in a while, but when they do, I figure we can deal with them. I'm too old and, God knows, too tired to play games unless its basketball. You were there for me with Cheri and I plan, with your permission, to be here for you with your mom or anything else that comes along. Now, I'm not talking marriage, not yet. I'm talking about two people getting to know each other and seeing where it goes. Marriage is always a discussion topic if you wish. But you're stuck with me loving you. You, or we, are just going to have to deal with that fact. Now, if I said something that scares you or intimidates—,"

"I'm not going anywhere." A calm smile came over her face as she spoke. Her ledges filled again. "Why me?"

"Dear, the list is too long. Now lick your fork and let's get back to your mother and Tony. This thing really scared him, too."

They got up from the table and Bull picked up the tray he had put on the neighboring table and put their used dishes on it and then the two of them walked out. As they crossed out into the hall to go back to the elevator, Hanna reached over and took his hand.

In every man's heart there beats a warrior, a poet, an athlete, and the world's greatest lover. Only through the heartbeats of time gives the man his wisdom.

Packard Thornton

Lyle Van Duesen had been the senior custodian for twenty years at Borman. He repaired, patched or painted just about every corner, outlet, light bulb, toilet, classroom, or office on that campus. Lyle was forty-seven and Tony worked for him. Tony, even with his slowness, never seemed to bother Lyle. He loved the older man as if he was his older brother. He looked out for Tony and, in his way and in his ability, Tony looked out for Lyle. They never went out after work together. Lyle had asked years ago if Tony wanted to go have a beer with him after work. Tony had quickly said 'no' and Lyle never pushed it or asked again. He figured if Tony wanted to go out with him he would ask. They spent more time together during the week than most married couples and they were very happy together. They didn't talk much about anything other than work and that suited both just fine.

Tony entered the office early in the morning. Lyle was sitting behind the small desk the district had given him. He looked up from the short stack of work orders by individual teachers to see his partner walk in. Tony was looking down with his hands folded behind his back and after he cleared the door he walked around the room where they stored the rakes, aimlessly wondering in deep thought.

"Morning, Tony."

"Morning, Lyle," Tony said as he picked up a shovel and felt the working edge of it as if he was checking its sharpness.

Lyle looked back up at Tony. He thought something in his voice sounded funny. "You're in kind of early, aren't you, partner?"

Tony looked over his shoulder from the corner. "Yeah, I guess. I couldn't sleep anymore so I thought I might as well come in and get some good work done." He looked back at the shovel and then put it down.

"You all right?"

There was a pause in Tony's response. "Lyle, you think that Gwen will be all right?" He had picked up a hoe this time and was feeling the edge of the blade in the same manner that he did the shovel.

"You mean Mrs. Jackson? Yeah, I think she'll be all right. The doctors say they just had to change her medication a little. She seems to be doing all right since she's been back at school."

Tony paused again as Lyle watched him. "I don't mean from when she was in the hospital. I mean from this disease she has. Do you think she'll be all right?"

Lyle sat back in his chair. He had known Gwen a long time, as long as Tony. He never knew the school without her being there. For the first time, Tony's question caused him to stop and think.

"Oh, Tony, that's a hard one. She's been sick for a long time."

Lyle could tell Tony was worried. Tony took time in his thinking but was able to usually come to the same answer an adult who wasn't slow would come up with. He was rubbing the tip of the blade. "Too many people love her for her to die."

"Everyone dies. No matter how much people are loved, partner—everyone dies," Lyle said as he leaned forward, resting his elbows on his desk.

There was a long pause. Lyle thought Tony had given up on the conversation and almost went back to the work orders before he could just barely make out Tony's voice.

"I know. But why can't I go instead? She's too important to die."

"What? I didn't hear you, buddy."

Tony looked over his shoulder at his friend. His hand still stroked the blade as he shook his head and said, "Nothing."

I shall grow old, but never lose life's zest,
because the road's last turn will be the best.

HENRY VAN DYKE

It had been a couple of weeks since Gwen returned to work. She had returned to her class against her doctor's orders but compromised with him and said since it was Wednesday she would take Thursday and Friday off, and return to work on the following Monday. The students were gone and Tony was out finishing his crossing guard duties. Lyle took his "CAT" ball cap off as he knocked on Gwen's open door.

Gwen looked up and smiled. "Lyle, what a pleasant surprise. What can I do for you?"

Lyle stepped into the room. "Do you have a minute Gwen? I need to talk to you about something."

Gwen got up and walked around from her desk and gave him her full attention. "Please, come in and sit down," she said as she signaled to a chair. He held up his hand to say he didn't need to sit.

"I just thought I'd come in and see if there was anything I could get for you?"

"No, hon', I don't think so. I think I've got everything I need. Why?"

"Tony and I have been just a little bit worried about you, Tony especially," he said working the brim of his cap.

Gwen's smile was delayed when Lyle mentioned their concern. Her eyes looked out the window to her right and he could see her looking over at Tony on the corner.

"Really? You boys shouldn't have worried about that little trip to the hospital. I told you it wasn't serious. Just needed to adjust my medication. That's all. I'm fine, really," she said as she looked out the window.

"Yes ma'am, I know, but Tony came in today and you guys go back a lot farther than me and he was just worried and got me to thinkin' also. We don't want you going anywhere. You can tell when Tony is thinking about something. He always walks with–,"

"—with his hands behind his back. Yes, I know. I've noticed that too," she said. Her smile melted away and she stood staring out the window.

In her mind, Gwen was watching a movie reel of images of her life, her experiences, sprinting through her mind's vision at an incredible speed. There were images of her on a merry-go-round as a child, being pushed by her father. Then, pushing her own daughter, at about the same age, on a similar merry-go- round; pushing students on the school's merry-go-round before it was removed. She saw Sonet teaching at her white board; Bull, walking through campus; Darrel and Barbara laughing and talking in the office. She saw her home and her daughter's face laughing and looking at her over toast and coffee in the early morning. None of it made sense and yet all of it did. She saw things that she hadn't seen or thought of in years. She stared out the window. Tony was walking out to the corner to cross the children. He walked with his hands behind his back.

The difficult we do immediately. The impossible takes a little longer.

United States Special Forces

Spring came with little or no incident. Oh, sure, it followed the tragedy at the Christmas play, actually called the 'Winter Play' for political correctness, of the fallen snow tree that was taken out by Johnny Kempler, who was playing a snow bunny. He was standing next to Susie Fedelstein whom he had a severe liking for and was poking her with his wooden cane.

Susie played a white and silver forest pixie and a beautiful one at that. She had creamy skin and her hair was a deep, deep mahogany red. She wore thick glasses only to see things beyond two feet from her face. Of course, young women like this, who also got straight A's, became lightening rods of passion for peers, like Johnny, who had short hair, freckles, and one ear lower than the other. His grade point average was okay if you counted P.E., which you always did. Susie only took P.E. because she had to. Johnny took P.E. because he was a ten-year-old boy and that's what boys did.

It was a well-known fact that all snow bunnies, especially the "Elder" bunnies, needed staffs to make them look wise. He poked her with the tip of his stick for the four-hundredth time; the tension in the pixie piled up. As a result of harassing behaviors perpetrated against her by Johnny such as chasing her at lunch, before school, and a little after school, the end came. She had enough of his dopiness and when he poked her with his stick again, she at first tried to look at him with a glare of 'If I could, I would set you on fire right now with a can of gasoline, if I could actually find a can of gasoline, and still get away with it in front of all these people.' But

Susie Fedelstein was a forest pixie. She was chosen for her beauty. Beauty was never known to be able to give a look of such vile anger as agreement to what she was thinking. She was stuck.

Her look at him only confessed to him that she truly, deep in her heart, found his attention wonderful in its own ten-year-old way. "She likes me," Johnny Kempler thought. "Look at the way she is looking at me. She's looking at me!" That was his thought just before she karate-chopped him in the throat, a technique she learned in a class she took on the weekends during the summer at the YMCA. He fell back onto his snow bunny tail and the staff flew back with him, hitting the cardboard tree, which knocked over the tree into the back stand, and the cascade started.

When it was over, the play finished, the parents had pictures of the unique performance. No one actually saw what happened because the two of them were behind "Boman," the friendly Forest Bear, and his body blocked most of the assault. Johnny Kempler and Susie Fedelstein, with a little help from their parents' photography, had a memory they would later scrapbook into one of three photo albums they made after they met again at Arizona State University, fell in love, and married years later. She would call him by his nickname in their times of love as her little "Snow Bunny" and he would do the same with her—"Zena, Warrior Princess."

February moved into March.

Bull arrived at school in his patrol car. He came into the office and smiled at Barbara who usually smiled back with a wink. This morning was different.

"Did you hear?" she said as she put down what she was working on and turned fully to Bull.

"Hear what?" he said as he took a sip of coffee.

"Tony fell ill."

"What?"

Darrel came out of his office when he heard Bull's voice. "Yeah, about an hour ago. He was out at the corner and he told one of the kids that he was feeling dizzy, then he just fell over. Mrs. Jackson was the first one the child talked to and she called the fire department. She followed the ambulance to the hospital and she'll call us when she knows anything."

"Where did they take him, St. Joseph's?"

"Yes. They said it has all the markings of a stroke. I have to go over to his apartment and get his insurance card and a few things. You want to go with me?" Darrel said as he pointed to the door.

"Sure, let me just put my stuff down." Bull looked over at Barbara, who reached out with her hands over the counter, and he gave her his briefcase. He kept the coffee and turned to follow Darrel out the door.

Darrel turned to Barbara and held up his hand-held radio and told her he would be on it if anyone needed anything. "Yes, sir. You have Tony's key?"

"Yep, right here," he said as he held up a set.

The two arrived quickly at Tony's home behind Gwen's house. Darrel didn't know how much Tony was paying Gwen for the place but knew Gwen well enough to realize it probably had never gone up. The house and yard, what Darrel could see from the street, always looked good. Tony had given a set of keys to his place to Darrel in case Darrel, or anyone else, ever needed to get into his apartment, like today. It was a red brick building to match the home. There was a screen door and then the front door on the north side, away from the main garage door wall that had been removed years ago so the building looked and performed more like an apartment than a garage. The front door was an older door with the small rectangular window in it. Bull was surprised to see a little curtain in the window of the door. He didn't picture Tony as a little curtain kind of guy. Bull held the screen door open while Darrel opened the front door. The door pushed open with the sound of a tight fit. As the two stepped in, they both removed their sunglasses to allow their eyes to adjust to the darkness.

"This won't take long. He told me once all his important papers are in a box on the floor of his closet," Darrel said as he moved to the right down a short hall from the main living room/dining room that they stepped into. There was a kitchen across from the open door and a hallway with a bedroom at its end and a bathroom on the right.

Bull looked around the room as Darrel left him. There was a freshly pressed white doily on the back of the couch. There were two other high back chairs opposite with a coffee table in between. There was a newer television on the opposite wall with a DVD and a small stereo component system on a floor-to-ceiling bookcase right next to the couch. The drapes were lace and doilies were again seen on the chairs. The walls were covered with paintings and pictures. There was even an old softball mitt on the top shelf. In a corner, nearest the door, was an easel with an oil painting of a country road and surrounding trees that looked about half finished. Bull called down the hall to Darrel. "I didn't know Tony was a painter. You finding what you need?" Bull called.

"Yeah, I think so; it'll just take a minute. He has a couple of insurance cards here and I want to make sure I got the right one."

Bull stared at the walls. There were dozens of color and black and white neatly framed pictures, mostly eight by tens.

"Tell me again why you have his key?" he said while walking along looking at the pictures.

"He left me a key to get in if I ever needed to," Darrel said as he came back down the hall to the living room holding a card.

"I don't know," Bull started as he continued to look at the pictures. It wouldn't surprise me if this is exactly why he gave you the keys."

"You're probably right."

Bull walked in front of the couch, looking at the pictures over the back of it. He found Tony in one of them as a young Marine. "Did you know Tony was a Marine, Darrel?" he said, still looking at the photos.

"You know, I thought I had heard rumors about that. He came so long before I did that I hadn't really paid attention."

Bull saw it first out of the corner of his eye. It was the color and the stars on it that made him look. It was almost hidden by the lamp next to the couch and bookcase. In a shadow box on the wall was the light blue ribbon and medal of the Congressional Medal of Honor. Bull's mouth dropped open without him knowing it. Next to it on the bookshelf was a framed black and white picture of a young Tony in a hospital bed, bandaged around his head and arms, with General Westmoreland shaking his hand. The medal had been placed around his neck. There was a letter next to it, also framed. It was the citation for the award.

CITATION

'By special proclamation of the Congress of the United States and presented to...'

Bull's eyes scrambled across the page. '...the Congressional Medal of Honor is hereby awarded to Elias A. Jackson, Gunnery Sergeant, United States Marine Corps, for actions he participated in on 29 March, 1969, at Marine Fire Base Six in the Mekong Delta in the Republic of South Vietnam."

Bull looked around the room. His eyes were darting from picture to picture. There was a small framed picture on the other side of the bookshelf. His eyes fell on it because he recognized it. "Holy Crap," he mouthed to himself.

Bull picked up the picture and held it. He stroked the frame and rubbed the image of the woman and man holding the small girl in his arms. The picture was the same one that Hanna had on her desk. The picture he held was clear, not as dark as the one on Hanna's desk. He hadn't looked at it that closely. Now, he could see the faces and see the youth compared with the aged. Elias Jackson was a janitor at the school Bull worked at.

Often, the shadows in our darkened rooms hold the toys we had forgotten about as a youth and are only discovered when the lights are turned on.

Author

A beautiful March morning

Barrows Neurological Institute was a wing at St. Joseph known throughout the world as the premier facility for brain trauma and brain-related illnesses. Tony had his own room. He had been initially treated and diagnosed by the emergency room and then sent up to BNI's Intensive Care Unit, where he was held and observed over night. Early the next morning, they were able to upgrade Tony and send him to his own room.

Bull kept what he knew quiet. He wanted to talk to Gwen but that day was not the day to do so. He drove Darrel down to the hospital in his patrol car so he could drop off the card to Gwen. There were no visitors allowed until the next day when Tony was moved.

When Bull eased open the heavy door and silently entered, Gwen was standing on the far side of the bed with her back to the draped window. Tony laid on his back with his eyes shut. Gwen was holding his hand. He had in an I.V. and a blood pressure cuff loose around his upper arm. He didn't open his eyes when Bull walked in but Gwen looked up. She began to lay down his hand onto the bed and then saw it was Bull and continued to hold it with both hands. Bull walked over to her side. "How's he doing?" he whispered to her.

"They think it was a stroke. Did Darrel get the insurance card?" she asked, glancing over at Bull then back to Tony.

Bull laid his hand on Gwen's shoulder while still looking at

Tony. “Yeah, he and I ran into Hanna on the way in through the lobby and the two of them went down to Admitting to take care of the paperwork.” He was silent for a moment as the two of them watched the sleeping man. “I know Tony is Elias,” Bull whispered. “I’m sure there is a good reason you haven’t told anyone that Tony is your husband.”

Gwen looked at Bull and then to Tony. “How?”

Bull held up the picture from the house. Gwen looked at it and then looked at Bull. She took it and placed it in the drawer next to his bed. She then returned her gaze to the man in the bed.

“His picture and citations with his name on it were hanging in his home. My dear friend here has enough medals in his apartment to last seven wars. He did more crap than Audie Murphy. Hanna has this same picture on her desk.” Bull paused. He could see the side of Gwen’s face. She took in a heavy breath and blinked slowly. Other than that, she had no change in her demeanor. “Why?”

“I have my reasons,” she said as she stroked Tony’s hair.

“Do you want to share them?”

She didn’t look up. She just kept stroking his hair, softly, gently, with the back of her hand. “They’re not important.”

“I think Hanna would argue with you on that. Does she know?”

Gwen turned now to Bull. She squared herself to him. “No, and she’s not going to know, either.” Her eyes looked deep into Bull’s.

“Dear, you can’t hide this from her. This is her father, for God’s sake.”

“Who else knows?”

“What?”

“I said, ‘Who else knows?’ You went to the apartment. Who went with you?”

Bull paused and continued looking into her eyes. He saw a fire there. “Like I said, Darrel went with me. He was in the other room and he doesn’t know anything unless he could read the numb look on my face when we left. Gwen, honey, you have got to tell Hanna.” He knew as soon as he said it that it was a mistake.

"She is not to know about this. Do you understand?" she said with clenched teeth and a death whisper that only the two of them could hear. "She is not to know about this, Bull. Do you understand? You are not to mention this to anyone."

"At least tell me why. Why are you denying your only child the knowledge that her Daddy is alive? Tell me why you want to do that to her?"

He could see her jaw flex and relax the muscle under her skin along the side of her face. She blinked, looked away for a moment, and then came back and locked his eyes again. "Elias Anthony Jackson died on a river bank years ago. She only needs to know that. You are going to have to believe that I have my reason for that being the story she believes." She stood up straight as she finished as if to reinforce the statement.

"Those reasons sound pretty selfish if you asked–,"

She cut him off. "No one is asking you. You're sticking your nose where it doesn't belong."

"It doesn't belong? It belongs right in the middle of this. The only people I care about are involved here. People are going to get hurt." He felt the tension in his jaw begin to form.

Gwen's eyes softened. Bull saw sadness in them as she turned to look back at Tony.

"People have already been hurt." Bull watched her rub the side of his head with the back of her hand. He could see her breathe a heavy sigh. She looked at the man in the bed with tenderness that only a spouse of a long love could give their partner. Bull saw her at the end of the breath, her face changed back to the firmness of a woman determined. "This is embarrassing enough, Tony's condition. I don't want to exasperate it further. I am asking you as a friend not to repeat a word of this to anyone. Hanna will go on living her life believing her father is a dead hero, not a living burden."

Bull's mouth fell open. He was witnessing a shift of character that he could not believe or comprehend. These words did not come from this woman. Or, and it concerned him almost to the point of fear, this was the heart of a woman he did not know. How could he have missed such a character issue with someone he thought he knew so well? He had trouble forming a response. He had seen more than most in this life of his and was not shocked by anything. This caught him by surprise. He couldn't put his finger on it but something was not adding up. "You think he is a burden? God, tell me you didn't say that. Tell me that you didn't just call this man a burden. I pray that I could live a life one quarter as courageously as he. We are standing before a damned American icon and you call him a burden?"

She turned to him again, eyes like cold steel. "Remember what I said, Bull, no one else. If you care or honor me as a friend, no one else is to know about this—no one."

Bull looked at her and then left the room. Gwen turned to the drawer and removed the picture. She drew her finger over the image and then returned it to the drawer.

Bull did his best thinking when he was jogging. It was cold in the morning but he went with his sleeveless Arizona State University Lacrosse Team shirt. He didn't wear it as much anymore, it was getting real thin from years of use and Bull didn't have the heart to throw it away. It still had the bloodstain from the USC player whose nose he broke in one of the earliest games ASU ever sponsored. USC players came over on a team bus and in full uniform. ASU players showed up in scrap equipment, old football jerseys found in a box somewhere in the athletic storage room, and cut offs. They proceeded to take USC to school. Then they all went out together and drank cold beer and ate burgers at the Chuckbox, a local beer joint and health department concern. But the beer was cold and the burgers were the size of Frisbee.

It was only on those occasions that Bull was insecure, frustrated, scared, or needing to, at his age, momentarily return to the womb, when he got it out and spent time in the softness that only this old friend provided. He couldn't even wash it in the machine anymore for fear it would fall apart. He hand washed it and laid it flat to dry on the increasingly rare occasions that he wore it.

But when he ran, things seemed to make sense. It was like blowing out congested pipes. They strangled him, the thoughts and words that he heard Gwen say two days before. He hadn't heard her say or think or do anything even remotely to that level of what he could only perceive as evil. That was contrary to her nature. That was contrary to everything he knew about her. Or was it? He thought that she would have given off signs of this character trait before this. This came out of nowhere. As he jogged he wound his way around the school again and again. The ideas and thoughts swirled in his brain. By the time the run was over and he was walking the last half block, he realized there had to have been something else he hadn't seen. Some piece of the puzzle was missing. He walked directly to Gwen's room. He knew she'd be in. He knew she'd be alone. There would be no need to whisper.

Her door was open and she was sitting behind her desk working. As he walked in he kicked the doorstop shut so it would close. He had finished sweating but the shirt was still wet. He looked out the window as he walked over to her, as if he was looking for the right words.

She looked up as he walked over to her desk. She was wearing a lavender dress with a single string of pearls around her neck. She had told him they were a special set from a long time ago that made her feel better. "You're wearing your pearls."

She looked at him and gave a gentle smile. "You're wearing your blood soaked rag."

"Will you just tell me why? Will you just trust me with it?"

"I have my reasons."

"You care to share them with me?"

"No."

"Come on Gwen, you and I have been through a lot together over the years. None of this makes any sense and you know it."

"I told you it's none of your—,"

"It's my business because I'm in love with Hanna. Her father is not dead, and he's working in secret with her mother. And all while, the daughter you idolize, while longing to be with her father, works with him! The man she thinks is dead is denied that privilege by her mother? You don't think that's weird? This isn't you, Gwen. This isn't the woman I know. This is some, some, God

I don't know who this is!" He gestured with his open hand towards her. He was frustrated and he was showing it.

Gwen remained calm, cold. "Don't try to analyze me, Bull. I told you the reason why she is not to know. Now are you going to respect me enough to honor my wishes?" She stood with her hands folded in front of her. Her eyes were firm in their statement. The ball was in his court because she wasn't going to move.

"Gwen, you are so wrong with this–,"

"Bull! Are you going to honor my request?" She was still calm.

He paused and looked at her. "You know I will. I love you, dear, but I have got to tell you this is wrong." He turned to leave, stopping halfway to the door before turning back around. "The doctors say he can go home tomorrow. I'm bringing the man back to his apartment." Bull then turned and walked out of the room. Gwen stood for a moment, unmoving. When the door shut again she slowly turned back to her desk, let out a deep breath, and sobbed.

What is left when honor is lost?

Publilius Syrus, 100 BC

There she was again, a teenager this time, walking towards whatever it was. Hanna was smiling and started to giggle again in her dream. When she is awake the one thing she remembers is how happy this dream makes her feel. She can feel the laughter as she watches herself in the dream. The grass she was playing in, some of it caught in her hair, was swept aside as it tickled her face. She was focused on the image she couldn't see. Her dress had the same small designs. Hanna woke up again.

Gwen stood in the kitchen leaning against the open door to the patio, feeling the cool morning air against her face and sipping on the mug of coffee.

Lyle was busy hosing down the sidewalks out front of the office while the temporary custodian from another school, filling in for Tony, was busy rolling out the crosswalk signs into the middle of the street.

Hanna decided to get up and, as always, she trailed her mother in showering and getting ready for the day. She thought that she would go see Tony right after school that day.

After school, she drove to the hospital, bought flowers in the lobby and made her way to his room. As she walked in she found the housekeeping staff had stripped the bed and the room was being prepared for another patient. A male custodian was backing out of the bathroom mopping the floor and didn't notice Hanna until she called to him. "Excuse me, but where is the man who was in this room?"

Just as she finished her question, Darrel walked in holding the same flowers from the same stand in the lobby. "Oh hi, Hanna," he said, looking around the empty room. "Where's our patient?"

"I don't know. I just got here myself."

"Do you know where the man is?" Darrel asked.

"No, I think he left. Maybe they moved him. I'm just supposed to clean this room," he said with a slight shoulder shrug.

A voice from behind Darrel asked, "Can I help you?" They both turned to see a nurse in blue surgical scrubs carrying a clipboard and bag of saline.

"Yes, we were just wondering where Tony Jackson went to."

"Oh, Tony, you're friends of Tony?" she said as she smiled. "Gosh he's nice. He was discharged about a half an hour ago. Actually, he was going to get one more X-ray in outpatient before he went home. A tall, older gentlemen, friend of his I guess, in a police uniform, took him down and then was going to take him home.

"He left? Gee, I thought they'd keep him a few more days. I went by his place and got some fresh socks and a bathrobe of his to help him feel more comfortable," Darrel said, holding up a bag in his other hand. "I guess that's good news, huh," he said to Hanna with a nod.

"I found a few things that were left here, too, that must have belonged to him," the custodian said as he went over and picked up a brown bag in the corner and handed it to Darrel.

"I didn't think he was well enough to go home," Hanna said. "Oh well, I guess I'll head back to school. Mom and I will probably go to his apartment this weekend or even tonight." She looked at Darrel with the flowers and the bags. "Those bags look kind of cumbersome. You want me to help you out to the car with them?"

Darrel handed her the bag the custodian had given him. "If you're going over there this afternoon, maybe you can take both of them back to him."

"Sure, I can take it," she said as she reached for the bag, still carrying the flowers in her other hand. They both commented that they expected to run-in to Bull and Tony on their way out. Darrel walked her over to her 1997 Toyota and put the bag in the back seat while she placed her bag in the front seat next to the flowers. Hanna told Darrel that she would probably run the bags and flowers home and then maybe tonight she would go with her mother and take them to Tony.

It had been a long day. She turned on her radio and listened to some jazz as she drove the short distance home, wondering if her mother knew Tony was coming home. She saw the intersection light change and had to brake fairly hard. The bag on the seat tipped over, spilling the contents on the floorboard. She stopped just short of the crosswalk. She was frustrated that the load spilled. While the light was red, Hanna put the car in park and started to collect the items from the floor. She saw it after she moved a box of Kleenex. It didn't make sense to her. She picked it up and looked at it. It was the same picture that was on her desk. Why was the picture from her desk in Tony's things? What was he doing with it? She looked closely at it. She held the picture up to her face and looked at the images in the photo, the clearer image from the one she had. She could recognize some of her own features even though she was so young. She could even see well-defined features of her mother. The man, the man's features—they looked familiar. She hadn't really looked closely at it before. The light changed and the car behind her honked.

"Oh, my God."

The character of a man in times of stress is not developed or created. It is exposed and shown to the world.

Dallas Hickman

Hanna's mind was racing. She startled at the car horn blasting behind her. She set the picture down and looked in the rear view mirror, waving her hand. She had never looked at the picture that closely. The picture, after all, was faded and dark. Nor did she even think to compare it to the man who was her crossing guard for years. She could put the two men's images in her mind side by side and now she could see the resemblance. She had seen the photo all her life. The man in it had been with her for as long as she could remember. But now that she compared it to the photo, there was no mistaking who that was. Tony was her father. She gripped the steering wheel and wiped tears away as they began to stream down her cheeks. The one thing in her life that somehow gave her meaning, the hole in her gut that she could never understand and that was probably a contributor to her divorce, had been there the whole time. But what really felt like treachery, feeling like the world's largest betrayal, was that her mother had known the whole time and yet did not tell her. Never, in all these years, did she say anything to her about the fact that Gwen's husband and her own father was in daily contact with her and yet had never been her father. Her tears responded to the building anger in her. "How dare she keep from me the one thing that she knew meant so much? How could she?"

She pulled down her street and, off to the left, could see her house and Tony's apartment. His door was open. She pulled the car to the curb and got out, carrying in the bags. The sun was setting earlier and the remnants of the last of the light were splitting two Lupine trees and entering the open front door. Hanna could see her mother inside, dusting. Gwen didn't hear her until after Hanna was in the room. She turned and saw the long shadow cast by the woman standing at the door. It startled Gwen. She was surprised to see her daughter standing there. She was able to place a smile on her face as if it was a pleasant surprise but Hanna could tell that Gwen wanted to have been done before Hanna was anywhere close.

"Oh, Hanna darling. You startled me," she said as she clutched her breast. "Did you hear? Tony got released from the hospital. Bull picked him up and had to take him over to get a follow-up X-ray but then he's coming home. I thought I would come over and tidy up the place before he arrived." She looked at Hanna and then at the bags and the flowers. "Oh, what pretty flowers," she said as she approached and reached to take them. "Here, let me put them in some water." She looked down at the bags as she turned and returned to the kitchen. "What's in the bags?" she said as she rounded the wall guarding the kitchen.

Hanna walked over to the chair next to a small dinette table and laid the bags down. She looked in one bag and then the other, pulling out the picture from the second bag.

"When did you talk to Darrel?" Hanna asked as she felt the images again in the picture through the glass.

"Oh, just this afternoon, before school let out. He came over and told me that Tony was coming."

Hanna's wheels in her brain were spinning. Her eyes moved around the room at the pictures and life that existed there. The doilies on the couch and chairs, she remembered when her mother bought several, she said for their house and then said they didn't go with the decor so she took them back. There they were. She smirked at her mother's answer and sniffed. "Huh, that's funny. Darrel and I met at the hospital just a few minutes ago. He brought one of these bags for Tony."

"Oh, that's right," Gwen laughed from the kitchen. "I tell you, this medication that I'm on is really trashing my short term memory."

Hanna was looking down at the picture. She held it in both hands. "How is your long term memory?" Hanna said.

"My what?" Gwen said as she came around the corner

"Your long term memory, how's that? Darrel brought a few things from here to perk up Tony's room. There were also a couple of things that were left at the hospital that the janitor bagged up. This fell out of the bag when I was driving home."

She held up the picture in her hand. "I was, needless to say, a little curious as to why the custodian at our school had our picture. Then I looked a little closer at it and noticed the resemblance between the man in the picture and the man who made me get off my bike in order to cross the street." She moved to the bookshelf. "The picture could have just been a wild coincidence but," she moved over and picked up a picture of Gwen and Tony dancing at some unknown night club. They looked like they were teenagers. "Then I look around his room now and I found this one, and then this one." She stood with pictures from the shelves. "There must be some mistake. Who is Tony?" She was shaking the pictures at her mother. "Why have you lied to me for all these years when my father lives in my back yard?" She was shaking as her mother approached her. "Stay away from me!"

"Hanna."

"You have lied to me my entire life, Mother. You told me he died. Shit, my father is living in the garage behind the house, my house, and my childhood home—my father. And you never told me?" Her eyes were huge, her face a deep red.

Gwen stopped her approach. She folded her hands in the dishtowel. "He did die; I didn't lie to you—exactly." There was a pause in her voice. She was thinking. Hanna could see there was pain in her mother's face. But then it faded to a resolve. As if she had an answer to this question already formed in her mind. "You have a right to be mad. You have an absolute right to be mad at me about not telling you. I am so sorry you are hurt. This is an extremely painful event and I'm not speaking just about you. You're father ceased being the father he was and became someone else that day. Every day since he recovered from that war he has tried to do the best he could for you and for me. He never stopped, but that day, that day we truly lost the man you thought of as your father. Bull brought the picture to the hospital, not Darrel. He found it here from the other day when he came over to get Tony's insurance card. It wasn't a mistake. Tony is standing where he's supposed to be standing."

Hanna shook her head. The tears were streaming down her face, mixed with eyeliner and make-up. "My father died years ago. You told me he died in Vietnam. How could Tony be standing in this picture where my father's supposed to me?"

There came a voice of a tired slur from the doorway. "Don't yell at your mother for something your father did."

Hanna turned. There, just inside the door were Bull and Tony. Bull held a small duffle bag in one hand and Tony's arm with the other.

"What do you mean?" Hanna said.

Gwen took a step in his direction. "Elias, don't." Elias moved into the room. Bull dropped the bag by the door. "I said, 'Don't blame your mother for the actions of your father'." He looked at Gwen. "Your mother wanted to tell you. Time and time again she tried to tell you. I made her stop." The room was silent as Elias took slow but precise steps to a chair at the table. His right arm was unusually limp and his right leg dragged behind the time of a normal stride. The right side of his face had slid a small amount. He pulled out the chair and turned to face the group as he sat down with a heavy exhale. He spoke in short deep strokes of breath.

"It was raining off and on most of the day before. But the night the NVA made their attack, it was crystal clear. The sky was always funny that way. It would rain and be sunny at the same time." He rubbed his knee with his left hand and felt his face as he spoke. "On a clear night you could see the center of the Milky Way. It was beautiful." Then we had some visitors. Fire Base Six was a pisser for the NVA. We came in one day, Daisy cuttered the area in the morning and had a fully functional mortar and howitzer firebase on line by sunset. It upset them to no end." He snickered with the thought of the NVA's surprise. "But I give a lot of credit to those sneaky lil' bastards. They came at us every night. We'd own the day and they'd own the night. We had been overrun twice in the two weeks before this last fight. Each time we had to kick them out of our own beds." He looked over at Bull, who was leaning against the door. "Bastards wanted to spoon with me." They both smiled.

"Well, this last one was the ticket. That night the weather and stars were beautiful. It was the rocket-propelled-grenades, mortars, and small arms fire that was—an awakening." He slowly tried to cross his legs and, discovering that he couldn't, he simply gave up and left them down.

"We knew that they were coming in. They really wanted that lousy beach and if it were up to me I would have given it to them. But the Captain said they couldn't have it. So we fought. The Captain knew we couldn't hold so he called for help but help said they could not be there until daylight. So we fought some more—all night." He stopped for a minute. He was staring at what looked like a spot on the baseboard of the far wall. Bull knew he wasn't looking at anything except the images in his mind and they were as real to him right then as if he were still there. He blinked a couple of times and then looked to each person in the room. "That was a very long night." He sighed again. "By morning, most everyone was dead or hurt real bad. There were lots of bodies. They ran at us in comp, comp," he stuttered.

"Company," Bull said.

"Company-size waves. We just mowed them down, one group after another. We'd use their bodies to reinforce the sandbags for our own fighting holes."

"Wasn't your foot shot off?" Bull asked. He got the 'Evil Eye' from Gwen and didn't even want to look over at Hanna who had been standing motionless.

"Not all the way. My boot held it on—anyway. I looked down the river and the sun was coming up, and there were the boats for us. They were right in the sun—it was real pretty," he said as he reached up and pointed with his finger to the far wall. "I've always liked sunrises since then. We had a lot of hurt people to get to the boats and they couldn't walk so I carried some, some could walk, but not too fast, we were all pretty tired. I was in charge of them. I was responsible. I had one more that I was carrying on my back. I had his gu-gun and mine in each hand and he hung on to my back. I got to the boat and they were dragging the Captain that I had just dropped off onto the boat. He was hurt bad. I turned and looked back to see if we missed anyone." He looked over his shoulder as if he was looking for wounded. He blinked rapidly and his breathing increased. Gwen moved to him and knelt beside him. One of her hands pressed against his face and the other folded on top of his two hands in his lap. He was looking past her and when her hand touched his face, he came back to today. His lip quivered from the emotion. He looked at her instead of past her. His eyes filled with tears, as did Gwen's. They looked at each other. Years of love moved between them without words, without thought. She smiled tenderly, his breathing slowed. His eyes blinked slower. "I could still fire the guns so that's what I did. The doctors asked me that later. 'Did you feel what hit your head?' I had to tell them 'not really'. They didn't know if it was a bullet or shrap—shrap"

"Shrapnel?" Bull said.

"Shrapnel."

"I think I fell backwards. At least that's what I was told. I don't remember much about it. I can still see the sky. The clouds were kind of pink. I thought that the boy on my back might be hurt, but I couldn't do anything, 'cept keep firing my guns. I just laid there and fired my guns. Someone said I was firing with one hand and holding onto the other marine with the other. Someone grabbed me and pulled me. Someone said it was the Captain when they dragged him onto the boats. I don't know. Someone else said I actually hit some of the NVA—bad people when I was shooting. That was good." The cadence in his voice eased. He nodded his head as if he was agreeing with himself.

"Then the bullets ran out but I just kept pulling the trigger. I don't remember much but I remember pulling the trigger and hearing a 'click, click' sound. So I let go of the gun." His tone was soft and smooth, like black velvet. "When I woke up, I was in a hospital and your Momma was looking at me." He looked at Gwen and smiled and then looked over at Hanna. "I did not recognize her at first but then I did. They gave me a medal for all that, for being scared. Your Momma is not to blame for this. I am." He sighed again and looked at Hanna. It was the face in the picture. It was an image that had been with her forever. She was looking at an older man now. A man that was in the last stages of his life but still there was a fire in the eyes that lit up a room, although they were tired eyes.

"The doctors said that I needed an operation that would take out part of my brain. The doctors said it would keep me from dying. I heard the orderlies say that it would make me 'stupid'." He almost spit the words out. "It was the sixties. No one wanted people from Vietnam with medals, especially stupid ones. I told your Momma that you needed to think I died on the river. You could not have a stupid Daddy. Your Momma fought me. I made her promise to never tell you that your Daddy was stup, stup, stupid. But she never stopped loving me. She convinced me to tell you—when you were younger." He paused and looked at Hanna. "Then, then something would be said about my brain, me being stupid, or retarded. You had a birthday one year." He stared at his daughter. Hanna knew what year he was talking about. She was a teenager. "That was the day you said you didn't want me to go with you to your birthday because I was retarded. I could tell. You were embarrassed to have me around."

She began to shake her head no, but she knew he was right.

"There were other times. Some earlier, some later. You would say something or be around someone who would say something and I could see it on your face. What the orderlies said was true; no one wanted to be around stupid people. I thought early about leaving you and your mother, that you two would be better off. But she said 'no'. She got me this apartment behind the house and got me my job and would come down here every night and fixed up this place while you thought she was out for a walk and we would talk and she would tell me about your day. Sometimes, we would go to your house when you were gone and I would just sit in your room."

"Why didn't you try to tell me? Grab me by the shoulders and shake me? Tell me this is the father I was looking for?"

Gwen stepped forward. "We did. Think Hanna, think of the times you heard him called a 'retard' or 'stupid'. What did you do? All those times at the corner, around school, friends at home. What did you do when you heard your friends say that to him? He saw your reaction. That solidified our thoughts but we kept hoping that something might change your feelings. Finally, we just thought it was too late. Too much time had passed."

"You're telling me this is my fault?"

"No," Elias said. "It's really my fault, I guess, if we were to lay blame. It's just life."

His lip began to quiver again. "Sometimes, sometimes, I would sit on your bed and just hold your pillow to my face so I could smell you. I got to see you every morning and every afternoon on your way to school and home again. And sometimes, during school, you would say 'hi' to me and that was nice." He began to choke up. He rubbed his good hand on his trousers nervously. "I am sorry for lying to you. I thought I was doing what was right. I could not thin–think that you were ever embarrassed of your Da–Da–Daddy. I saw the way you felt when those words were said to Tony who wasn't your father. I couldn't bear the thought of those words being about your father in your mind. I love you a lot. Your Momma would put your pictures that you drew in school up in my hospital room at the V.A. and that would make me feel better. All I thought about was coming home to you and Gwen. You would think that your Daddy was a hero who died a long time ago. You wouldn't be burdened with someone who was- was—stupid. This way you kind of had two daddies, one you could admi—admi–,"

"Admire," Bull aided.

"Admire, and the other who would watch over you every day that I could. I would always make sure you got to school okay." He looked into the eyes of his daughter for the first time. For the first time since her youth she looked into the eyes of her hero. He was an old lion now, scarred and aged but still, a lion.

The tape in her mind ran with thoughts. She couldn't focus on any one thing. The image of him during her life, the lie, the image of him always there, the lie, the years she thought he was dead—the lie. Then, there they were. Her own thoughts and words. She heard herself as if it was that morning when she spoke them.

The room fell silent. Gwen walked over and put her arm around Hanna, who began to cry. She looked up at him as she cried. She let herself be held for a moment and then shook her mother off.

Elias walked to the bookshelf and pulled an old mitt down from the top shelf. It was freshly oiled and there was a Borman softball in it and three large rubber bands wrapped around it. "I found your mitt and fixed it. But by the time I did, the season was over. So, I guess I just kept it." He reached out to her with the glove in his hand. She looked at it and then took two steps back, turning her back to the room. "You fixed my mitt."

His hand holding the mitt dropped slowly to his side. "That's what daddies are supposed to do," he said, almost in a whisper.

Bull leaned against the door, processing the story. He saw the whole picture. He could see why Gwen lied. He could see why the story went the way it did, although he would have gambled on the compassion of society rather than decades of the heart. He was in the presence of what love was about. Love had nothing to do with sex, the house in the Hamptons, changing the diapers, or breakfast in bed. It had everything to do with sacrifice of the heart. Against one's own best interest, against one's own self worth, for the good of someone that one might not even know or worse, rejected when they received it. Love was a sacrifice word. It meant the breaking of the heart and body for someone else. 'What a glorious place to be,' Bull thought, and a smile came to his face.

Bull started to move in his direction, but without looking at him, Elias raised his hand to stop him. "I think I am sorry for asking, and I would understand if you didn't want to, it being such a long time the other way, but I would like to be your father that you can say 'hi' to. A father that you can call your father.

Hanna stopped crying. She looked at him so long that Bull thought she didn't hear what was asked. "You want me to forget the past and call you 'Daddy'; is that what you're saying? You want me to forget that you and mother intentionally lied to me?"

"Hanna, we didn't—," Gwen started.

"Yes, yes you did. You should have forced me to hear, forced me to listen."

"No one was going to force you to hear something that you yourself didn't want to hear. We saw how you reacted when others said things. Your father was a hero in your eyes. Why would we want to change that? Your father couldn't bear that."

"He couldn't bear it? He couldn't? What about me?"

Gwen stood right in front of her. "Play back the tape of your life, Hanna." Gwen's voice was firm. "When did you ever defend him when you heard what he was called? When did you ever want him around? Then think about this. He could have left. The pain might have been eased for him but he stayed. Believe it or not, if you look back on your life, he was here. He fixed your bike; he cared for us when we were sick." She looked at her husband and smiled. "He was here, in this house, caring for us both, even when one of us didn't want him here. He cared for you every day, even though you were embarrassed by him."

"I wasn't embarrassed—,"

"Gwen, that's a little—," Elias started.

"Play the tape, Hanna. When, when did you care about him, show him compassion, smile at him or even want to stay and talk to him? What the doctors told us, what he heard so many years ago—they were right. Yep, we tried. We thought the world had changed around us and we could tell you who your father really is, just the guy who loved you all these years. But time and time again we were reminded that if we did, we, especially your father, risked losing you forever. So, he took what he could get." Gwen looked her husband. "And I took what he could give me."

Hanna looked at him. "I never thought you heard. You never acted like you heard—anything."

"No, I heard most of it," he said nodding his head. "Plus a few things you never heard."

Hanna looked at her mother and then at Elias; lastly, she looked over at Bull. She left the apartment without saying a word.

"She'll be all right. She just needs time to process this," Bull said, wondering if he would ever see her in the same room with the other two again. He walked out after her, calling her as he cleared the front door. She was almost to the sidewalk. "Hanna, wait up," he called to her back. He jogged to catch up with her. He said nothing. She said very little. She cried; she ranted; she shook her head. He said nothing.

There was a long pause and then Elias turned to Gwen in the now empty room. "Mrs. Jackson, it seems like our secret is over. I don't know how much longer we have together but would you hon— hon— honor me again and marry me? All over again?" He reached out to her with his good hand.

"I would be most honored to marry you again, Mr. Jackson," she said taking his hand in both of hers. She let the tears run down her cheeks for the first time with someone else in the room.

To love and be loved is to feel the sun from both sides.

David Viscot

It had been two weeks since Elias' hospital stay when Hanna's dream arrived again. She again found herself in the long grass and wearing the same cotton dress that she has always worn in her dream, the one with the little cherry design on it. But this time the dream was different. She was fully-grown. She again turned to walk toward the image that caused her to smile. She started to laugh, her hand coming up and partially covering her mouth but she didn't care. Her pace picked up. She woke. Her eyes, like countless times before, opened, but this time they snapped open. She was wide-awake. She knew.

She jumped out of bed and slid her feet into Elsie and Nadine, names she finally settled on for her slippers, and grabbed her robe off the foot of the bed and slid it on as she moved down the hall and out the front door. She hadn't really noticed it before, but there was a little cluster of cherries on the robe on the back label. "Odd," she randomly thought. The sun was just breaking the horizon, although the house across the street was blocking it from hitting her home. She walked down to the sidewalk while she finished tying her robe; all the while looking down the street. She didn't see him but she knew he was there. She started to walk quickly in his direction. She began to trot, a smile came to her face as she passed her neighbor's house and then she began to giggle. As she got closer to the corner she could see him.

He had already put out the school crossing signs to slow traffic in the middle of the street. It was early, but he was an early man. He stood with his back to her, watching the sunrise. She stopped when she saw him. She was looking at the same image that had always been there. She laughed like a little girl watching her daddy watch the sun rise. She was free and loved, and at that very moment she felt whole for the first time ever.

"Daddy," she yelled at his back as she continued her walk. He didn't hear her. "Great," she said to herself in laughter. "Now, his hearing is going." She put two fingers in her mouth and whistled like a Longshoreman. "Hey, Dad," she yelled after the screeching shrill whistle.

He turned to her. It took him a moment to recognize her. He wasn't expecting it. His face, questioning the noise, was slowly replaced with a smile. The closer she got the grin grew. He began to move toward her and she began to run and reached out as she came to him, stopping only when her arms were around his barrel chest and his arms wrapped around her back. "I love you, Daddy."

There was a pause. She could feel his chin on top of her head and he kissed the part in her morning hair. "I–I-lov-love you too, dear," he stuttered. The two stood like that for a minute and then both, as if they planned it, turned and watched the sun come up.

....the most powerful of these is Love.

Apostle Paul

A late April spring day

Elias and Gwen decided to get married at the school. It wasn't such an odd place considering that was the world their love orbited. It was a Saturday. For weeks the school staff had worked like their own family was celebrating. The image of sickness and twilight years was sure to have crossed some minds on campus but most only saw this as a freeing, of sorts, once they heard the story. It inspired them. It humbled them. It encouraged them that love like this could still exist. It gave many of them hope that their run in life was worth it.

Bull took the lead, along with Barbara Gaven. There was secrecy, intrigue, misinformation, and downright lying going on regarding the wedding.

Bull convinced Elias that he needed to get married in his old Marine uniform. They promised each other to keep it a secret from everyone else. Elias, in turn, told Bull he needed him as his best man and he would have to wear his uniform as well. On the wedding day, the cool morning was being warmed by the freshness of the sun. The entire district staff was invited and all had contributed in some way to the wedding. White chairs were rented and placed on the open amphitheater lawn. Daisies, Gwen's favorite flower, were in bouquets around the stage. Bull came out of one of the classrooms where, it was alleged, the groom was housed. He was in his full dress whites. He walked down the sidewalk; Hanna came out of the bride's staging area. He stopped in his tracks. She was wearing a cream white tea length dress with open beadwork wrapped around her neck that dipped under her throat. She looked at him and smiled.

"You didn't," she said with a smile as she walked towards him.

"Yes, ma'am, I did." Whatever it was, he might as well admit to it, he thought.

She paused and looked at him up and down. The last few weeks had been the developing moments in their relationship. Both knew that there was more to this than luck and their own stamina. They both knew that this was going somewhere and that a power greater than their own was driving the train. That freed them. If they were going to do this relationship thing, they were going to do it right.

They went for walks and talked. They went out to dinner and talked. They sat on each other's front porch and talked some more. It wasn't to learn the other's favorite color but to discover the color of each other's hearts.

"Packard Thornton, you are downright handsome in that uniform," she said as she walked up to him and fingered the buttons on his coat.

"Well, you should have seen me twenty pounds ago. I was drop dead handsome." He took his hand and palmed her cheek, pulling some loose strands of hair off her forehead. "You should see your father."

"No— you didn't," she said patting him lightly on the chest.

"Stop saying that. Yes, ma'am I did."

"Can you even wear this thing if you're not in the service anymore?" she said as she brushed the jacket and straightened the ribbons on his coat.

There was a pause and Bull looked down at her. "I got a special dispensation. Besides, once a marine, always a marine."

"What did you do?"

Just then Darrel came out of the classroom in his Navy dress whites. He stood for a moment and looked at the two of them as he put his white cover on. He was a lieutenant commander when he rotated out of the service. "I'm going to go check on the minister," he said.

Hanna and Bull looked back at each other. Hanna's mouth hung a little open and Bull closed it with his finger. He rested his hands on her shoulders and looked into her eyes. She had no clue, and Bull and Gaven's plan was about to come full circle. "Remember Jen'ot at the restaurant? Remember when I said a couple other pilots went with me to Europe?" Hanna nodded. "When we were in France we all became friends and one of these other Marines was a Marine Captain. Good guy, straight-laced, good drinker, dirty fighter, all Marine, remember?"

"Yeesss, so?" she said hesitantly. "Bull, are you going to get us in trouble with the Marine Corps?" There was a noise in the distance. It was faint, but Bull recognized it right away and looked up trying to find the source of the noise. From a distance, a helicopter made a low approach. As it got closer, Bull could see the twin blades of the Chinook and the battle gray used by the military. Hanna looked over at the ship as it was making a circling pattern over the ball field just south of the amphitheater. There were orange cones, a lot of orange cones, marking a large circle in the field.

"There's a whole bunch of cones—where did all the—,"

"I don't know," Bull shrugged.

Hanna looked back at the landing helicopter. "Packard Thornton, what did you do?" Hanna said as she watched the copter land.

"I had Jen'ot make a call to an old friend," Bull said, taking her hand and starting to walk towards the field where the Chinook was kicking up grass and dust. "I got your father a wedding present," he said with a smile.

Bull waited with Hanna until the pilot feathered the blades and the dust settled. The side door slid open and uniforms, big uniforms, jumped out.

Bull looked at Hanna with a smile. "The captain stayed in when Jen'ot and I got out."

Climbing out and standing outside the helicopter was a Marine Captain Tom Ratcliff, Jen'ot in his French uniform, a Colonel, and General Fletcher Rimza, Commandant of the United States Marine Corps.

"Bull?" she squeezed his hand while they walked towards the men.

As Bull approached he came to attention and saluted. All the men, including Jen'ot, responded. The Colonel, whom Bull figured was the General's aide, started to make the introduction. "Lieutenant," the deep-throated Colonel started. "This is General–,"

"Thank you, Colonel, but this Marine needs no introduction to me. This man and I have thrown up in more French pilot's boots then any two men alive. Isn't that right, Lieutenant?" shaking Bull's hand.

"I am proud to say I witnessed such action, yes, General," Jen'ot said while waiting his turn to shake his friend's hand.

"Damn Fletch—I mean General. It's good to see you again."

Bull turned to the Captain standing next to the Colonel. "You must be the Captain I've heard so much talk about."

"Yes, I am. Ben Ratcliff," he said as he reached out to shake Bull's hand.

"Boy, am I glad they found you," Bull said.

"Not nearly as glad as I am at being found. You know how that war was. I haven't seen Elias since that day we were shot up together. I wasn't in very good shape to find out how he did. After I submitted his name for the Congressional Medal of Honor, I was rotated out." The Captain took a breath and smiled. "He called everyone under his command his 'charges,' even me." Bull looked over his shoulder at Hanna. "When the Colonel called with this story and your plan, the fires of Hell couldn't keep me away. The man saved my life."

"How much does he know, Bull?" the General asked as they walked from the helicopter.

Bull smiled. "He has no clue, General. When he asked me if I would be his Best Man, I asked him if he wanted some groomsmen to be with him. He said to do whatever I thought would be best. I told him I would have a few guys available."

"Hot damn, Bull," the General said. "I bet he'll crap his pants. This is going to be great!"

"I think you could be right."

While he walked the officers back to see Elias, Hanna kissed Bull on the cheek and went in with her mother. She was in a classroom, sitting at a desk converted to a makeup table. Hanna looked at her mother in the mirror while Barbara put the finishing touches on her hair.

Gwen's eyes met Hanna's in the glass. Then Gwen said, "Are you happy? You look as though you're a million miles away. What's wrong?"

"I guess I was just thinking that there aren't a whole lot of people who get to watch their parents get married, especially two who aren't in the best of shape. You haven't mentioned if you're planning a honeymoon or even a wedding night."

Barbara stopped what she was doing and turned to Hanna.

"Well, I hope to say we're having a wedding night. You don't think we should, dear?"

"Mother, Dad's had a stroke and you're fighting each day for the next day. I don't think you need to stress yourself anymore than necessary, do you?"

Barbara put her hands on her hips. Hanna noticed and started to wonder if she was actually having this conversation.

"You don't think that your father and I have been intimate over these last few decades?"

Barbara's eyebrows went up.

"Well, I didn't think–,"

"Come on dear, you know as well as I do that a woman has her needs."

"I didn't say that you–,"

"Here I am on one of the most romantic days of my life and you want me to worry about whether or not I'm going to give your father another stroke? I'm going to do my best to give him another stroke tonight."

Barbara nodded and pointed with the end of her hairbrush. "You tell her, sister."

"Mother, I don't think I want to hear this," she said as she backed up a step.

Gwen turned to Barbara Gaven. "Barbara, do you think I got

some juice left in this old body for a few more years of sweaty sex with my old man, who, by the way, really is an old man?"

"Mother, I KNOW I don't want to hear this."

"Honey," Barbara started while turning back to Gwen's hair and talking to her in the mirror. "If you were three years younger, they'd declare you a national security risk. What a way to die, coming and going all in one motion."

The two women started laughing hard.

"Don't encourage her. I'm sorry I brought this up," Hanna said.

Gwen stopped laughing and turned back to Hanna. "I did forget something."

"What?" Hanna asked with a sigh.

"Well, if I'm going to be with my lover tonight, who's going to watch my kid?" Hanna laughed as well.

Elias was looking in the mirror when the men walked in. He had just put on the last medal. The light blue ribbon of the CMH lay perfectly around his collar. He was checking out the dress blues that he hadn't had on formally since before he went in country. He pulled the white cap slowly down on his head as if scared to break it. The door opening startled him.

It was Bull. He stuck his head in. "Tony, I mean Elias—hell, what name do you want me to use?"

"Tony's fine."

"The groomsmen are here." He then pushed the door open to allow the uniforms to enter.

The first one in the door was the Colonel, who took up a position just inside the door. "Attention on deck, General on deck." The bark of the Colonel hit a file far away in Elias' head. He responded automatically by coming to attention. The General entered the room with the power of his position. He came in just a few feet and then stopped.

"General!" Elias said and quickly gave a salute. It was his left arm. The right was still weak from the stroke but some how that didn't matter to anyone in the room.

"God Damn it Gunnery Sergeant, you wear the Congressional

Medal of Honor. I have the honor of saluting you," the General said as he came to attention and offered a crisp salute. The General held his salute until Tony was able to respond. The General reached out with his left and shook Elias' hand. "I am damned proud to be groomsman at your wedding, damned proud. I've heard about you, and a few of us old dogs want to be here with you. We have one more marine who would have cut off his own leg to be here.

Captain Ratcliff came from around the edge of the door and entered the room. He walked within a few feet of Tony and saluted. "Semper Fi, Gunny."

Tony stared at the man after the salute. His mouth dropped open while he tried to form words. "Cap- Captain Ratcliff?"

"It's good to see you again, Elias."

Elias looked at the other men in the room. "This is the Captain, you brought me my Captain," he said as he choked up and he walked over and hugged his former leader.

Darrel walked in the room just as the two let go. "Gentlemen, it's time."

The men gathered out on the sidewalk just behind the back wall of the amphitheater when Hanna walked up to Bull. She stood close to him and looked up into his eyes. "I can't believe you did all this."

He looked around and smiled. "Yeah, well you do stupid things when you're privileged enough to get to hang out with a bonafide hero and his daughter whom you are falling desperately and madly in love with."

"You are?"

"Desperately."

"Desperately?"

"Madly."

"Madly?"

Barbara came out ahead of Gwen and barked at the men in uniform as if she herself was a Sergeant. "Bull Thornton, you get those men lined up out there. We got a wedding to do."

Bull looked up from Hanna's eyes to see Barbara. "Yes, ma'am. We are moving." He turned to the others and said with a smile,

"Gentlemen, we have our orders." Then, before he left her, he kissed Hanna so hard that her eyes rolled back in her head. "I love you, Hanna," he said to her.

"I love you too, Bull," she said to him.

Printed in the United States
94513LV00004B/49-60/A

9 781587 369551